These Dark City Streets

Dave Anderson

AN INTRODUCTION IF I MAY

Hello friends! My name is Mighty and what you are holding in your hands is the only copy of the cult classic '*These Dark City Streets.*' I want to give a brief rundown on what you are about to read so hopefully you're not confused at any point.

Time is short and not to be wasted. I don't want you reading a bunch of pages and thinking, 'What is going on? I am confused. Should I read those pages again? This is why I don't read, it's always confusing and ends up being work instead of pleasure. I'd rather watch Netflix instead.'

So, let's try and avoid these pitfalls, shall we?

This is a real story about a real event. Don't worry, it's not some boring documentary or history lesson that's been done to death a billion times in schools while the students day-dream instead. I did my best to write this so it's quick and fast paced to prevent you from drifting away and thinking about other things.

My name, like I mentioned, is Mighty. I wrote this book along with Nails. I do the third person passages while Nails does the first person. For the most part it's Nails telling the story in first person while I do the other passages in third person.

Imagine us has a hip-hop duo like Dr. Dre and Snoop Dogg. Andre 3000 and Big Boi. Sage Francis and B Dolan. Not to act too confident, but if you like, you can add us to that list as well. But instead of rapping, we are a writing duo. Writing can sometimes feel like rapping minus the funky beats. Anyway, you get the gist of what I am slanging.

So back to the point of this introduction. I want to plant a few seeds in your fertile brains before you begin reading. Some terms that are key to the story and you will hear often are the following: Dark side, Light side, Thought wind, Nails, Faith, Statue of Hero, Molly, Mighty, Sunshine Smoothies, Corey.

I don't want to give too much away so sit back and relax and grab some popcorn. Actually, don't grab popcorn since that will stain the pages from the grease. Is there a snack that accompanies reading a book? I am starting to ramble. Enjoy this book and please make sure to put it back from where you found it. More on that later. I am going to research snacks to munch on while reading a book. Hip-hop, Mighty and Nails in the building and we refuse to stop!

FLASK OF FAITH

The black ashes twist and twirl in the tangy autumn wind, softly landing on his skin, turning it ashy black to match the colors of the clothes on the human named Nails. Each foot moves onward, propelling the human to his final destination to gander at the girl he loves and cherishes.

He gazes through the murky window as she paints another masterpiece. A cigarette dangles between Nails' blackened red lips-a tall tale sign of a digestive system refusing to digest its surroundings-the smoke lingers for a moment celebrating its freedom before it's abrupt departure and ultimate demise.

Inhale. Exhale. Freedom. Death. Ad Nauseum.

He rubs his beard and breathes a laborious sigh. In another lifetime, perhaps, they would laugh and love and grow old together, sharing with each other thoughts and theories about the bittersweet planet they call home. As always, he contemplates trying to communicate via touch, since language does not work. He wonders what will happen if he tries to kiss her.

Will she reciprocate?

Is love the missing factor that causes her and the others to only have a limited arsenal of phrases to choose from? He promises himself that his first kiss and embrace of skin would only occur when she is fully coherent. To abandon this could cause a chasm between them that would prevent a future together.

She is his anchor to this life. Without her, or rather, the prospect of them being together, he probably would have drowned in a sea of black by now.

His soul burns daily knowing that something sinister is keeping her and everyone else from communicating freely. It causes him great strife and anxiety to see them all verbally paralyzed by the hand of something black-hearted and sadistic.

Upon awakening each morning it is a primary motivational tactic he forges inside himself: Never rest until the perpetrators of the crimes against him and the others were dealt with by having hands handcuffed behind them so they would see the world through grimy grey iron bars.

Nails extracts his glasses to whip the black ashes off so he could continue watching his perfect girl create her art. He recalls the first time he saw her and how his eyes were glued to her trim torso. She seemed to be born to wear the color black, and he seemed destined to watch her wear that color. Every time he contemplates touching her and kissing her, a stop sign flashes in his brain. He believes that once her wicked spell is broken, they will be together. Don't rush it and regret actions made.

An hour and five cigarettes later, he decides he has procrastinated enough, and it is time to hear that bittersweet voice—the voice that says the same few lines every hour of every day of every month causing half his body to melt in pure bliss from her beautiful tone and grace while the other half sinks lower and lower each time those same words echo and bounce inside his lonely sheltered skull.

"Hey Faith. It's Nails. What are you painting?"
"Hey, I am busy painting. How are you?"
"You're so beautiful. Can I kiss you?"
"Hey, I am busy painting. How are you?"
"You're doing an amazing job. I would love to buy this painting."
"Hey, I am busy painting. How are you?"

Each time he speaks, it feels like a defective needle trying endlessly to find a vein.

FLURRY OF FOOD

I slowly stroll into Faith's kitchen and am always surprised with the bountiful supplies of food. A dull tug on the refrigerator door showcases endless premade meals.

Meatloaf. Chicken parm. Hoagies. Salads. Lasagna. Steak.

I grab a hoagie and slap it on the table, tearing into the transparent lining. The salty meats line my stomach, providing a tab of energy and drip drops of dopamine.

Who supplies this food?

Faith is too busy painting to shop for groceries. In fact, painting is all she ever does.

There is so much I don't understand about the dark side that this mystery is just added to the long list that causes my blood pressure to bubble and bounce.

I toss the remnants into the shiny silver trash can and begin to feel unsteady.

Equilibrium slightly skewed.

The "beast" is rising from slumber. Yawning and stretching inside of me. Soon it will need to be released from the cold cracked cage.

I swat at the remote in a feral fashion and turn on her fifty-inch TV, which towers over my thirteen-inch one. I watch a reality show about something so stupid my mind drifts away to claw and dig around for some peaceful mental vibes.

A few hours pass and the nervous energy from the beast begins to cause some discomfort. Reluctantly, I stagger to the door, but before I open it, I crank my head sideways to get one last view of Faith before I depart back home. I take a dozen or so mental snapshots that I can store in my brain to retrieve when I feel alone and despondent.

I know the feeling that is brewing inside. I call it "the beast," attempting to release any responsibility or association to myself. This is something foreign that has no passport and enters with no advance notice—an uncontrollable, rambunctious and insane energy that is the product of isolation and agony.

Inside my body there is an organ like the bladder that gathers all my grievances, and when that organ is full and overflowing, it invades my entire body, slowly creating a raving lunatic. When the organ is emptied, it feels like a reset button. Crashing waves level out into mellow ripples. However, only a few options exist:

> *#1 Drink myself into another state of mind.*
> *#2 Step into the ring with the thought wind.*

Each plan provides a way to temporarily exterminate the beast.

The problem with the first plan is that a cloudy mind yields cloudy results, while a sharp mind generates sharp results. The days following a heavy booze bender makes my entire body feel like a broken clock. Gooey goon gears that leak tears instead of time. A pathetic pendulum that barely rotates as the minute and hour hands refuse to communicate with the barrel and dials, causing a stagnant stew of traffic.

If I am to escape this bombastic attack of black, I need to be awake and alert—a panther tracking down its prey.

It seems like it is an obvious decision to pass on the first plan. However, holding a mug of poison suds and sipping on many of them offers a euphoric sensation that wakes an army from slumber inside me where the Sergeant's only goal is to make people feel alive and full of zest and ready to conquer everything in its path. This is a much-needed feeling, even if it only lasts for a few hours as it works well to keep me afloat in these treacherous seas.

The problem with plan two was the lack of any joy involved in it. The drink at least lifts my spirits and makes me more merry and delightful. Sure, it is a false feeling of security and bliss, but it is one that feels as important as oxygen.

The thought wind provides none of that. It is punishment with no satisfaction. It creates a tornado of cocaine chaos pulverizing my entire body causing a weakened flu-like feeling.

There is, however, a walloping benefit of the thought wind: it retrieves thoughts and patterns and shapes and information about the dark side that my suspicious mind tells me are clues and leads that could give me some sort of answers to why I am on the dark side and how I can escape.

The thought wind also, oddly enough, is my source of income, as it wrangles my stagnant brain into creative blasts of inspiration.

Was I mentally prepared for the abuse it launches at me? The beer, vodka, and whiskey offer a mental vacation while the thought wind was the complete opposite. It made me face the ugly realities that is my life.

Ready or not, something has to be extracted from me. If I did nothing, I fear I might lash out in violence against my fellow humans. That was something I promised myself would never happen. Faith and the others remind me of a pet in a sense. They rely upon an outside source for survival and only demented demons would capitalize on such innocence.

I decide to entertain the thought wind tonight and then, tomorrow, have a few drinks to try and keep the anger at bay—a daily dose of medicine in hopes of preventing the feeling currently residing inside me from building up into an emergency state, causing my dam walls to crumble.

Like clockwork, my brain quickly reminds me that there is no escaping the thought wind. It feels like a parasite that feds off my misery. Like a roommate you never see but they always made their presence known from supreme sloppiness.

Anytime I come up with a solution on how to stay positive and strong, I would think about the evils of the thought wind and feel defeated again. It became a hate anchor that I was determined to remove.

I force myself each morning to say my mantra's even though my progress in finding a solution to my problems felt slower then a slug.

Each new day is a opportunity to grow stronger.

Each new day I will flex my mental muscles and break free.

A WAR AGAINST THE WIND

Inside my closet contains the necessary armaments to wage war with this mysterious foe. I grab a bag and walk out of the apartment. No need to bother closing the door or locking it, since nobody tries to peek inside or steal the measly antique possessions inside—Nintendo. Atari. Thirteen-inch TV. Boombox. Cassette player. Computer. Record player. Fax machine. Gameboy. Lasertag. VCR. Typewriter. Synthesizer.

I go to the normal light post I use for these battles and unzip my bag. The components inside consist of a rugged silver chain, a lock with a key, a thermometer, a digital clock, and an audio recorder. I carry a poster board separately that does not fit inside the bag.

I take the chain and wrap it around my wrist and pole, locking it firmly into place. The key finds a temporary home inside my pants near a thicket of lint.

I position the thermometer and video recorder gently on the concrete slabs. I take the poster board and put it up against the pole so I would always be able to see the vital message it contains.

"3489 Salvation Street is where you live. It's located ten feet away. It's the house with the door wide open. Put on your headphones. If the thermometer reads above 101. Go Home ASAP. Do not go anywhere else but home. Your name is Nate/Nails and you are doing this to find answers to leave the dark side."

I remove the headphones and stare straight into the poster board.

My ears begin to tickle and twitch as the electronic radiation in the air begins to enter and increase, as if it knew there was a fresh victim and it was feeding time.

I trained my subconscious to trust the sign even when I was in a position similar to an LSD trip where nothing made sense and nobody could be trusted.

The thought wind begins as a predictable foe. It would request me to unlock the chain and walk the dark city streets with no headphones and then have a drink under the two-hundred-foot Statue of Hero. I always refuse. Never surrender and become zombie drones like Faith and the others is my motto.

When the thought wind knew it wasn't going to have a meet and greet with its adversary, it then begins the next rounds of attack. This consists of comments on current events occurring on the dark side or with myself. In typical dark side fashion, the news it presents has to be given in an angular and artistic way.

The thought wind then digs deeper, frustrated that it does not get its wishes. Like a company mining treasured natural resources, it enters crevasses of the brain that are covered in cobwebs. I am never sure if phase two and three is the thought wind implanting these thoughts or just removing them from my subconscious. It is probably a combination of both.

I speak into the audio recorder with what my brain and eyes witness. This can be a challenge as I will have to talk while my brain is flashing up images that appear dangerously real.

Sometimes it's simply not possible. My brain is so overwhelmed with stimuli, I turn comatose and surrender all movement and responsibility and only can shake it off when my body begins to feel heated and harsh.

I look around at the various buildings of black as the thought wind begins. I can maintain a connection with the physical world the first five minutes or so as the thought wind operates in a creepy crawler mode of invasion. Eventually my eyes close and I get lost in the images.

My brain waves show me unlocking the chain and walking the streets with no headphones on with a confident look sprawled across every facet of my facial features. I arrive at the Statue of Hero to see it sitting on a bar stool surrounded by a full bar stocked with tons of beer and liquor.

The Statue is wearing a kilt and talking in an Irish accent and hands me a mug which contains the sweet nectar of the gods. The Statue tries to clank mugs together in celebration but his thirty-foot mug is too large creating an awkward mismatch of sorts.

Then the audio part begins. It tries to make me think I have accepted the thought wind's proposition. Luckily, the chain and sign will prevent me from actually giving into the twisted demands.

"Nails the Nihilist, you made the wise decision of ripping to shreds your former life. Why torture yourself daily knowing you're only delaying the inevitable—losing at the hands of a master showman like myself. You will wonder why you waited this long and added so much unnecessary stress to your life."

"If you think you are being brave and becoming a stronger person by denying my wishes at any point and trying to stab me in the back, you will pay dearly. This is the way of the future. I am the future. We are the future."

At this stage of the mental hijacking, I am able to convince enough brain cells to articulate a message.

"We will never be friends, you sick fuck. Why would I want to be your sidekick? To live in a world of black and subhumans? I want to love and be free. Start a future with Faith."

I am no longer drinking at a bar with Hero. Instead, I am just a head sticking out of crunchy grey gravel. I try to mutter the normal "Fuck you, asshole," but speech and independent thought dwindle away. I see my other limbs scattered around.

My legs begin to move and I wonder if they will run away. Instead they assemble below my head in a skull and crossbones formation.

"Why don't you get a real job, you bum? Those stories you write are so lame. Faith really can talk, but she knows you're some weird stalker guy with no future so she just pretends to act this way and convinces everybody else to do the same. They laugh at your sorry ass endlessly."

The thought wind goes deeper and deeper into my brain, yanking out random bizarre thoughts that makes me wonder whether they could be clues to my former life or help me escape this current one.

Ultra-violent white static that sounds like all the voices in the world jabbering at once.

White blood leaking from blown-out eardrums.

Laser-long legs dripping ivory-colored flesh running on top of drums creating booming blasts.

Bins and crates filled with rusty smiling skulls, oozing milky venom.

A needle filled with sprinkles breaks the barrier of skin as the arm morphs into a vanilla ice cream cone.

White eyeballs fall from the sky as junkies pulverize them with white Doc Martens, whipping out rolled up dingy dollar bills to snort the vision of a thousand albino snakes.

I snowboard down a mountain, but instead of a snowboard, I am riding Faith as she stares back at me in terror as an avalanche of snow races behind us.

I notice a shed nearby. I snowboard into it. I quickly remove my feet from Faith and try to warm her up. She breaks free from my embrace and says, "My name is Faith and you're going to die."

She raises her hand up and points it towards me. A fingernail sharp and pointy that goes on forever like a Stretch Armstrong, plunges deep into my chest. A sadistic wild grin populates her face.

I feel the cold of two winters rush across me as snow leaks from my wound instead of rosy red blood. I touch the snow expecting immediate frostbite, but instead, my fingers turn into hydrogen and helium and become mini suns. I try to flick the thermal energy off since it's the hottest feeling I have ever experienced, but my legs catch on fire, and within a minute, I become a human sun screaming in agony.

I start to feel uncomfortable as my ears and cheeks begin turning fire engine red from my temperature rising like volcano ash ready to erupt. Twitching and turning my body like a water moccasin releases the reverie from its death grips just long enough to see the poster board.

HUNGRY HUNGRY HIPPO

Struggling to move, he thrashes around in a panic state and manages to unlock the handcuffs and lollygags to his apartment covering both ears like a child who isn't supposed to hear what adults are saying.

He lays on his couch exhausted while the brain still feels aftershocks and residential ideas ricocheting off every crevice and corner of his stoic skull.

He sits up and slams a few glasses of water that lubricates his rusty joints.

Laying back down, he stares at his ceiling watching the lines and patterns ever so slightly merge and melt into each other. He finds it so comforting, twenty minutes pass in the blink of an eye.

Still exhausted and desperately craving the remote control to his ancient artifact television, he must first begin the act of free-form writing instead. This is a time when his brain is brimming with creativity that he will use for his newspaper *Nihilist News*.

He pulls his wooden cracked chair out from his desk and turns on his old computer. The Suicide Machines spin on the record player. His fingers tap away endlessly while his brain is caught inside a hazy fertile daze trying to capture feral ideas and organize them into something that would yield a story or two, and thus pay his rent. Like a drug, he feels the effects start to diminish, so he quickly reviews his writing haul. Ten pages. He will trim it down and such tomorrow. Enough for now.

One final part is left, however. He plays the audio recording and haphazardly takes notes like a hungover college freshman. The audio usually doesn't yield much, but sometimes when he's mentally AWOL he will spit some supremely strange gibberish that finds a way into his newspaper.

He walks over to his wall. What once held paintings and a mirror is now a madman's journal. Today's session yields a singular clue.

The color white.

He looks at his wall and wonders where it fits in. Perplexed and confused as always, he walks away feeling like he ate a steady stale bowl of sorrow.

He sits down on his cushy black couch and stares blankly ahead. The Nintendo system is on his radar. He picks up *Bump 'n' Jump* and slams it inside the groovy gaming system.

Nothing appears on the screen.

Exasperation and irritation as he removes the game and blows on its insides for ten seconds.

Playing the game provides a break from the madness and a small sense of elation.

When his hands feel warped and achy, he takes a break. He scans his apartment for anything else that might occupy his mind. He grabs a Speak and Spell and touches a button. After a few seconds of the strange electronic voice, he begins to feel irritated and drops it to the floor.

He roughly handles a Mr. Potato Head doll and quickly rips its head off.

There is a collection of Snork plastic figures that did lighten his mood briefly from their irresistible cuteness.

He plays a Simon Says game for a few minutes until the game annoys him.

He picks up Rock 'Em Sock 'Em Robots and starts to play it until he realizes it's a two-person game.

Hungry Hungry Hippos proves to be a two person deal as well.

When his eyes meet with the Teddy Ruxpin, he knows there is going to be trouble for these dolls.

He grabs the Care Bear doll and with great fervor attempts to rip its arms out. Noticing his strength, or rather lack of it, causes the head to remain intact so he grabs a pair of scissors from the kitchen drawer and cuts the arms off and then stabs it over and over in the chest until nothing is left except white fluff all around him. He then repeats this action with the Care Bear and Cabbage Patch Dolls. His apartment mirrors a graveyard of eighties dolls and toys.

He is a man, not some child. He doesn't need these toys. How dare they insult his intelligence. He would remember this when he tracks them down. Let's see how they like playing with dolls and old-ass games as he creatively tortures them for what they did to him.

He feels mentally drained and would investigate the color white and what clue it could possibly yield, tomorrow. It was good to give each day a purpose and something to wake up to when living in a place such as this.

LIMITED EDITION

"Hey, it's Mighty, if you found this single copy of 'These Dark City Streets,' you can skip this chapter if you like, it does not involve you. Take a break and go outside and soak up some beautiful nature."

"Hey everybody, sorry to interrupt but please put down the book and listen up. So, you've had a chance to read some chapters and get an idea for what kind of book this is. I need to take a vote now. Please make sure you are honest with the response."

"How many of you think you might finish reading this book if you brought it back home?"

"How many of you think you might not finish the book at all?"

"Take a few minutes to think about it. There is no right or wrong answer, just be honest with yourself."

"Ok I have some bad news. All the ones who are not positive they will finish it, please give me the book and leave this room."

"What the hell Mighty, this is some weird bullshit, all we ever said was we wanted to know more about you."

"Yes, I understand, and I wrote this book with that in mind. The problem is the information contained here is sensitive and top secret so I can't trust people who may or may not read it."

"Indecisive people who have no willpower to finish a three to four-hour book most likely will leak information to the public without finishing the book and truly understanding the bigger picture of it all."

"It's not a big deal really, a lot of people are not readers anymore with Netflix coming out with new shows and movies daily. It's fine, whatever, I get it, I guess. After a long day of work, you'd rather watch Netflix that read."

"The two of you remaining please continue reading. You have four hours to finish and then I need the books back so I can burn them. There shall only remain a single copy of this book."

"You asked and asked for my background and here it is. There is a lot of serious highly confidential stuff in this book, so I have to be careful with who I allow to read it. I need to know you are not going to tweet about what you read."

"I know it's weird to present it in a book that you have to read while I am here, but that's how they do it on the dark side bitches! Sorry, you don't know about the creative dark side, yet. But continue reading and you shall find out and once you are done, we will have a connection and bond. I expect a friendship that will never cease. Blood brothers forever. Ride or Die. You get the point."

If you're lucky enough to have found the single volume of this book, I do apologize for the quick intermission, but like I said, I have to make sure the few people who read this can use their big brains to realize they should digest the material and leave it inside them and never try to expel it incorrectly with theories and conspiracies about stuff they learned from the mainstream.

That being said, whoever found this book, please be careful with it. Do not make more copies. Do not share it. Put it back from where you found it and let others naturally discover it from their curiosity and travels.

Please continue reading. I will do my best to not interrupt the flow anymore. Sometimes I will try and brighten the mood since things can get a little dark here. Shit, the book is called '*These Dark City Streets.*' Does the world really need another new art piece that's dark and depressing and only makes us feel worse about our predicament on this spinning planet?

So, I will do my best to add some humor and hope when I can. Just remember the sun will always shine if you allow it. Anyway, back to the story about who I am and how I came to be.

SKATE OR DIE

There was something about that sound. Wheels that are smoother than a baby's butt rolling and rolling against the crunchy crackle of seasoned concrete. As if every swipe of your foot against it, to propel the board forward, was absorbing all the souls that touched the same ground before you. The lungs act as a vacuum cleaner sucking in fresh air and aborting any toxic particles that snuck in through an unguarded exit.

Freedom has been defined and fought for since the second a cell was able to wiggle and waddle, but in my mind, skateboarding is the definition of what freedom is, was, and always would be. To be living in a land of 'do this' and 'do that,' skateboarding is one of the only things that gives me purpose in this strange plight I am on; the antidote to their ocean of rules.

I spend an hour working on a heelflip down a flight of three stairs at the local skate park when I hear my stomach gurgle and bark. I pick up my board and survey the surroundings. Darkness engulfs all in site at 1pm on a Tuesday in October. The concrete, trees, buildings, and skate park are all different shades of black. Smoky black. Raven. Onyx. Leather Jacket. Licorice. Black olive.

I try to rack my brain for the millionth time on how I ended up on the dark side living amongst this odd collection of humans, but I knew I would arrive at the same dead end.

Sighing deeply and feeling like I am an actor in a black and white film, I begin to crave a sliver of light that would hopefully act has a ray of hope to crush the clouds of gloom and doom that was rising from foot to head from living on the dark side.

However, the thought wind told me on the very first day.

"If one chooses to visit the light side, they will be considered a traitor and dealt with accordingly."

I wasn't terribly concerned about any repercussions since the dark side functions about as smooth has an engine with no oil. Where is the proprietor of this odd island? He who designed it is nowhere to be seen. When the substitute teacher is teaching, who cares about rules.

However, in the back of my mind, I ponder what the punishment would consist of? And if the thought wind is the one who enforces the laws, doesn't it need a physical presence to slap handcuffs on in order to conduct a trial?

Was I already being punished for something I did in another lifetime? Karmic debt and shit.

So, I pick my battles and only broke the rules when I felt I could no longer tolerate the isolation and agony of my blackened soul.

I ruminate about the previous day's thought wind session. The color white was pronounced and striking. Each blast of images centered around the dull shade. Was it pushing me towards the dreaded enemy mainland? I owed it to myself to investigate the color further and if punishment is walloped against me, I would handle it like a man.

I categorize this visit as a skate session in my mind in case I am mentally hijacked at some point and they find out I traveled to the light side for investigation purposes. Whatever happens on the light side will be used strictly as information in my quest to find an exit from the dark side. Do the work. Get the hell out.

There is a skate spot next to the river under an overpass that has a nice transition spot and curbs to grind that I visited a few times before, so I slap my board onto the concrete and begin moving towards the bridge that connects the light and dark sides. I have The Restarts blasting in my ears giving me extra confidence.

Arriving at the light side, my eyes always took a few blinks to become accustomed to the white, tan, and khaki that devours all in site. It reminds me of walking into a fifties ice cream parlor that only serves vanilla ice cream.

I skate the spot for an hour until my empty stomach finally withdraws its application to be a functioning organ.

I never really left that skate area before, not because I am scared of others opinions piercing into my soul and causing a ruckus, but because there really isn't any reason to. I didn't know of anything the light side has to offer besides it being light instead of dark. Which when I reflect on it, the light did seem to ward off that pesky pest called depression.

Perhaps that's why I skated this mediocre spot in the past? Like metal to a magnet, my body subconsciously knew it couldn't survive without some softer, brighter tones. My feet briskly move using the stomach and nose as the GPS.

A store with a sign plastered on the front reads 'Sunshine Smoothies' and my body decides to hit the brakes and park it's hungry pile of bones there.

The door opens and the menu is studied intensely. Nothing fried. No meat. No cheese. Essential food groups are missing in action. Puzzled and a little frazzled on what to choose, I finally randomly settle on a mango-pineapple-flaxseed-almond milk smoothie, along with a pomegranate peanut butter creme donut.

The line is long, and I stare straight ahead trying to blend in. When it's finally time to order, a cute but very plain girl mans the register. I fumble a little with my words but finally gain possession of them again, delivering an order.

I saunter down the street drinking my smoothie and am in awe of the flavors. Bright, zippy, and exotic.

The donut is next. Crunchy, smooth, and rich.

I savor each mouthful swishing it back and forth like mouthwash so all the flavors reach every crevice and corner of my mouth. But unlike mouthwash, there was no spitting this out, for it was swallowed and meant to absorb and melt into my cells and organs.

I feel invigorated, like a dying plant given water after days and days of roasting in the hot summer sun. Before I know it, I am already back on the dark side. Time passes without notice from the supreme slushy melty meal in my hands.

I passionately skate around the city the rest of the day. A set of stairs I always pass on, I land almost effortlessly from my cells soaking up all the beneficial nutrients from the smoothies.

As I walk home, I notice something shiny up the street that moves in my direction. I pause to gather my thoughts and figure out the threat level. I decide to move slowly with caution as it appears to be a man with metal legs. The closer I get, the more I am able to get a clearer picture of it all.

The knee area contains a skull with a wide grin. On top of the knee is a large gun pointing down towards the skull as if it's ready to blow it's brains out.

In the shin area, there is a large bayonet pointing upwards towards the skull like it's ready to carve some skull slices to make a sandwich with.

All around the objects is shiny metal creating a fantastically evil looking human creature. It walks with big, giant steps like a spider who is not comfortable with being a spider.

This is not the first time I witness metal where flesh should be. However, it is the most extreme. The times before, it was usually one or two feet of metal protruding from elbow or skull. This time, it's both legs devoured by metal mania.

I could never quite figure out what these wounded people's deal was. They didn't live anywhere I was accustomed to. Their speech is a jumbled mess. I assume this is what happens when you lose to the thought wind. Seeing the metal humans always serves to enforce the decision I made daily—never mingle with the voices in my head.

Empathy thick as morning fog plagues my mind as I reach inside my messenger bag and pull out a cassette player and headphones. I slap them onto the person's head and press play.

The human spider thing seems to perk up and find direction like a refurbished compass after being left alone in the corner of a dingy basement. A few times, they were able to mutter some words. Something about evil assholes and such.

I knew that I didn't want to end up like them, and yeah, it was risky giving them my main protection against the thought wind, a set of headphones, but my inventory of this item is strong so I felt it was my duty to give them any assistance I could. It was the least I could do as I feel like we are kindred spirits, except I am lucky enough to have all limbs still intact.

Each day I try to focus on core activities that I believe will help keep me sane and facilitate finding a way out of here. Skateboarding keeps me in shape and distracts my mind from blown out wild wacky thoughts.

Faith's existence makes me want to stay alive and start a future with somebody. Ideally her.

My wall of clues makes me feel like a detective who will not retire until he solves one last case.

These activities fill up my day fully but ultimately, I can't silence the curiosity about what everything else Sunshine Smoothies has to offer.

Perhaps I am getting sidetracked from my escape model with this amazing food, but Sunshine Smoothies isn't something I am willing to ignore quite yet. I didn't think the light side and their food would yield any positive results to help me get back my life before this blob of black, but you don't know, sometimes the smallest, stupidest things are the ones with the strongest highest yields and will help you escape.

I expect stares and glares from the light side people, but my first visit to Sunshine Smoothies was smooth enough that I felt I could visit again with no repercussions. It was like they were so anxious and focused on inhaling whatever Sunshine Smoothies has to offer, they didn't care if the creator of the dark side, Hero himself, walked in giving them his famous middle finger while telling them all the reasons they were inadequate and unsatisfactory humans.

I stroll out the door lost in flavor city with a pineapple-blueberry-strawberry smoothie with a double-Oreo-caramel-crunch donut when I hear somebody talking to me.

"Hey, how are you doing? Would you like a free sample of a potential new donut? I noticed how much you enjoy them, so I figure you would be the perfect candidate to give me an honest answer."

I remove my headphones and look around to see who is speaking. It's a woman who's demeanor presents itself as being management at Sunshine Smoothies. Feeling comfortable enough with the circumstances, I respond to her.

"Hey, yeah I'd love to sample a donut. You guys pummel all other bakeries."

I remove the donut morsel from her calloused hand and eagerly enter it into my mouth. I padlock my mouth and chew slowly as it is a feeling I want to last eternally.

"Stunning, no surprise. You guys bake art."

"Thanks so much for your compliments and business. We will make this donut then. My name is Molly and I am the owner."

"I am Nate, but people call me Nails. It's nice to meet you. Please don't ever go out of business or move. I would soak in a tub of sorrow for days, weeks, and months."

"Ahhh, ain't you sweet? How old are you Nate?"

It's a easy question. But one that I honestly just don't know. I look at the palms of my hands for some answer and knew if I wait any longer, I would be back on the dark side, involved in a one-sided conversation that is slowly driving me bonkers.

"I am twenty-five," I proclaim with a rusty shaky grin.

"My daughter, Corey at the cash register, is around your age, as well. She's a gentle soul who's very cautious and reserved so she doesn't date much. Would you be interested in hanging out with her?

"She's shy? She's beautiful."

"Come back tomorrow. I will talk to her tonight."

"Sounds good, thanks. You do know I am from the dark side though?"

"Yeah, I concluded that pretty quickly."

I could see my reflection in the glass resembling the man in black, Johnny Cash.

ALIVE & WELL

I pick up an extra smoothie for Faith to try. Instead of my normal walk that is tense and rigid, I move with the grace of a human who is not dead yet and very much alive and well.

"Hey Faith, I picked up this amazing food that's all chewed up like a mama bird does for its young. Have you ever had a smoothie before? I am sure you have. Stupid question. You have a perfect body. You don't achieve that without healthy food. So, what are you painting?"

"Hey, I am busy painting, how are you?"

I am feeling so good from the smoothie that I wasn't going to get depressed this time. My nerves relax and I watch my future soulmate apply paint to canvas. Her favorite thing to paint is nature scenes where animals have skulls instead of normal faces. This painting is squirrels with Day of the Dead skulls. She always gives the animals a different type of skull. Everything she paints is amazing.

I begin to wonder how she sold them since she really couldn't communicate. Or did she sell them? I didn't see any of the finished product lying around anywhere so I conclude they were sold somewhere. Maybe I could be her manager and we would slowly fall in love. At first, she would only see me as the manager and nothing else. Then she would slowly see how generous, kind, and awesome I am and we would all of a sudden kiss one night and be glued at the hip forevermore.

I hate how my mind would constantly make up scenarios like this but when you are alone with a brain churning and chugging seeking answers, it's bound to constantly happen.

The next day, I have a tough time concentrating knowing a potential date with a cute girl is on the radar. Sure, she is from the light side and it would most likely never go anywhere between us but I was sick of the dark side's half-baked rules and knew in order to stay sane, I would have to bend those rules, and if the bending broke me as well, so be it. Either I go insane or break some of their rules.

Plus, I feel I could basically do anything on the dark side these days. Authority is autonomous. The driver fast asleep behind the wicked wheel. Nothing had happened yet, breaking some rules here and there, so perhaps they are lenient in their beliefs. There are no police to make arrests—instead just the constant cloud of threats that loom in the sour air via the thought wind.

I decide not to skate in the morning in attempts to vanish showing up with a body lathered in droplets of sweat that would produce an uninviting odor.

Approaching Sunshine Smoothies, my body is mixed with feelings I rarely feel on the dark side. Optimism, hope and nervousness launched inside a blender, buzzing loudly like a motorcycle engine.

My attitude and mood on the dark side is a steady diet of annoyance and tolerance of the so-called utopia called home. Leaning heavily on the former.

I remind myself daily not to get wrapped up in the pleasure and vice and remember the first and primary goal is to find a way out of the dark side. Look at this rendezvous with a pretty gal as a way to gather intel like a squirrel gathers acorns. And not a black squirrel, but a normal-looking squirrel.

I take a deep breath, grab the door and pull it open. Does Corey know what I look like? Should I say something to her? Before I could make up my mind, I hear, "Can I help you?"

"Oh hey, yeah um, I will take a coconut lime donut and the paradise smoothie."

I think about saying more but my jangled nerves might stumble and trip and instead of coherent sentences it would be a befuddling tangled web of miscellaneous letters and sounds.

I take my food outside and let the sun shine its healing rays on my forehead and face. After fifteen minutes, I start to feel crestfallen. Then the door swings open and out comes the owner Molly. She is covered in flour and food ingredients looking like a crazy scientist of the food world

"Oh hey, sorry you waited so long. I gave Corey an early lunch so you guys could hang out."

"Cool."

Corey walks out wearing light blue jeans, a white shirt, and tan shoes. Even though her clothes are the dictionary definition of plain, the hallmark of the light side, she has an innocent pure glow about her that is sublime. Or maybe I am just happy to see a girl not wearing dark clothes and acting like they are the envy of the galaxy while barely speaking at all.

I instantly regret the statement about my dream girl Faith. I know that her afflictions along with everybody else's on the dark side is out of their hands. They are victims of a sick mind. If they could, they would break free and hang out with me and behave like people who are hip to cool shit and took pride in their communication skills.

"So, Corey, this is Nate. I mean Nails."

"Hey," she said, forcing a slightly awkward fake smile. Even though the smile doesn't appear genuine it shows that she is not close-minded about their date, which at this point feels like a victory. All I want is conversation with a real soul.

I respond back with a shaky but coherent enough, "Hey."

There is a mile-long silence until Corey says, "My mom gave me $40 so we might as well go get some lunch."

"Cool."

We wander aimlessly with Corey pointing out various establishments to shovel amino acids and vitamins into our hungry nervous mouths.

"What about a bar? We can sip on a beer and get a burger or something?"

"The light side is mega healthy for the most part, so we only have a few bars, none that are close," says Corey feeling like Nails must think her and the light side are so lame.

There are bars on every block of the dark side

"This place is pretty good actually; they have a nice selection."
"Cool."

I look at the menu. Everything comes with a salad or fruit or a superfood. I go with a cauliflower-sprouted-crust pizza with broccoli rabe and mushrooms.

I can feel a thousand eyes watching me. Their eyelashes trying to stab me in the chest with every blink. Maybe Sunshine Smoothies is like a neutral peace zone. Outside it, the people on the light side were less accommodating. I tried dressing less macabre, but all my possessions are different shades of black.

Then there was my middle finger. To live on the dark side, you have to tattoo your middle finger black to show praise to the leader Hero, then each day raise the middle finger towards the light side. On holidays it was done in unison with everybody on the island. I should have worn a band-aid over the finger.

Maybe I should have dyed my hair blond as well?

Why didn't I think this through more? These kinds of mental glitches would never rescue me from this bizarre prison. I need to be razor sharp with every action and move. Outsmart the enemy. Then when I taste the syrup-sweetened flavors of liberty and freedom, I could let the boxing gloves fall to the floor. But until that point, I have to over analyze every situation looking for potential potholes that could flatten the tires of this moving car.

When looking at Corey, I did my best to gaze at her with respect and admiration. I still am in awe that I am on a date with such a pretty girl from the light side. Even though the conversation is fuzzy and shoddy and seems to reside at the bottom of the barrel, to just talk to a girl or anybody feels amazing.

PUNISHMENT FOR THE UNKNOWN

How long had it been since I had a functioning conversation? An equal exchange of pleasantries.

I feel a slight ping of guilt betraying Faith, but no matter what happens, I would always have a special place in my heart for her. At the very least, I would eternally enjoy her art. But I knew we would be together soon enough.

This is all just a test to prove my love for her. But is it? Perhaps it is purgatory for a vicious crime produced in a past life. It is very possible it's a punishment since I am all alone and surrounded by humans who can barely communicate. It feels like a new age type prison invented by some guy with a fancy education.

At least I am not in physical pain. There is no torture to my body. Mental torture sure, but nothing physical. So in that respect I feel lucky. If I was in a legit prison there would be no freedom to create my own amusement and joy. I just need to become better at handling the obstacles that seem to constantly flash in my face.

Stop!

I yell at myself. Be in the moment, not lost inside again contemplating it all for the millionth time. This encounter will be over, and I will have spent the majority of time lost in thought.

"So how long have you worked at Sunshine Smoothies?"

"We opened up a year ago. Before that, I worked at a catering company with my Mom. It's nice to work with her and the food she makes is so delicious and healthy, I feel tremendous all the time, so it's not a bad deal," she said with a more relaxed tone. "Check this out." She stands up and climbs on a table and does a backflip.

I stare in awe of her acrobatic performance.

As Corey sit's down, she glances at me and see's a man puzzled at her strange random act. She knew this would happen. It was tough for her and other customers at Sunshine Smoothies to control their abundance of energy at times. She knew something strange was brewing and that her Mom was part of it, but when she questions her, Molly just ignores her. Corey doesn't have any other friends, so she can't investigate it any further unless she wants to risk eliminating her only friend.

"I know that was weird, sorry, I just want to show you that when you eat healthy all the time, your body is able to do amazing things."

"Wow, yeah, that was impressive." *And super weird, who does that? I shouldn't judge though since I come from the strangest place of them all.*

"Anyway, how do you like living on the dark side? It seems like such a cool, hip place to live."

Before I speak my brain ponders the statement—*I assume the dark side is portrayed as a fascinating place around the globe and that nobody really knows what it morphed into. I am so lonely and desperate to talk to somebody that I have to answer the question without scaring her away.*

"It's an interesting place for sure. An artist's paradise," I say trying not to sound guilty at my white lie.

"Since they only accept artists there, it's really cool to be surrounded by other people who share your same passions, you know? That was Hero's dream, to have a place where everybody is an artist."

"Yeah, I always wish I was creative enough to live there, but I have never been the art type. What is your talent?"

HERE WE GO AGAIN

Another brief interlude to dive into Nails thoughts? Isn't this becoming overkill? We get it. Isolation forces one to look inward and all that crap. On with the story, Mighty! Less you and more Nails! I agree folks, so I will just make this one short, okay? Compromise, the give and take that makes any relationship not sink or stink.

So, like I was saying, Nails thought about the word "talent."

The dark side is a breeding ground for those who have talent. Talent is not something he has.

He is an average skateboarder at best and his newspaper is juvenile bullshit. This is the one time where he is glad the word "fair" is not in play. He does not belong in a place that consists of only talented people. So, the question arises like the moon and sun, why was he here?

BACK IN BLACK

"I, um, skateboard and produce a newspaper."

"Oh cool, I was always curious how people actually got paid on the dark side? Since everybody does art, do you just buy each other's stuff or do you depend on mail order?"

"It's a little of both. Hero is big into developing new artists, so he tries his best to subsidize them until they can make their own money. As for me, since I am an amateur skateboarder, I make money with my writing. So, I am the owner of *Nihilist News*."

"What is that?"

"Instead of normal news, I tell a story and that story is the news. People come in from the streets to rant and vent and then I type up something creative."

I take a pause and know I have to tread carefully. The release of too much information and it will spook her, forcing me to return to watching Faith and becoming more depressed and anxious.

"Really? Wow, and you're the owner?"

"Yeah, I was always good at being creative and coming up with tall tales, as my teachers and parents call them, so when the dark side opened up years ago and I had nothing else showing any promise in my life, my parents pushed me to enter into the dark side's Amateur Artist Development Program and I was accepted. Then Hero liked my newspaper idea so much, I ended up being the owner."

"It's a pretty cool set up. I skate in the morning, then after lunch, people stroll in off the streets and we hang out; crack a couple beers and just talk about what's on their mind."

"I tape record the entire conversation, and if something interesting is discussed, I type it up for the paper. But it has to be creative and different from a normal newspaper. So, I type stuff up and let the people figure it all out. We don't have normal news here. Nothing is really normal. But in the past year or so, business has come to a crawl from the thought wind."

Ok, that was a whale of a lie. I never interviewed anybody, but if there were normal people or when people become normal again, that is the plan, so really it's just a future business plan. I did mention the thought wind, at least. My mind then wanders yet again to that day over a year ago.

HE'S DOING IT AGAIN!

At least my tangents are quick and kind of interesting? Don't worry we will get back to the meat and potatoes, but first, a little vegetables. Don't kale me!

Nails wakes up on a couch. He feels rested but thirsty. No headache or damage to the brain. A quick survey of his surroundings indicates he is in an apartment and water can be found in the kitchen.

He opens the creaky cabinets and grabs a glass. Suspicious of everything, he rinses the glass with soap to ensure it is properly cleaned of whatever could be inside it. He quickly downs the lukewarm tap water and can feel his body perk up like a plant that's been neglected and banished from water. He walks around the apartment for a few minutes and decides he needs some fresh air.

After only a few steps outside, Nails is transported into an old drive-in movie theater where he is sitting inside the driver's seat of a convertible car.

Machine-gun blasts explode in the air-blocking out all other sound as the screen appears liquidated and vaporized. But when the smoke clears, the act of senseless violence is really the dark side's way of conveying a message. The bullets form holes in the screen that read.

"Welcome to the dark side. A utopia for the creative mind."

He is then transported to a castle from the 1800s. A scroll appears in his hands.

"Always be creative and dress in black. Never mingle with the lame light side."

"Good things will come if you stay evil and dark. If you choose not to get a normal job, you will have to make money creating art. Submit your art and if your bank account becomes bloated, then we approve of what you are doing."

"Curious about how we have invaded and infected your mind? That's how we operate here. Deal with it. Nothing is normal. Why would anybody want to be normal? Normal is for the light side. Stay weird. Embrace it. Don't fight it. This is your complimentary welcome kit. Tomorrow will be different."

A few weeks later he was hungry and broke. Rage and Fury spun around inside him like a tornado. This made it problematic to slap on a fake smile and be a commendable worker bee. Procuring a job at a bar or any place else was probably not going to happen. He would have to embrace whatever creative tendencies that resided inside him.

After a few months or so, he knew good things would not materialize. It was a sick game by a perverted mind. They most likely convulsed in screams of giggles that generated a pleasurable buzzing in their brains courtesy of his complementary buffet of misery.

Refusing to let them win, Nails was able to find some value and pleasure in skateboarding. He felt free like a bird soaring in the sky when his feet were on that wooden board. All his worries faded away like the setting sun when the board was in motion.

He stumbled upon his newspaper, *Nihilist News*, after he decided to skateboard one evening with no headphones on and figured he would just say "fuck you" over and over in his mind so the thought wind could not invade.

When he got home, he felt confused and cornered. His plan did seem to work slightly but the thought wind was able to sneak in and ignite some mental grenades. He couldn't stop thinking about how much better life would be if there was no life at all.

While planning how to end it, his brain, in one final last-ditch effort, began leaking ideas and images. His fingers typed away as if he had morphed into a marionette.

So began the writing of a weird story about ping pong eyes. Upon completion of the strange story, he began taking pictures of the architecture around the dark side and pictures of art produced by Faith.

He stayed up for two days straight, surviving on adrenaline, cigarettes, and a newfound sense of purpose.

Suicide left the radar and was replaced by the joy of art.

Slumber so heavy a bear would be jealous, followed. During his twelve hours of sleep, his brain dreamed of wild scenarios and scenes but when he woke and began to make food, only two words were noted: Nihilist News.

He found the name fitting since the newspaper was created in a time where he hated everything and believed in nothing.

Not quite sure how to distribute the paper and how it would earn him an income, he dropped them off at bars and coffee shops and a few days later his bank account flashed three thousand dollars.

A smile crept across his face, something he almost felt guilty of since he wanted to maintain a steady diet of aggravation to keep him on edge so that he would never accept this as his home.

He tried writing the stories when he woke up or at night or really any time of the day, but they all came out stale and lacking anything interesting. He simply couldn't write the stories unless there was something desperate and hazardous wrecking his brain. He felt like a chef unable to cook food unless there was a grease fire spitting flames towards his face.

He did begin to enjoy being surrounded by creative things and being creative himself. However, when you are unable to share the magic of art with others, it can feel flat and frustrating.

RETURN

I am brought back to reality when I see a woman ripping a tree out of the ground. What is wrong with these people? Has the entire world now entered a new phase of delirium? I am glad the light side is able to communicate but they now appear to be far from normal.

"I always romanticized the dark side has a place for outlaws and rebels— like the wild west meets the twilight zone. Where if somebody gives you crap for your art you could destroy them and it was perfectly acceptable. Well, as long as it was done creatively," said Corey.

"Well, you are correct about art being the most important aspect of the dark side and human justice and well-being being number two."

"The biggest problem is this place has so many rules and constant suggestions that it seems to conflict with the concept of art. Art is about a free expression of ideas and the dark side is all about art but with extreme limits attached around it, like a spider web engulfing a mosquito."

"I can't stand it. I am a skateboarder and there's no rules in skateboarding and I am surrounded by rules. It drives me crazy sometimes! For example, I was told to never visit the light side, if I did, I would pay severely."

As if I could pay more than I do now, being surrounded by the living dead.

"They say you must always wear black. Even your socks have to be black! You have to do everything in a creative way. Brushing your teeth? Well make sure it's done differently than the light side. And your toothbrush better be black. Want to add some color anywhere, you better get approval. Oh, you want a cat or dog? It better be black. You want to open a business? It better be odd and strange. Milk, it better be chocolate milk.”

Ok calm down your ranting like a lousy lunatic lush.

I take a deep breath through my nose and out my mouth and continue in a more zen like tone. “So basically, be creative and think outside the box, but follow our rules and get approval first.”
“If they ever allow visitors over, I wouldn’t mind witnessing it firsthand.”
“How about tomorrow?”
Her perfect pale skin blossomed a rosy red at the invitation.
“Maybe, I will let you know,” says Corey, now feeling the pressure of what she said nonchalantly a few minutes prior. Not knowing if she really wants to visit the dark side, she gets defensive in nature. “But I thought the dark side has a strict rule about non-artists visiting?”

Shit.

“Well, the dark side isn’t exactly how it’s portrayed around the world. Things have been off lately. Skewed and slightly crooked. Like, imagine a person walking normally and then imagine them walking with a drunken swagger. The dark side is a drunken swagger right now. So that thundering gate with the big bold lock, it now swings back and forth instead of remaining locked in place.”
“About six months ago is when things started getting strange courtesy of the thought wind. See, the thought wind basically hijacks your consciousness to get what it wants. Nobody is quite sure what it wants.”
“Wow, that’s not good.”
“There are so many theories about why it arrived in the land of paradise, but from what I can gather, it’s the ultimate authoritarian dream. Total control over the people with no violence or police. No judge and jury. No prisons or death penalty.”
“Or maybe Hero installed it because people were always getting sidetracked from their art. Cell phones, internet, and tv. Instagram, Facebook, and Netflix. So, the thought wind was installed so people could focus on their art and be the most prolific artists ever, like Picasso and Banksy.”
Corey nods and gently smiles while I talk.

"I have been invaded by the thought wind many times and it's not exactly a pleasurable experience."

Careful with what you release.

"It immediately wants you to feel guilty about anything you have done that the dark side feels is not art worthy. So, if you're just doing your art and being a good person, it's tough for the thought wind to affect you too much."

"With that being said, every time you go outside you need to wear headphones. It has a really tough time competing with the music. And even if you are the perfect person in the thought wind's mind, it can still bring up very old things you did. It's very sadistic. It knows what you're thinking and uses it against you."

"Another theory about the thought wind is that maybe it was invented so people would listen to music more, since music produces dopamine and motivation."

Shit! Release of excessive information has occurred. You cracked a safe and now the cops are en route to bust your stupid ass!

Who the hell wants to hang out with a stranger they just met and then go to his home where their brain waves can be hijacked?

Ruined—the one chance at escaping loneliness. Back to stalking Faith, and eternal agony that was bound to crack me like a pack of crackers under the boot of a fifty-foot tall monster.

Calm down, at least you didn't mention the worst part. That the thought wind can easily hijack you via cell phones.

Corey's heart begins to beat rapidly and swiftly causing her face to show concern. A normal person would have run fast and far, but she doesn't exactly have a list of friends she can hang out with. In fact, her only friend is her Mom.

She silently stares at the boy in black while he talks. She listens and digests his words as she tries to figure out if he's cute or not. He looks to be in good shape, but when one wears all black, it can hide things. He has a handsome face and Corey can see that face being pressed against hers, with lips locked and not being turned off by the idea of it.

"So, I would just have to wear headphones. Sounds simple enough, I pretty much do that right now, anyway."

I feel a burst of energy again when Corey doesn't rule out visiting my sadistic twisted home.

"The first few times you visit the dark side, write down what you're here for and where you're going. Then constantly look at what you wrote down and repeat it over and over. After a few times here, you will learn how to focus on the music and your brain basically adjusts to how the dark side operates."

"Right."

"Make sure you listen to music you can sing along to as well. If it's catchy and the rhythm and bass are infecting your soul, the thought wind has no chance of getting you because good music takes precedence over everything— even powerful brain thoughts being flash flooded inside your skull. If it's not catchy make sure to focus on the instruments or the emotion and vibe the band is emitting."

"Gotcha, yeah."

"For example, say you are going to the movie theatre and you have directions written down and your brain tells you different directions and suggests you do something else. Most likely, the thought wind found a way inside like a pesky rodent and it's now ready to lead you elsewhere."

"Stupid rodents."

"Now, I will meet up with you once you get off the bridge and through the gate, so in that regard, your fine. But if for some reason we get separated, I want you to understand how the dark side works as of late. I am sure any day now it will go back to being the normal artists paradise."

I doubt it though.

We eat our food and make some minor conversation when Corey looks at her watch and says she better get back to work.

"I will text you tonight about tomorrow."

"Sounds good."

STRANGE MESSAGES ON THE SCREEN

I hope that my cell phone still works as I turned it off months ago after the endless text messages kept coming from who the hell knows where. Well, it was the thought wind. But some humans had to be sending them to him, right? Or was it a division of the thought wind, like when a company starts another company?

He thought about the first time he got a text from "them."

"Bees will get drunk if alcohol is available and the bouncers at the hive will refuse to let them in until they're sober."

"You know, I thought my family was a little kooky and crazy until I met yours. I can't imagine having your DNA. Your brain constantly turning sour thoughts into action. Real bad action, too. Stupidity at its finest."

"Who the hell are you and what have you done to my family?"

"Calm down, spaz. Did you know banging your head against the wall burns 150 calories a day? If you want those perfect abs for your girl, it's something to consider."

"Fuck you, where am I?"

"Pteronophobia is the fear of being tickled by feathers."

"I hope you choke on some feathers."

"Now, now, like I said, calm down, spaz. Can't we have a civilized conversation like the gentlemen we are?"

"That's fine with me."

"If you lift a kangaroo's tail off the ground, it can't hop."

"I thought we were going to have a real conversation."

"Pardon me, where have my manners gone to? Right, so let's talk. Why don't you come outside with no headphones and we can talk without that silly phone."

"Fuck you, I am not stupid."

There is a species of spider called the hobo spider. Now, come outside and try and find that spider."

"Like I said, I'm not stupid. That loser piece of shit thought wind will just infect me like the coward it is."

I throw my phone against the couch where it hits the cushion and bounces off as if telling me this will not end as simple as just pulling a plug.

DESIGNED FOR FAILURE

"So, how did it go?" asked Molly, assuming it would be a disaster or the light side people would deter Nails from ever coming over again by throwing an avalanche of stares and dirty glares at the forbidden enemy.

"Congenial."

"So that's all you're going to say?"

"He invited me to the dark side tomorrow, actually. I just don't know if it's a sterling idea."

"Corey, I love you more than anything, but you need to break out of your shell."

You're the reason I am so shy, what you do to me, she wants to scream from mountaintops.

"Fine, I will text Nails that I will meet him on the dark side. You do know about the thought wind, though, right Mom? It could electrocute and eradicate my very existence. Is that what you want? Your precious daughter to meet her fate in front of a guillotine like a gooey goon?"

"Corey why are you talking so weird?"

"I wish I was weird like Nails. I am just trying to break from my shell and not be so boring. Isn't that what everybody wants from me now?"

"Well, yes, sort of, but you don't have to talk like that. Anyway, didn't Nails say he would protect you and give you guidelines on how to remain safe?"

"He did, yes."

She had set up Corey with a guy from the dark side knowing it would backfire.

#1 Set Corey up on a date
#2 Shows you care about her being an ordinary traditional girl who goes on   dates.
#3 Have it be with a person who it will fail with
#4 Poison the well; aka make sure your daughter does NOT date anybody
#5 Things will go back to the way it was, which is needed.

Molly needs Corey to work as many shifts as possible, since she didn't think anybody else could be trusted. People were already suspicious on why Sunshine Smoothies gave them so much energy. The more employees, the more chances of somebody sabotaging her legit business that, in her mind, wasn't doing anything really harmful—just serving up fun food that isn't necessarily conventional.

It was vital for the plan to be successful to keep her business afloat. She couldn't have Corey be dating anybody, let alone somebody from the dark side. Time to act on #4.

"Well, I do understand if you don't want to go, Corey. Like you said, it's potentially dangerous."

"Whatever, I will just go then."

"Corey, I think between the thought wind and this boy you barely know, it's best to avoid the dark side. I could set you up with our flour supplier, Jake. He's handsome and seems very into you. Plus, he doesn't have his middle finger tattooed black."

"Oh, so now I should just go back to being a hermit, Mom? You always mention Jake, but when I talk to him, he seems to only look at my chest and nothing else. Total creep. I will just go, maybe the thought wind will give my boring life some excitement."

"Corey, I forbid you to see Nails. If you love and respect my authority, you will delete Nails' number immediately."

But Corey is already briskly marching away with a newfound sense of self and purpose.

Corey drives her car and parks it near the bridge. As she is walking over the bridge, the first thing that catch's her eye is the two-hundred foot "Statue of Hero" painted in all black giving the light side the middle finger. She smirks a bit as she focuses her eyes on the badass Statue. It is basically identical to the Statue of Liberty, but it is giving the finger to the light side and of course it is all black. It sparkles and shines the way the sun walloped it this time of the day.

She is approaching the end of the bridge so as a cautionary act she put on her headphones early. She isn't a huge music fan but knew that Nails was really into punk so she creates a mixtape of the pioneers of punk she discovers on the internet. She thought the Ramones were the catchiest, while the Misfits seem like they would be the soundtrack to the dark side.

As she exits the rusty gate, she frantically looks for Nails. Her eyes dart in many directions to find the weird cute boy in black. She keeps telling herself once she gets past the iron gate, she would not do anything else, for that could be the thought wind trying to get her.

She has written on a piece of paper, "I am here to meet Nails and Nails only. I do not need to do anything else."

She studied lyrics the night before and was doing her best to remember the choruses so the thought wind could not crack open the safe and rob the mental bank.

As she begins walking towards a bench, she couldn't believe everything really is all black. The trees, the concrete, the buildings. Even the squirrels—black!

Her heart begins to accelerate, causing the palms of her hands to sweat when a text message comes in reading.

"Did you know no matter how ticklish you are, you can't tickle yourself because your brain is expecting it and processes it differently?"

"Let me ask you a question, who the hell do you think you are, coming here? Use that cute little brain of yours and go back to where you came from before it's too late. Or else the only art you will be making is your blood and guts on the concrete."

Her entire body erupts in goosebumps. She is so caught up in the moment, she forgots to just stare at her note and not engage in a mental war that she would surely lose.

"Hey, be nice, I am not causing any harm. I am here to visit your beautiful creative town," she responds back with.

"You're really starting to piss me off, you know that? Why don't you follow my middle finger and we can settle this dispute there? Did you ever find out if breast cancer even runs in your family like your Mom told you all the time before she stole your breasts?"

Her shaky fingers punch in, "My Mom wouldn't lie to me. You don't know her or me. So buzz off."

"Like I said, which you're too stupid to digest, come to my finger and we can discuss this over dinner. Wear something cute, too. In England in the 1800s, pants were considered a dirty word. So, no pants. Show some skin."

She gets more and more annoyed at her phone and contemplates smashing it. As she waits for Nails, her phone buzzes and burps in her pocket. She doesn't want to get caught up in this head game, but curiosity is her new vice that she quickly surrenders to.

"So what fruit will it be next week? Do you think that was the start of your problems? No friends, live with Mommy. Never been on a date. Or maybe that's what you always wanted. You think you're going to hang out on the wrong side of the tracks and that will cure your ails? Bitch, welcome to Hell. Either walk home now or prepare to die."

Goosebumps shower her entire body and invade every cell like an amphetamine-laced group of soldiers whose commander is persistent and resistant. How did this thing know such secret information about her?

She is a stranger in a strange land. Lost and falling apart mentally, she is shaken from her requiem with the words, "Hey Corey."

Oh, thank god, she tells herself. She runs and gives me a hearty hug.

I can tell she is shaken up.
I remove one of her headphones.

"Are you okay? You can remove your headphones for a minute. It takes about a minute for electronic winds to cross the blood brain barrier and start messing with you."

She removes her headphones and immediately a creepy scant electronic buzz flows in the wind. As she opens her mouth to speak, it feels like the thought wind is inside her mouth coating her tongue and perhaps getting a little frisky.

"Yes, sorry, I am fine, this is all just a little new to me." She doesn't want to mention the text to Nails, as she is already broadcasting to him that she might not be able to handle the dark side.

"Ok good. Yeah, I know it's a lot to take in. I mean, even the water here is black."

They both turn to the large volume of black water as it sways back and forth like a drunk at last call. It is the most eerie thing Corey has witnessed as she is so accustomed to the bone white that is the hallmark of her side. It feels like all the darkness in the world was collected and dumped into the river. If one is to swim in it, they would instantly become the most wicked person ever.

What had she gotten herself into? She should have just gone out with Jake and lived a simple good life working with her Mom and eating the best food ever. Instead, she volunteers to date a guy who lives on an island of black where you can get your thoughts hijacked.

As she said that to herself, she did feel a tiny thrill pulsate through her body telling her brain that playing it safe, and knowing the future, one that will be boring, is not the path to travel.

"How about we go for a walk? It's a nice day out."

"Sounds good."

I really enjoy taking walks but walking and talking is difficult with the damn thought wind. Every time I am about to stay something, we both have to pause our music and move our headphones behind our ears and make sure the conversation is brief and airy and under a minute.

As we are walking, instead of being present in the moment with Corey, I retrieve inwards unable to stop my reflective brain.

Living like I did, with headphones constantly on, feels like living in a world and not wanting to be a part of it. But that is not the case here, I yearn to be a part of it, but everything and everyone seems designed to make that impossible.

I commit an act of social alienation every time I slap the headphones on, but it is a necessity and I do feel like I am in control of the situation knowing I have several back up pairs. Being able to control my environment to a degree, by choosing to block out the thought wind's corrupt sounds, does empower me.

I dream of a place where humans walk and talk with no headphones. During a thought wind session, it showed me a city where there were no headphones needed but people still didn't know their neighbors and hide inside all the time watching TV or playing on the computer.

It does scare me a little, that when I finally do escape the dark side, my new home would consist of this kind of anti-social behavior. I pray that does not happen. Everyone should know their neighbors and value camaraderie over technology and isolation.

I have to find a place like that to live.

VINTAGE IS NOT HIP IN THIS SCENARIO

"The gargoyles on various buildings have zero meaning. They just look cool. The more you observe about the dark side, the more you will notice endless things that are far from pragmatic. The island is designed to look hip and operate in a way that's completely opposite from how the light side operates."

"It definitely is opposite."

"As you can see, the entire vibe here is vintage with a film-noir atmosphere. I do dig it, but when it's July and ninety-five degrees at 1pm and your city still looks foggy and dusty like the basement of an ancient antique store, it can be a bummer."

Corey nods in awe of her new surroundings. So accustomed to her assembly line consistency that living on the light side provides her—when that uniform is ripped off, leaving her exposed and raw, she surprises even herself when she feels vivacious and animated at the idea of something newfangled.

She is shaken from her pleasant daydreaming when a ventriloquist and his dummy seem to burst out of a building. Both are dressed in suits with newsboy hats like they were from the 1930s.

As they continue walking, more and more people seem to be leaking from buildings. They all have the same markings as the buildings. Corey could feel fear invade more and more cells in her body. Was she hallucinating? The thought wind must have got to her. But she doesn't hear voices. Or is it the thought wind telling her this?

She tries to reach for Nails, but he seems just out of reach each time. Then the side of a building randomly crumbles beside her and runs away. She saw it with her own eyes, that building ran away!

With tears running down her face and on the verge of fainting she is finally able to grab Nails. He quickly hugs her and removes the headphones from her right ear and says, "Don't worry, you're fine, it's not the thought wind. Let's get to a safe building."

We enter a thought wind-safe building. It is $30 for each of us to enter. I could feel my blood begin to boil paying $30 just so we could have a conversation without our minds being hijacked. Whoever was responsible for this would be hunted down like a hungry shark who spots a soft, oily, chunky, succulent seal and tears into them leaving nothing remaining except the color red.

Immediately, I ask what happened.

Wiping tears from her face, she says, "The buildings were just, I don't know, they were moving and jumping and falling apart and then running away. It was the most terrifying experience of my life."

"Oh no, I am so sorry, I didn't see any of that to warn you."

My phone then beeps and before I have a chance to even unlock it, a video pops up along with a bunch of words. Then a text message appears *"Together we could be a great team."* I try to ignore what this all means and explain to Corey what happened. I decide to use the video and words that just appeared since I have no other explanations.

"Let me explain. What you just experienced is a troupe called The Falling Buildings. They're tattooed to look like buildings. It's one of the most extreme art forms on the dark side. Anyway, they randomly assemble in the morning to look like a building and then they just arbitrarily fall apart and it's supposed to be one of the coolest, hippest art forms right now."

"Wow."

"Since you were not expecting it, I could see how easily that would invoke terror upon you. They were falling out of those buildings just feet from you. So crazy. I am so sorry I forgot to mention that."

I grab my phone and show her the video that was just sent to me to prove I am not just bullshitting her.

"Wow, they really are tattooed to look like buildings," she says with a smile as serotonin replaces cortisol in her brain.

"Yeah, the dark side is obsessed with art. So, you're used to walking down the street with no issues. Well, the dark side finds that to be humdrum, and since it absolutely must do the opposite of the light side, it strives to make your walk be hip."

"So The Falling Buildings is a performing arts troupe that gets subsidized by the dark side. So that's their profession. Once they can make money on their own merit, Hero will stop paying them and look for other upcoming artists to replace them. Look at how well they blend into buildings. Newer buildings are actually built with them in mind so they can easily blend into them."

She couldn't believe how talented they were.

A fresh text message invades his phone.

"Inviting a guest to our home without approval what 40% of women have hurled footwear at a man."

That is a first. It was like they were about to say something and got interrupted. Are there two people sending these texts, then? It's like one person does the serious ones and one person, the so-called funny ones.

"So anyway, what is this place?" Corey inspects the cafe and it is not what she is used to at Sunshine Smoothies or any place in general. She feels an ominous feeling creeping up her spine.

"It's like a coffee shop but you have to pay to enter since its thought wind proof."

"What I really meant was why is there no menu? Instead people get their palms read?"

"Everything has to be creative and different. So, in Hero's mind, an ordinary coffee shop is boring and something to be found on the light side. He won't let that kind of thing operate. In order for this coffee shop to open, they had to get Hero's approval and apparently he thought having a psychic predict what food is best for you, along with predicting your future, is creative enough."

We both impersonate sloths as we trek towards the psychic as all we want is some peace and quiet, not a prediction on the rest of our lives.

We position our palms facing upward as the psychic commences the activity. After a few minutes of our palms getting gently touched, a pack of tarot cards is presented.

The psychic asks me to choose one. I spend twenty seconds looking at them and finally select a random card.

The psychic looks terrified. She starts to tremble a little and then begins a wailing of words. It isn't a language we know, but the intensity and magnitude of the tone portrays it as having significance. She then picks up a double chocolate brownie along with peanut butter cookies and hurls them against the glass.

As we bolt from the cafe, Corey takes a quick glance back into the coffee shop and notices two men subduing the woman.

After getting far enough away from the coffee shop, we both stop running and look at each other in shock over the bizarre incident.

"Wow, that was crazy! She read our palms and it was all fine until the tarot card caused her to short circuit."

I reflect upon what Corey said. The physic saw the tarot card and it shook her from whatever state she was in. Which means there could be hope for Faith returning to her normal self. However, it would have to involve something colossal. Something so influential to jar loose the current zombie-like state and remind her that she is a human and not a subhuman.

"What language do you think that was?" asks Corey.

"Sounded Italian. Did you hear the word run, as well, at the end?"

"You know, I think I did, so she was telling us to run," said Corey.

"Well, can't say I am surprised, the dark side is a conundrum. Did you happen to see what tarot card you picked out?"

"I kind of remember it, yeah. Let me look on my phone to see if I can find it. Oh shit, this is the one. It's the Fool. It means a new beginning."

The thought of this makes all the hair on my arm spike up like a mohawk.

"So that's cool at least. This is your new life or something," said Corey.

"Yeah, I guess."

IT AIN'T HARD LIVIN' IN A GRAVEYARD

Voluminous drums and bass enter the ears and shoot directly into the brain, suffocating any outside voices so Corey and I would glance at each other repeatedly in attempts to feel like a single organism instead of two distant ones. It was important to use your other senses when your ears were preoccupied soaking up sounds so the visual side of life becomes something we have to embrace more and more.

We approach a large stretch of flat land where endless epitaphs peak out from the ground. I shuffle past the graveyard hoping Corey would not comment on it and want to stop. The more curious she becomes the more she would grasp the reality that the dark side is a discombobulation of hodgepodge and the boy in black's brain is a version of Jekyll and Hyde. She would discover it's in her best interest to abandon both without hesitation.

The less she knew about the dark side, the better.

The quicker she trusts me, the better.

I am an admirable person. I am positive about this.

I recognize that the more we hung out and click into place, like a key into a lock, the more she would accept the dark side because she would grasp the bigger picture of them jiving well together. We would build a future and be the cute couple in black who wore headphones all the time. But my aspiration slightly shatters when she pauses and her feet get stuck in the concrete slabs causing her to not go anywhere.

Then those pretty little lips uttered, "This graveyard sure is strange."

Great, here we go. Curious like a kitten.

She steps over a weathered iron fest with ease and enters the graveyard. I reluctantly follow behind.

"I can't believe they would disrespect the dead by painting the grass and tombstones all black," says Corey.

"Well this isn't a real graveyard. See, look."

I am easily able to rip an epitaph out of the ground. They even have dumb dark side slogans written on them.

"Dark Side Never Say Die."

"Light Side are babies that cry."

I grab another from the rain-soaked grass, "Hero Is Our Hero / The Light Side Is Full Of Zeros."

"Black Is The New White."

I chuckle a little at how stupid this graveyard is. What purpose does it serve? If I am pretty much the only true soul around, the graveyard would thus have been created for me? It just doesn't add up. Which sounds about par for the course.

As we are leaving, Corey casually goes to grab an epitaph out of the ground, and when she went to yank it, it doesn't easily become separated from the dirt. This is not a pseudo one like Nails has lectured her about. She wonders how many other real ones are mixed in? She is about to say something when she notices I am already on the street pacing back and forth impatiently waiting for her to get over this and just accept that the dark side is simply a strange place and the less you question it the smoother your life will be.

I move at the pace of a slug down the street. I don't want to appear like a jerk but also want Corey to give up her fascination so we can move on with the evening.

As Corey is leaving the graveyard, she doesn't pay attention and bumps into another person. She goes to remove her headphones to apologize when I dart down the street to prevent a wayward conversation with these so-called humans.

We stop at the first bar we see, dreading the interiors and what strange tone it would occupy to satisfy Hero. Corey reminds herself that she would stay strong and trust that whatever happens—Nails will protect her.

We open the door and it feels like we are swallowed by moving darkness. Waves of black invade, covering every crevice and corner of the interior.

"So, um, what is this one about?" inquires Corey, somewhat dreading to hear the response from me but also feeling like she is prepared to handle it.

"It's called Ink and Drink. You get a tattoo while you drink. However, I am sure you already know, it's not as simple as that. When you enter with more than one person, then you have to tattoo each other."

"Yeah, no thanks, I just want to relax, and plus, I can't tattoo."

"Well, see, the problem here is that once you enter, you can't leave until you have some ink on you."

She surveys her surroundings and feels like a rat in a cage. An internal alarm blasts sirens that bounce off each organ like a pinball inside a machine.

"I know this is the most extreme of stuff so far on the dark side, but we can just do small tattoos, it will be fun."

"Did you know we were entering this place?" asks a slightly annoyed Corey.

"I did, but I wasn't paying attention, sorry."

She did believe him and decides to just deal with it.

"So, how do we decide what to tattoo?"

I have no idea, so I walk up to a table and grab a tattoo gun. I then grab a few beers. The less Corey interacts with the drones the better. We sit drinking a beer when a person stops over and drops off an iPad so we can watch a video about how to tattoo. After the video we both seem to say at the same time, "So what are you going to tattoo on me?"

"I don't know. How about we take the next twenty minutes to think about it?"

"Ok, sounds good," says Corey.

Twenty minutes later we both have our ideas ready.

"Why don't you go first?" I tell Corey.

"Remove your shirt."

"Give me your arm." Thirty minutes later there was a new tattoo on the inside of my upper arm.

"It's a nail, I love it! You did a great job."

Corey manages to smile a little. But still a bit on edge about the wicked needle that would dig into her skin by an amateur with little to no training.

"Ok, give me your leg, please."

An hour later, Corey see's four black bars on her ankle.

"What is it?"

"It's the symbol for Black Flag. They are one of the first hardcore punk bands and have a cult following. Even if you don't end up liking their music, just having those four bars is a message to the world that your a free thinking badass who will fuck shit up!"

She chuckles and gives him a light jab on the shoulder.

"That was kind of fun," she said.

"Let's go get some coffee, I am exhausted after this."

After finishing half the assorted snacks, I take a sip of coffee and say, "Your Mom's food has spoiled me. This now tastes subpar."

"I know, right? Like, this stuff tastes stale when it's obvious it was just made today. My Mom's food really is unparalleled. But to achieve that kind of superiority, it sucks all her time up. I think she might be a perfectionist or something."

"So what are your hobbies Corey?"

"Well, I like to exercise a lot. Run. Swim. Walk. Bike ride. I like reading books and eating my Mom's awesome snacks. How about you?"

To my knowledge, that is all the light side cares about. Being healthy and enjoying nature. Not creating anything. They did seem to have energy and strength that is extreme. They probably used that strength to kick Hero out. I can picture some woman in her forties picking Hero up like a baby and walking him over the bridge and dropping him off.

I could see why Hero had such a distaste for the place, being such a creative mind as he is. They just seem so abnormally healthy here. I remember the first time we met and how Corey randomly performed a backflip. That's not something you do on a first date.

"That sounds like fun. Skateboarding is pretty much my only hobby. Well, and creative writing. I already told you about *Nihilist News*."

"How long have you been skateboarding for?"

I dig around my brain for the answer but as always end up chasing ghosts. I wasn't really good, but I could do some tricks down some stairs, so I must have started at a somewhat early age.

I recall when I first started skateboarding on the dark side. I was having a particularly frustrating afternoon. The type of day that felt like entering a jump-roping contest using your shoelaces. The constant rules were overwhelming causing a feeling of suffocation. I needed an outlet that was independent of all these rules. I wandered the city listening to music that would make me want to skate—Street Dogs. Cock Sparrer. Pennywise. Blanks 77. Lagwagon. Career Suicide. Agent Orange. Kid Dynamite. Dag Nasty. Bars of Gold. Mischief Brew. Bad Religion. Destruct. Pears. Concrete Elite. Days N' Daze and Off With Their Heads—singing their loud, robust choruses or harsh melodies—when I saw a skateboard park and, like it was coded in my DNA, I bought a skateboard and it's been my trusty sidekick ever since.

"Since I was eight. I wish I could go pro, but skaters these days are so gnarly and always pushing the limit. I could never be that good."

I point out the window to a building across the street and say, "A skater would ollie off the top of that building onto the street without a second thought."

"Well, luckily you like your job, at least."

"Yeah really, good point."

We finish our snacks and coffee. We both are wired from the coffee, so I suggest we get some more beer to counter the caffeine. I hope this back and forth of caffeine and alcohol doesn't cause me to get all unbalanced mentally—we seem to be having a good time—so I will just have to cope with whatever side effects show up.

SKULL MUGS

We stop at the nearest bar while Corey explains to me that she is not a huge drinker and will need to be careful. I tell her she can drink a light beer slowly while drinking water as well.

"I will take an IPA."

I looked over at Corey. She just stares straight ahead paralyzed about what beer would best suit her.

"And a session IPA, too."

We walk a few feet to a small table where Corey again feels a strange sensation brewing in her soul sensing this place is the strangest yet. I sit down without hesitation while Corey is skeptical of the sitting situation as it looks like we are sitting on the scales of an animal.

Light pink, bony, and smooth. It briefly reminds her of pink lemonade that Sunshine Smoothies sometimes served. Knowing she has to just suck it up, she finally reluctantly sits down. The scales poke at her butt.

I return with the beers only to disturb Corey even more.

"Gross. What kind of glass is this?"

"You're drinking out of what looks to be a skull of some sort. Not sure the origin."

"Is there another bar we can go to? Why the hell is the beer served out of a skull and the seats made out of animal bones? Oh I think I just answered my own question. It has to be creative," she says with a slight annoyance of the current establishment and its use of skulls as mugs. She enjoys the dark side being so off-the-wall different, but there were some invisible lines you don't cross and the dark side seems to cross them more often than not.

"Correct. So, this particular bar also doubles as a kind of a museum." I hand Corey a pamphlet that describes the bones and skulls used in the bar.

She quickly glances at the pamphlet. She might be sitting on the bones of a Woolly Mammoth.

Not impressed, Corey stares at her skull beer and then back at Nails. She doesn't want to look weak, so she forces a sip down. I am sure the skull is clean she convinces herself.

"This is pretty good, what kind is it again?"

"It's called a session IPA. I am drinking an IPA now. You're drinking a lighter version. Then there's also double, triple, and quadruple IPAs. Here, take a sip."

She takes a sip and her face cowers and cringes.

"Yeah IPAs take some time to adjust to. It's a good sign though that you enjoy your session IPA. It means, in time, you will progress to a normal IPA followed by a double IPA."

"Is this place thought wind proofed, then?"

"It is, yeah. They don't charge you an entrance fee either. Bars are very popular on the dark side. That can also be a problem, though, because the easiest way for the thought wind to get you is after you are drunk and forget to apply your headphones to ears. So, you have to monitor your intake. That's another so-called benefit from the thought wind. People are more careful about their alcohol consumption.

But beers also cost ten dollars each. I am going to be out of money by the end of today at this rate.

Corey feels great after two beers, and without hesitation, orders a third. I am on my fourth IPA and feeling fantastic. We both give the finger to the thought wind and order beers as if it never existed. Conversation is steady and abundant. We share stories and I am able to make things up on the spot when it is called for. I don't want Corey to get sick from all the beer, so I suggest we call it a night.

As we are leaving, Corey sees a rugged, faded, wooden sign buried in the corner that resembles an epitaph reading "Junkie Bones." Her swollen brain tries to register it as it bumps into its skull like an overstuffed subway car. She then blurts out, "Can we go to the graveyard place we passed earlier?"

"Sure," I say feeling slightly annoyed at her request.

We enter the gritty graveyard that is not like any graveyard built before.

Corey's boozy brain thinks about "Junkie Bones" again and begins kicking some dirt around with her black shoes.

"What are you doing?"

"I don't know."

She keeps kicking the dirt and then drops to her knees and begins digging into it like a punky possum. She adjusts her head upwards to notice me watching her with a slightly worried look. She stops and stands up brushing the dirt off her face and jeans and quietly mutters "Sorry about that, must be drunk."

We leave the graveyard and wander back to my apartment. Corey walks over to the couch and flops her drunken bones onto the black couch.

I look over my record collection which consists of close to a 100. I've been trying to collect as much as possible lately to keep me occupied. Each new record entertained me for a full week. Looking at the artwork, the lyrics, and then listening to the warm mahogany-rich sounds a record generates. I am looking for something mellow and when my fingers touch *Dear You* by Jawbreaker, I knew it was the right album for the occasion. I sat next to Corey and when I look at her to say something, she begins kissing me.

It had been so long since I had touched another's flesh that I want it to last forever. First the shirts come flying off, and then I seem to notice something odd protruding from Corey's bra. The alcohol overrides my suspicion and dictates my hands to attach to fabric and remove. As I clumsily fumble around, Corey stands up with tears in her eyes and crosses her arms over her chest in an attempt to prevent me from seeing something that could potentially cause discord and dilemma.

"Nails, I really like you, but there's a reason why I am the way I am, socially. I just want to warn you so you don't freak out."

"It's cool, I promise I won't be a jerk." I stood up, as well, and touch her hand in a supportive manner.

"Ok thanks. So, I don't know how to say this really, but my breasts are grapes."

So that's why they always looked so perfectly round.

She studies my face for a response to see what kind of man I am. I don't say a single thing and begin kissing her again. Her bra drops to the ground and I begin touching the grapes. They feel so smooth and warm that I become overzealous as one of them becomes loose and falls into my hand. An empty vacant space appears before me. I began touching the other grape breast knowing I shouldn't but I lose all discipline. We continue to make out when the other breast falls, forcing Corey to try and save it from hitting the floor and thus forcing a separation of bodies and skin.

"Why do you have fruit instead of breasts?" I ask, trying to act casual and concerned instead of drunk and rude which would cause her to feel even more self-conscious.

"My Mom says breast cancer runs in the family, and if I removed my breasts it would save me from potentially going through chemo."

"That makes sense, yeah, but how did you get grapes to grow?"

"I don't really know. My Mom has me take some pills and drink some stuff. Next time she said they will be strawberries. They change every few weeks or so. In the past they have been apples, oranges, pears, tomatoes, and pears. She says when the fruits grow, they absorb any potential cancer cells."

"Wow, that is really wild. You would fit in perfectly on the dark side, ya know? Doesn't get more creative than this."

"I guess, yeah." She then covers her face in embarrassment trying not to cry. A minute later, she removes her hands from her face and puts her head on my shoulder.

I try my best to stay calm and not erupt into a volcano of hate. I finally meet a real soul and her breasts are fruit. Somebody is fucking with me big time. I should have known nothing would be smooth anymore. I have to expect obstacles and challenges at every turn.

I survived so far in this creepy land being self-employed, which is something I never imagined was possible due to its ups and downs. Then somehow, I met a girl from the enemy mainland who seems to like me. If I could overcome all those obstacles and stay upright instead of drowning on my back, then I would not let something like fruit breasts defeat me. Every failure is an opportunity to learn from defeat and become a stronger person.

The booze begins turning into melatonin and after such a crazy hour we crawl into bed and instantly fall asleep.

DEAD END

"How did it go, Corey?"

"It was so embarrassing! I hate you so much Mom!!"

"Would you just grow up already? You look flat, where are your grapes?"

"Nails ate them. He said they tasted disgusting."

"Sweetheart, I only want what's best for you. Now where are your grapes? You know I need to inspect the harvest for cancer cells."

"Don't have them. Told ya, already. Nails ate them. Said they were disgusting. He said whoever grew them is a loser and they should never be allowed by law to grow fruit again and should have to get a real job and be a normal mom. He said a lot of other things too. I will text you later as I remember them."

"Corey, I don't like your attitude. I really need those grapes to dissect them."

She storms off leaving a pair of grapes on the table. They began to roll off the table when Molly bolts over just in time to catch the precious valuables.

Corey flung herself on her bed and stares at the ceiling. Immediately she thinks about junkie bones. Could there really be a person buried in the graveyard? Nails said it was all just the normal dark side vibe of slapping black paint on stuff and doing the opposite of what the light side does, but could he be lying to protect me? Or is somebody lying to him?

It's like somebody put that sign where the employees wouldn't see it for a few days or weeks in hopes that somebody else might notice it and investigate it.

She reaches her phone and types in "missing persons heroin crack meth." Endless webpages shower her phone. Feeling a bit overwhelmed she takes a deep breath and begins clicking on each page. An hour later she couldn't believe how destructive hard drugs have been on society.

This is a dead end. She has to physically remove dirt and debris to see if there really is a dead person decaying before she could move forward on whether it was worth investigating.

SINISTER BREWS

Nails knows the time has come to write another edition of *Nihilist News* since rent is due and with the dark side being so expensive the hundred dollars in his wallet would only last a few days especially if he continues hanging out with Corey.

If you want to have a girlfriend, you need money, he told himself. At least while living on the dark side you do. He dreamed of living elsewhere, where things were cheap and he could work a normal job and live a simple quiet life.

Whoever he was selling *Nihilist News* to, their demands are somewhat strict. He couldn't just sit down in front of his computer and knock out a story. He tried that a few times before and his bank account never registered a chunk of cash.

He knew failure was part of life, but thoughts of violence and destruction still spun around inside his skull that his hard work was being rejected. He so desperately wanted to see them or it or whatever face to face so he could pounce on them, ripping throats to shreds, that he ripped of his headphones one day ready for an invisible battle against an opponent he couldn't see.

With his headphones removed and fists in the air, a physical person never appeared. Instead, the thought wind enters his brain and spun a strange tale.

Skeleton hands type on a typewriter. Body and limbs missing and absent. After it was done typing, the hands remove the paper and when Nails eyes focus on the paper it erupts into flames.

It let loose of his brain and he was able to scurry back inside his apartment like a scared rat. Lesson learned. Subpar stories will be rejected.

So off the wall ideas and stories that were supremely weird was the only solution to his cash quandary. He just didn't have those ideas built into him or he wasn't motivated enough to spawn them. In any case, like corrupt sports athletes, he needs a little boost. Letting the thought wind invade him was his version of steroids.

He always dreads this part of his existence the most. But if he wants rent money and a girlfriend and to avoid the fate of others who couldn't afford anti-thought wind gear, it was a necessity, for it was excellent at generating ideas and gave him news about the dark side, and possibly, it was giving him information about his old self.

He goes to his closet in a irked mood and removes his bag and poster board. In a rushed annoyed fashion he sets up shop. He removes his headphones and tenses up in anticipation.

At first, the thought wind, being a predictable foe as it was, would suggest meeting under the middle finger to talk things over.

Nails had walked to the Statue of Hero many times with headphones on and it appeared to function and resemble a normal statue. However, he knew there was something sinister brewing inside.

The thought wind then enters his cerebrum, cerebellum, and brainstem to harvest memories to blast him nonstop, trying to create a narrative that would want him to go to the middle finger. The middle finger was always the central theme. It was so predictable. Go to the Statue and middle finger with no headphones. Get there, and they could talk. They would solve all the problems there.

He would never accept that proposal. He needed to crack open the safe and get the hell out of there quickly before the cops want to arrest him. He constantly thought about that analogy while living here.

"These are really good. Relax. I am not eating your girlfriends breast grapes. Because I already ate them a few minutes ago. There were only two of them and I am a big fella. They were tasty I must say. You showed great discipline not eating them. A true gentleman you have developed into. Well, minus the anger issues. You are pretty much the angriest guy I have ever seen."

"Wouldn't you love to just reduce all the complexities and complications of life? Live next door to Faith. Have simple conversations about art. It's a real easy solution. Just remove the headphones and let's party at the Statue of Hero. 2pm. Let's do it."

Hero is now doing some weird dance and he eventually begins to melt away into two bowling balls. Another statue appears, picking up the bowling balls and applies them to their chest. The new Statue's skull oozes steam as black spaghetti sprouts and grows like human hair as it morphs into a real woman.

The bowling ball breasts then turn into eyes blinking over and over. The woman rips them off her chest and begins eating them.

Nails can see the insides of the Statue. It is filled with purple eyes. The woman sticks her arm down her own throat to retrieve the eyes and instead pulls out globs of black spaghetti. She put it on a plate when two tarantulas appear on the plate and act like meatballs.

She twirls the spaghetti hair with a fork and punctures the two tarantula's. They scream with anguish.

Two black birds violently swarm the woman Statue. She grabs the two birds and bites of there heads and tosses the bodies to the ground.

Tarantula heads grow on the birds bodies.

Nails watch's in horror as the new species tries to function. He shakes and shakes until he wakes.

BLACK LUNGS & SILENT TONGUES

I review the thought wind session for clues. The two is interesting, because when added to the end of the other numbers in the thought wind hijacking, it reads 2690, and last week, there was the street name of Calumet I had written down. 2690 Calumet Street I repeat over and over. Hoping the thought wind was not bluffing, I proceed to investigate 2690 Calumet Street. If such a street even existed. My brain says to find a map and I oblige.

I walk to the local library which is five miles away. The walk feels refreshing but also works up a sweat. I hope there is a water fountain inside. I open the door not in the mood for any bullshit and find it all dark with candles everywhere. A sign reads:

Let the books do the talking. Hush Hush Keep it Down. Black Lungs and Silent Tongues.

Two librarians appear dressed in dominatrix outfits wearing gas masks slapping their rulers on palms in a sexual manner.

I can feel a feeling I don't like churning inside me. Can't some things just be normal here? Everything has to be bizarre at every twist and turn.

I walk around for an hour until I find a map of the town. I open the dusty antique and mutter a quiet cough.

A dominatrix librarian appears and removes a ruler and slowly taps it into the palm of her hand, as if indicating she would be using it in a sexual manner if I continue to make normal human sounds.

I fight the urge to run towards her and grab the ruler, snap it in half and with the sharpest edge gouge it into her eye. Then when the blood runs red instead of black, I would punish her by saying "Bitch's blood ain't even black, what a snitch witch dumb bitch."

Then I would gouge her other eye out and bury her in the plethora of books. The ultimate punishment. Surrounded by the things you love with no way of embracing them. Payback for what I currently feel while living on the dark side.

But then my brain reminds me that these are dominatrix librarians so they would most likely enjoy this punishment.

Goosebumps pop up like a bag of ripe popcorn when I see the address is legit and within walking distance. I fold up the map and eagerly walk to the location from the brain rob.

PERFECT PEOPLE

It is an all-black building. Signs of a functional company a thing of the past. My heart drops like an elevator after aging cords finally snap.

However, resistance to failure flows up my esophagus like a bubbly burp as I turn my attention to the dingy dumpster.

Digging through the noxious objects, I stumble upon a paper that reads "Perfect People, LLC."

All I pluck from it after reading the entire soggy stained dead tree is that they made computer chips at one time. I dig around further until the smell becomes overwhelming, forcing a hastily departure.

Walking home provides ample time to review what I discovered. I put in the new Daughters album I just got and turn my cassette tape volume low for a quick minute to fully concentrate and ponder over the new findings.

Computer chips. Perfect People. Faith and others acting like robots. Did Perfect People install chips on the people from the dark side so they could focus entirely on art? It seemed like a realistic conclusion. Why was I the outcast then? How could every single one succumb to it but me?

Maybe they volunteered and I was the only strongest-willed one to say, "No thanks, I don't want some creepy chip inside me denying my animal urges and desires. Vices and virtue would not be removed causing a human void of emotion. The rollercoaster that is the human existence is part of the journey. I want to feel it all. The terrible lows and glorious highs."

NIHILIST NEWS

A few days later, I return to the light side for a skate session and to meet up with Corey. This time, I bring an edition of *Nihilist News* that is my favorite. I know the stories are dumb, but I want to at least bring Corey a copy to prove I am not lying about them.

"How was skateboarding today?"

"Yeah, it was fun. Great weather. So, I brought a copy of *Nihilist News* for you to check out."

I give her a brief rundown first.

"The front cover with the black cat who's fur is spiked out with a oversized skull face is a painting by Faith. She's a talented artist and friend of mine, so I use a lot of her art in Nihilist News. Then I go around town taking pictures of other stuff and develop them at the camera store."

Corey holds the newspaper and carefully scans it over. At the top is "Nihilist News. Your source for off the wall news and analysis."

Corey flips it open and the first page has WAR then another page has WITHOUT then A then WAR on each page. Followed by another of Faith's paintings. Then the feature story titled "Ping Pong Eyes."

Corey begins reading it.

Culo launches spit at the time clock and hopes it finds an empty spot to register his name. Saliva splash's on plastic, clings to it, and begins to trickle down to the floor with the rest of the workers' spit, forming a puddle. It reminds him of a bunch of clouds that gave up. With identity theft on the rise, saliva was now used as a form of identification, causing puddles to pool around time clocks, ATMs, and gas stations.

The punishment for getting caught stealing one's identity was being locked up in a public place for two days straight while everybody in the community spits on them. They were given no food or water, as well. Identity theft dropped eighty percent from this new gross law.

His daily prison sentence is finally over. Another day wasted earning dead trees. As he exits the building, the fall foliage imprints a tattoo on his eyes. Those electric colors. So bright, so mesmerizing. There's a park close by that will continue this visual orgasm.

Culo paces around the park, looking for the perfect spot to park his body. He finds a crumbling bench that appears to be on its last leg of existence and decides it's the ideal spot to witness more of those righteous orange, red, and yellow swirling colors. Usually he put on headphones, but today, his entire focus was on the epic fall colors.

He was soon lost in the east coast's best season, the colors reminding him of dive bar signs burning through a rainy night. They pop and rumble like fireworks in his brain, burning brightly against the dull shades of black and white buildings.

After an hour of this technicolor show, he gets back into his car to continue his journey home. But wait. There's an ingredient needed for his sinister evening. He drives north. Dilapidated buildings litter the street, causing Culo's heart to beat a bit faster and beads of sweat burst through his skin, only to live for a few seconds.

He parks his car and immediately the chaos begins. A person with a pumpkin on his head is running down the street, while another person with a bat chases him. The bat hits the pumpkin. Pumpkin shrapnel lies around the fallen human. Holy fuck, thinks Culo, is that Eddie?

The man gets up and appears fine as he walks towards Culo.

He says, "Hey man," as if what just happened is perfectly normal. Eddie is a squatter that inhabits one of the buildings. They had met during college and became friends due to liking the same bands. They were both obsessed with The Clash, Rancid and Crass. After graduation Eddie ended up choosing the life of dirty floors and rotten teeth while Culo chose the life of landlords and bosses. They still hung out here and there, at the occasional punk show, but for the most part their relationship had become more of a business transaction. Culo pays Eddie as they discuss an upcoming show briefly. They then go their separate ways.

When Culo gets home, the party begins.

Beer and Meth. And lots of it.

Instantaneously, he is taken far from sobriety. He starts frantically flipping through his records, taking out the ones with rad artwork and giving them a thorough stare down. Remembering the late drunken nights, he would play the records loud, seeing the band live and how those words and images had helped him through some rough times. He grabs some vinyl that will be listened to that evening—Nowherebound. Enzyme. Fried E/M. Snuff. C.H.E.W. Goddamnit. The Hold Steady. Authority Zero. Suck Lords. Catbite. Chubby & The Gang. Doc Rotten. Better Oblivion Community Center. Those Poor Bastards. Millencolin. Grade 2. Extended Hell. Starving Wolves. Be Like Max. No Use For A Name. Cro-Mags. No Time To Waste.

A loud noise awakens his dog, putting him into a barking frenzy. The noise is Culo throwing his empty beer bottles against the wall in reckless abandonment.

He puts on some porn and turns up his stereo. A mixture of moans and songs about unity filled the room. Culo dumps all his stash on the table for easier access.

He stumbles around his apartment looking at everything, trying to snap mental pictures of it all. The toxic rollercoaster in his brain makes it painfully difficult. He grabs a few porn magazines haphazardly, flipping through them and then returning to his records. He tries to block out what will be done shortly with nostalgia about his life prior to work and bills. It feels liberating to think about the good ol' days.

An orgy of chemicals run rampant in his body. 5:00am flashes on the clock across the room. What the fuck is going on? His apartment is cluttered with booze, drugs, porn, and vinyl.

He reaches into his pocket for his smokes. He opens them up and notices an odd one. It must be a joint! "Fuck yeah," he thinks. He removes it and grabs his lighter, excited to get even more mangled up, mentally.

Instead of a joint, it's a rolled-up piece of paper. Culo unrolls it and it reads *"ping pong eyes will expose all lies and make the man with the tie fry and cry"* Huh? He thinks blurrily to himself.

His body begins to move and tells his brain not to worry, to enjoy the buzz. Culo then goes apeshit when his favorite song oozes from the speakers. Screaming as if he's in a dingy Jersey basement circa '78, whipping sweat at the crowd with his devil lock, screaming the chorus with so much intensity his vocal cords become raw from the rage.

The next thing he realizes, he is in his room fumbling for two ping pong balls. He then goes into his kitchen and seizes an ice cream scoop from a drawer.

Excruciating pain and blood. One eye out. Numbness spreads.

Second eye out. Fingers slick with blood pick up the ping pong balls and insert them gingerly into vacant sockets.

His brain flashes a memory of youth. Hanging out in the woods. Hiding above the train tracks watching the trains skedaddle like scared rabbits with no worries or burdens.

He calls for his dog and a taxi.

Culo tries to chug a beer but the movement of his skull is a relentless fury of torment and misery.

Arriving at work, Culo isn't even sure what day it is.

His boss says, "What the fuck is this, Culo? How many times do I have to tell you, we're not having a 'bring your dog to work' Friday?!" Ahhh, so it is Friday... "Now, get him out of here and get some sleep, your eyes don't look right."

Culo retaliates triumphantly, "This is my seeing-eye dog! I lost my eyes an hour ago. So not only will he be here Fridays, but every day!"

Quietly, Culo thinks to himself, "if that asshole would have just let me bring my dog to work on Fridays like I requested, all this could have been avoided."

Before the next story begins, I added some more art with some slogans. Each page has one of these words. NEVER SURRENDER NEVER GIVE IN. Along with some artwork. It seemed to give the newspaper some well-needed bulk to it. Corey then begins reading another stupid story of mine.

I never really gave a shit about the afterlife. Why ponder and mull something that nobody has yet to shed proof of existing? When I think about it, I figured you died and that's that. And God, if he existed, kinda sucked for making alarm clocks.

So when I did die at age 36 from a heart attack after learning Ignite finally released a new album and it was all Acapella—I learned there was an afterlife and it was a wee different then what I thought it would be if it existed.

The first thing I heard after dying was somebody shouting, "I love drugs!"

I look around and see a ten-million-person orgy. At first, I thought it was a dream. A pretty badass dream! But then a man approached me and said, "Hey dude, welcome to the best damn party in the world. There's a drug table over there. Feel free to smoke, drop, inject whatever you want, and go grab a hottie to get your groove on with. I'm Van Vanilla by the way, the proprietor of this joint!"

I decided to take a stroll and see if any other stuff is happening. It took a full day to just walk past the million-person orgy.

When I finally pass it, I encountered an ocean of cell phones with people swimming in there as if it was a legit ocean with waves and jellyfish. A guy tells his buddy, "You surfed that iPhone wave mad crazy good, bro."

"Thanks, brah. I thought I saw a shark on one of those Blackberries, so I just made sure I had my anti-shark app installed, and I was good to go."

I didn't stay long at the ocean of cell phones since it was fucking retarded. I continued my stroll and then started seeing things flying through the air. It is food. 'Welcome to the Crew Cutters Food Fight' the sign read. It is thousands of people throwing food at each other while Van Vanilla runs around singing his awful generic lyrics. I seriously couldn't imagine anything worse than this. My stroll turned into a sprint to get far away from the scene.

I stop running when I see on the horizon different colored bombs on the road. "What now?" I thought, getting annoyed at my new "home." They were beach balls where potholes and sinkholes were in the road. So instead of fixing them, they just put beach balls in there. "This place is insane," I thought.

I couldn't mentally handle the beach-ball road, so I randomly start to walk into a meadow. The grass is about 3 feet high, and after ten minutes of walking through it, I began to hear chirping sounds. Is that crickets? It keeps getting louder and louder until I am surrounded by thousands of chirping crickets. They all stare at me while releasing their orchestra of sounds and then one speaks to me in an Australian accent.

"Hey mate, can you tattoo a tribal armband on me?"

I was not expecting the cricket to ask me that. I respond with, "I am not a tattoo artist and tribal tattoos are the worst ever, you don't want one of them, only meathead sheep get those."

The cricket tells me that Van Vanilla had told him that they were hip. Figures. Van Vanilla is probably the architect of this entire place. That guy is the worst.

I decide to keep walking through the meadow. I hated my new home. I should just go find the million-person orgy.

After 5 hours of searching for it, I finally found it. I take my clothes off and went to touch a chick when she asks what my favorite Crew Cutters song was. I told her, none, they're a terrible band. "Sorry," she said. "No endless ass for you, then. We're all huge Crew Cutters fans and you have to love them to join our orgy."

I was beyond furious at this place. I went to the ocean of cell phones and began breaking all of them. People started screaming at me like I was killing a real live thing. I didn't care, I just kept breaking them until I was exhausted and sore. A beautiful thing, I thought, as I stared at the carnage that surrounded me.

For a year, I wander around encountering stupid thing after stupid thing. I look angry and felt angry. I broke whatever I could and yelled at everyone I could.

I saw an old building one afternoon and just aimlessly walked in with nothing to lose. I saw a tall lamp near the door that I was planning on smashing when a man with a curled mustache approached me and said, "Before you walk any further, what's your favorite Crew Cutters song, young fella?"

I thought about his question and how my last answer cost me endless ass. My heart raced. My hands sweaty. "Just say, every song," my soul said. "You can't continue along this path of anger and alienation." But I just couldn't admit such a thing. I said, "None, I hate that fucking band. Let me guess, I can't come inside now and have access to a mile-long buffet."

He smiled and laughed and said, "We fucking hate that band, too. Welcome to your new home."

A hundred years later, and life was great. I would wake up and read in complete peace and then partied with all my Crew Cutter hater friends in the evening. I even met a girl who I think hated Crew Cutters more than me! We got along great. All of us did, really. Every day, I was so glad that I didn't lie and pretend to like that shitty band.

VAGUE LIKE A VIKING
AFTER VATS OF VODKA

As Corey reads it, I think about how trivial and idiotic my newspaper is. It is creative yes, but who likes this? Or maybe they just make fun of me while reading it. I began to get infuriated again. Calm down, I tell himself. It can't be healthy to be this bitter all the time.

Deal with the cards you were dealt like a real man does. Figure out how to leave this place and don't just wallow in self-pity. Millions have it much worse than you. This was all true, no doubt. However, there was one humongous difference. All these people were at least surrounded by others who could communicate more than just a few pre-selected lines. At least they can talk to others, even people in prison can, well, unless they're in solitary confinement.

"So, this guy just wants to bring his dog into work and his boss repeatedly says no?"

I let her words resonate for a minute. Did I desire bringing a dog to work in my life prior to the dark side? Was Culo somebody I knew in a previous life? Who was the man in a tie who wanted to fry and cry? Could I piece together my past life through these stories? I suppose it was possible. But it was also possible that whatever thoughts my brain was telling me were not mine. They were just implanted and not retrieved from my brain. I felt a rush of cynicism, yet again, at having to cope with this bullshit.

What did I do to deserve such punishment?

Maybe I lived in the future and committed a crime and this was a virtual reality punishment and I was really just in a chair right now in an air conditioned room while a qualified person in this arena monitored me to make sure all is well.

My brain is constantly entertaining different scenarios on why I was alone in a city of black.

"For the other story, did somebody approach you about how they hate a popular band? Well, I mean, you pictured somebody discussing this issue with you?"

"Correct. Colossal hatred towards this band for their generic music and brainwashing society into thinking you were strange if you didn't like their terrible music."

"So, it's telling people to think for themselves and come to judgements about things with their own brain and to reject mainstream narratives."

I wanted to kiss her for understanding my art, and I did, since nobody is really alive in my mind.

"Yeah, everything has to be creative and different on the dark side. In the past, somebody would have told me this story, but nobody really visits me anymore. They are scared that if they talk about anything other than art or complain about stuff, it will give the thought wind more ammo. So, I had to make this one up."

"Yeah."

"Screw the thought wind. I am not afraid of it. I know who I am. Even though it's really good at hijacking your consciousness, I am even better at flipping that shit and tossing the thought wind out of my brain like the worthless bum it truly is."

I try to act, ironically, tough as nails, to impress Corey. To show her that she doesn't have to be apprehensive about the thought wind and doesn't have to constantly figure out if it is really worth it to hang out on the dark side, for I'm an able-bodied and enlightened dude that would protect her. That was the plan at least. For better or worse.

"Every few weeks or so, I drop a newspaper off and they deposit money into my bank account. Once a month, I receive some feedback. It's generally positive. A few times they told me simply 'try harder.' They surprisingly pay me enough so I can afford all my bills and then have some leftover for groceries, beer, fun, and all that stuff. So I can't complain too much in that regard. Getting paid for my stories is pretty badass."

Of course, they also reject some of them. Forcing me to fry my brain via the thought wind. Bastards.

"Who are they? Like can I order a copy of it?"

Who are they? Great question. One that I have asked myself a thousand times. But I just didn't know. The thought wind told me to get a real job or do something creative and you might be able to get paid. It's good I didn't know anything more or else I would spend the rest of my life making sure they lived a life of bad luck. I envisioned constantly fucking with them. Popping their tires. Random attacks causing broken noses. Broken windows. I don't want them to die, but to experience the day in and day out misery that I felt.

"Yeah, I am not really sure who they are. I don't need to know either as it seems like a good enough set up for everybody involved. They like the stories. I need cash. Everybody wins."

"Well, I really like your strange newspaper. The dark side is such a stimulating place, well, besides the thought wind."

"They have all the right ideas about being creative and offbeat and all that, but something isn't genuine here. Balanced conversations don't exist. If I tried talking to a friend like we are now, at some point real soon, they would change the subject to art or music, which is fine, but it's not smooth, it's with this panicky feral way."

"Ugh."

"I don't get it. I mean, maybe it's the lack of light? The thought wind? The black ash? I definitely get the annoyance itch as well, so I try and leave the dark side as much as possible to remain sane."

Soon she would find out their communication skills are limited like the menu at a steakhouse. I just need to do a supreme job at delaying this discovery.

Debilitate the details.

Decaffeinate the coffee.

Bend honesty like metal under flame.

Vague like a Viking after vats of vodka.

Shit, then there's the thought wind perverts who are mostly likely the mob and never miss an opportunity to make a quick buck at others expense.

I bumped brains with a guy who was loaded at a bar once and he disjointedly explained how they force artists to march the city streets with no headphones.

They hook them up with audio and visual. The audio sounds like a paranoid schizophrenic as they battle with a foe who can't be defeated.

These clips are mostly sold to musicians who produce industrial music as it adds a whole new level of realness in their already intense music. As for the visual it always goes black at some point.

Static replacing clarity.

Then days, weeks, months later, they return with a metallic limb. They figured out a way to have the audio and video linked to a website so they didn't need the devices back. It generated a plumb income for the underbelly of society workers.

If I fail at this mission of limiting exposure of these obstacles from Corey, then it's back to watching Faith and praying each day that she and the others snap out of whatever trance they are in. Unless Corey is okay with all this and finds it thrilling. Too much of a risk to hope she lands in that camp, however.

"So, what should we do?" asks Corey—shaking me from being stuck inside my head pondering it all for the millionth time.

"Oh hey, yeah um, the weather is so inviting today. Do you have a park nearby we could hang out and have a picnic at?"

"Indeed we do, Mister Nails."

"Nine Nihilistic Nails.

"Nail the Nimrod."

"Nifty Nails and the Spider Snails."

We both laugh large at Corey's ramblings.

As we strut our stuff on the concrete slabs, I tilt my head when I spot something uncanny.

Black crows on white buildings?

Panic invades like doors opening on Black Friday. Hallucinations must be causing this vision. Too many battles with the thought wind is now causing me to see things that are not there. Should I announce what I see like a sports announcer during a game so I could assess whether I was officially losing my mind?

"So *you do* have some dark over here," pointing at the birds.

"Yeah, they have been here for the past few weeks. Sloth crows we call them. They don't seem interested in flying in the air like a kite. It kind of feels like they just stare and judge us. I don't know what their deal is. It's pretty creepy, really. A lot of people believe it's a prank or some experiment from the dark side."

"They look so out of place amongst all the white and vanilla. Do you think people will try and get rid of them?"

"I don't think so. Not sure if you have noticed, but we really only care about being healthy on the light side. So when the black birds show up on white buildings, we just continue along with our day. The dark side is the one who started this feud. Yes, we also contribute to the problem by removing any dark colors here. Anyway, the light side has a lot of people who are big on animal rights as well. So even though they throw a wrench in our gears by adding black to the white, nobody will do anything about it. We're too busy living our lives instead of fighting small wars."

I study the birds. It's possible they flew over from the dark side. It wasn't a long distance. Animals migrate all the time. Especially birds.

Maybe they share my affinity about craving a color and atmosphere that is opposite of what they currently witness all day every day. It feels like going to another country and having your native meal prepared for you in advance, so you don't feel homesick. I study them further. Are they brewing something sinister? Impossible. They are birds with bird brains. They don't inflict harm intentionally like the bigger-brained humans do.

I brush off their presence like crumbs on a plate. These birds will not be an obstacle that derails my moving train. Every cell in my body is full of strength and stamina from connecting with Corey that I would not let broken wings break a dam I spent so much energy building up. The tides are turning. No more salt in the mouth.

We hunker down on a sturdy, rusty, brown bench holding hands bathing in the prime weather.

"This is the lights side's beloved season. The sun is shining from an angle where you don't have to take notice of a two-hundred foot Statue giving your homeland the middle finger. Five months from now, if we want some sun, we will have to face the statue."

"Sorry about that," I say with a slight smile.

Corey begins laughing and then kisses me on the cheek.

"You know, once Hero put up that Statue, everyone on the light side basically wanted him on trial for every injustice on earth. They could accept the island being turned into a dark ink spot, but he really crossed the line when he had the middle finger facing us. Honestly though, it just makes me laugh every time I see it. He must have really resented the light side to put that up."

Corey thought about that statement and wondered if there was any truth associated with it. Did they care at all? How could they? They seemed to only care about Sunshine Smoothies and exercising. Her mom, when she reflected upon her character, maybe shouldn't be trusted blindly simply because she was her mom and best friend.

"He was, or rather is, a passionate guy from what I know about him. Heart on his sleeve. Live and die for the creation of things. Growing up all he ever heard was that he couldn't have a career in art. But once he got a sunglasses advertisement deal it made him substantial cash."

"Sunglasses?"

"Yeah, he searched the internet for pictures of the ugliest animals and then used a program like Adobe Photoshop and put sunglasses on them. Some of the animals he used were the naked mole rat, blobfish and the vampire bat. Then put sunglasses on them with the caption of 'Sunglasses Online. Turning cute faces even cuter.' Everybody loved it so much, he was in high demand from other companies. Once he was a millionaire, he then quit the commercial art business and focused on developing young talent and creating an artist's utopia."

Corey reached into her pocket and Googled "Hero's sunglasses" on her phone.

"Oh wow, there's so many ugly animals that now look less ugly because of him," she said with a loud robust giggle. I release a loud chortle as well.

As the sun starts to fade away like an old photograph, Corey casually mentions crossing the bridge and entering the island of black. Her intentions are slightly narcissistic for the dark side seems to have ignited a burnt out flame inside her. When she visits or thinks about the dark side she feels alive like being hooked up to an electric outlet and plugged in—her legs bouncing and bopping nervously like she is dancing on a table during an Oktoberfest celebration.

GOTH MARRIAGE

As they exit the gate, Corey soaks up the new visuals that devour everything in its path.

Dark chocolate, fig, and nicotine colors invade and conquer all in sight. Some color did peek out from the shadows, but it was usually from the black paint falling off, showcasing the former colors. All the humans are dressed head to toe in black. Some variations of black at various places on their uniforms did appear such as grey and dark blue.

She walks past a building and catch's a glimpse of herself and what she sees is a person who looks miles away from her previous plain self. A wiggle of confidence pulsates through her body like a worm on a rainy day.

She wants to remove her headphones and battle the thought wind for a few minutes, to give it a heads up that Corey and Nails would not let some non-human entity break them, but she forces herself to silent the adventurous side that is aching to escape.

They march on the black concrete holding hands as black ash splashes on various parts of their body due to a strong wind. The paint job, most likely performed by amateurs in a quick fashion, caused it to rain down black ash when the wind did what wind does. Perhaps that was Hero's vision? It did look badass. Corey imagines they are a goth couple who requests black ashes rain down from the sky after the officiant introduces the married couple for the first time.

"Get your ears tattooed black."

"Learn how to breathe black fire from your mouth."

"A free guide to creating black toothpaste."

She observes the kooky chaos around her with a confidence and assurance that she is not a visitor but instead an occupier.

We stop at a bar and order beers.

Corey glances around trying to figure out what bizarre theme this bar would be. After a few minutes she gives up and decides to engage in conversation.

In the corner of her eye, she sees a faint image of a lady with a mohawk and leather jacket who floats through the air with majestic grace. She rubs her eyes assuming exhaustion has caused visual lies even though she feels rested and in the right state of mind.

The mohawked lady floats towards her.

Corey stands up and screams, "Ghost!!"

In a normal bar, patrons would have glanced up at the screaming human but nothing was normal about the dark side, so her outburst causes no alarm.

Nails rises quickly in concern.

"Corey, calm down, this is the theme here, it's a ghost bar."

"Oh, okay." She feels a sudden relief like losing your wallet in a crowded space only to discover it seconds later.

"My fault again, I should have prepared you."

"So how did this happen?" she says with a slightly shaky voice.

"Well, from what I heard, she was a die-hard punk rocker and wanted to be the most creative person who ever lived on the dark side. So, she studied ghosts and figured out how to become one."

"That's so crazy."

"Yeah, so to be a ghost, you can't plan your murder. She needed somebody to actually murder her for real. That is super tough because it's just artists living here so nobody is really into jealousy and all that. So from what I heard, she had sex with a couple of woman's boyfriends and husbands and one of them got drunk one evening and hung her from the ceiling."

I have no clue if this is the truth or not. But I didn't see any harm in a white lie if it opened a locked door and let me out of this black bone-headedness.

"Oh, my God."

"Yeah this place really took Hero's vision to the next level."

"And Hero was okay with that kind of behavior?"

"Apparently, yeah."

A PLACE LIKE NO OTHER

"I just can't believe how much different it is here compared to the light side."

"The dark side is designed to be a place like no other. It's all about the art and attitude. Swagger and sway. Hero designed it so that every person who lived here is creative."

"He grew up loving art, music, and literature, but so few people around him shared his interests. They made fun of him instead. He always told himself if he became successful, he would design an artist's paradise. So, everybody on the dark side is creative. Even if you're just working as a cashier or a plumber or a cook—you're into art, and thus, you are constantly inspired by those around you and every day you're excited about life, even if your job sucks, because you are surrounded by people like you instead of being an outcast."

"It's really a great idea," said Corey.

"When you get done with work, instead of doing chores or other stuff you don't want to do—Hero pushes you to do art instead. He motivates everybody by letting them know that if their art is superb enough, there's a chance they could quit their day job they have on the dark side."

"Hero spends half of his day reviewing everybody's art to figure out which ones he will subsidize. Which means, they can create art all day and he makes sure they have all the money needed to survive."

"He really wants to help young artists flourish and blossom their talents without worrying about people constantly telling them to give up and get a real career. So if he looks at their art or music or writing or whatever other talent they possess and thinks it's really good and they're not making any money, he will have them quit their day job on the dark side and just focus on their art full time."

"I would love to quit my day job and do art all day," said Corey.

"Sometimes established artists move here simply to be surrounded by others like them. They don't expect or need anything from Hero as they are already making money."

"Hero then began a campaign to emphasize how different and better the dark side is compared to the light side. He felt he couldn't accomplish this without a Statue giving the light side the finger."

Corey stands up and gives the sky the finger and they both laugh.

"He also doesn't like tourists or even artists friends coming to visit the dark side. He wanted to make it as pure as possible so people could focus on nothing but art."

"With the appearance of the thought wind, young artists discovered a new set of issues because your house has to be insulated with thought wind protecting walls. Some starving artists come here and they can't afford to protect their living quarters with anti-thought wind walls and start to lose their minds. Every three months or so, you have to hire somebody to come in and clean or replace your anti-thought wind filters in your walls because they eventually get saturated with the thought wind."

"That's really creepy and gross."

"Sadly, some people can't afford that, so they have to rely on headphones every second of their life. Then if the headphones break or get lost and can't afford to replace them, the thought wind is able to invade them."

Maybe that's where Perfect People fit in. They offer you a chip to become the perfect artist. One that could focus on art from morning to night and never get distracted by social media and TV and chores and was safe from the thought wind.

The thought wind regularly reminds me during our sessions that a perfect solution waits for me. I just needed to discuss it at the Statue of Hero. But I knew the deal—give up my freedom in exchange for artistic bliss. I just don't want to become a zombie like everyone around me.

I pieced together all this information I tell Corey from skating around and observing and soaking in everything I could, and obviously the thought wind. What I don't know, I just make up.

I heard of people living outside the city, as well, who rejected all the dark side has to offer but I wasn't positive about that and didn't want to mention it to Corey.

"So, who designed the thought wind? Shouldn't Hero do something about it?"

"Exactly!" I say ready to burst from enthusiasm from another human besides myself who finally grasps the reality of the situation.

"Nobody ever discusses where Hero is. I mean, he would never allow this. I assume he doesn't live here anymore. So instead of discussing where Hero is and how to stop the thought wind, they just discuss what new art project they're working on."

"I have heard people theorize that the thought wind is designed so people would listen to music more. Since music is known to be great for the brain, the theory is, it would be a safe alternative to meds. That's why music is huge here. But it's such bullshit. You don't ruin an artist's paradise to make people listen to music further. Everybody already has a passion for music."

"Oh cool, the beer is not dark here," says Corey in a cute quirky burb of letters.

"If you decide that the inside of your building is not going to be black, then Hero has to inspect and approve of the colors you use. If he doesn't like the way it looks, he gives you thirty days to fix it and add more black. He loves things that are just totally off the wall, so you really have to be creative and bring your A game if you are not going with the color black."

"Nobody has seen Hero so he can address the thought wind?"

"Yeah, I really don't know what's going on with him."

Corey is busy on her phone. She is excited to show me a picture of Hero but to her surprise, nothing shows up online. From what she gathers, I have never even seen a picture of him.

We go back to my house where pans are heated, garlic is crushed, and water is boiled, causing the apartment to flood with pungent smells.

Post dinner see's the TV flashing images of humans that were very much alive, causing subconscious jealousy.

An hour later, we begin to make out.

Medium-sized strawberries pierces my eyes.

Not sure if I should touch them or not, I chose to just ignore them.

Later that night, I feel I should at least address the issue. "So…strawberries this time, huh?"

"Yes, strawberries this week. I know you think it's very strange. I can see it in your face, so you don't have to pretend or hide from the subject."

"Sorry, it just seems like from my experience on the dark side that when somebody claims to be doing something good for your wellbeing, it's generally not. They have some alternative motive in mind, so I don't want to see you being just a subject for their experiment, is all."

"Thank you for your concern. Trust me, I have thought about this a million ways and concluded to just trust my Mom."

"Yeah, I hear ya, your Mom wouldn't try and screw you over."

"I hope she wouldn't."

I kiss her on the cheek.

YOUR CONCERNS ARE VALID!

OMG Mighty, please no more of Nails being angry and Corey trying to act tougher while black birds perch on vanilla buildings. We get it already. Nails wishes he wasn't on the dark side making him super aggro. Corey is mainly focused on what's shaking on the dark side. Can we just gloss over this by now? Netflix is starting to look more and more appealing then this crap!

I hear your concerns valuable reader and trust me, there is more to the book than just that. I simply am writing how I saw it, and this is how it went down. So, patience please.

POP SHUVIT

We meet up on the light side the next day to see more and more black birds appearing. They are starting to act more aggressive. Sometimes flying down while people are walking.

"So, is there any more information about what's going on with the black birds?"

"Well obviously we blame the dark side. We think they released the birds here."

"I still don't get why they don't just trap them or kill them."

"I told you already. The light side is big on animal rights, so they won't do anything about it. Plus, crows are intelligent animals. They are not just some dumb bird. They remember faces, hold grudges, and can figure out if certain humans pose a problem and can imitate human's personalities."

I let the list of things she said resonate deep within.

"But they could carry diseases and parasites, and if the light side is so worried about being healthy, why not just catch and release them somewhere else? You know what, I will kill a few and give them to your Mom. It can be a new smoothie flavor. Chocolate Crow Oreo Caramel. Yum."

"Gross, and that's a dark side way of thinking. Plus, we only kick out artists and these birds don't appear to be artists," she says with a laugh while gently punching Nails.

Maybe you shouldn't have kicked out all the artists, this place is boring as hell.

Just then, a black bird swoops down from a building and takes one of the crackers Corey holds in her hands. It flies away making an obnoxious squeaking sound.

We both look at each other in somewhat disbelief and stand up at the same time indicating we are ready for a change of scenery.

"So, can I watch you skate a little? I have never seen skateboarding before."

"Yeah, sure, it's such a nice day out, I wouldn't mind a little session anyway."

I take her to my spot on the light side.

As we are walking, Corey asks me about my name—Nails.

"Well, as you already suspected, the dark side doesn't do anything normal. So, names given at birth is not allowed. I always thought nails were tough and kind of badass. Just how they can go into anything and stay there forever, so Nails seemed to fit. I wish I was badass like a nail."

We both chuckle. Corey plants a kiss on my cheek while saying, "I think you're plenty badass."

We get to the skate area and I do my thing for an hour. As I skate, I explain to Corey what the tricks are called.

"This is called an ollie. It's one of the most basic skateboarding moves. It's you jumping the board over something.

"This is a manual."

"Oh, it's like a wheelie. I have seen motorcycles do that on TV."

"Right, yeah."

"Tic-Tac is really easy. Just back and forth."

"That does look easy."

"The kickflip is my favorite trick. It's like an ollie. But you use your toe to flip the board one full rotation."

"Oh wow, you landed it! That is so awesome."

She runs over and gives me a big hug and kiss. I feel warm and welcomed as I am not used to this attention from a female for skateboarding. Since art is the main vibe on the dark side, people tend to take for granted the beauty of it. Sure, they talk about it nonstop and breathed it, but it never seemed legit due to their mental condition. This is genuine happiness for another person succeeding. It feels charming and simpatico.

"Pop shuvit is a fun move, to. You're just rotating the board 180 degrees."

Corey claps her hands and smiles wide.

"Do you want to try and ride the board? I will make sure you don't fall."

Her shy, cute smile shakes a resounding "Yes." I want to kiss her for hours.

"Ok so put your left foot at the front and the right foot at the bottom of the board. Don't worry, I will hold you up so you don't fall."

"Oh wow, I am moving, this is fun!!"

I could see some people stopping and staring at us. I want to give them the finger or something but knew it was best to stay calm and avoid trouble.

I help Corey off the board. We go to Sunshine Smoothies for lunch. It's super busy as always.

"Hey, you two, are you having a good day?" asks Molly.

"Nails showed me how to skateboard!"

"Well, be safe. So, what can I get you?"

"Just surprise us with lots of donuts and a smoothie for each of us," I reply.

We eat until our stomachs are overflowing with joy and satisfaction. We leave Sunshine Smoothies and go to the park to watch the sunset.

"This view is phenomenal. I just never get to see stuff like this on the dark side." Corey rests her head on my shoulder. As we are both getting lost in nature's Picasso, a black bird lands in front of us.

"Shew, get away from here," says Corey.

The bird just stares at them and will not move. I try to ignore the bird but instead find myself focusing on it. Emerald green eyes followed by fluffy midnight oil feathers. I get a eerie vibe that we share some sort of kindred spirit.

We both continue staring at one another trying to figure out each other's intentions. Neither side willingly to break. I am finally shaken from my requiem when Corey adjusts her position.

We get up and the bird makes a loud sound and flies away. Anger courses through my veins so I hold Corey's hand and feel the annoyance dissipate.

We go back to Corey's apartment and muscle memory flips the TV from off to on. It's the weekend, so Corey has to wake up early for a busy day slinging addictive snacks. With her fast asleep, I feel the need to burn off some nervous energy so I go outside and take deep breaths through the nose until the oxygen reaches a dead end near my belly button, then flies upward like a man deep in the ocean running out of breath.

I walk to the park where a dozen birds surround me making loud noises and flapping their wings. I remain in place while they inch closer and closer. I feel a bit threatened so I start to yell and shout and move my hands around like a bigger, bolder bird. They finally retreat.

As I am walking back, it's the usual vast amount of people exercising even though it is nighttime. Jumping jacks, yoga, playing with a glow in the dark frisbee, and comparing who has the best abs. One person even uproots a small tree and the crowd cheers him on as darkness is no obstacle for them.

What the hell is wrong with these people? Don't they own a TV or have beer or pot or anything that will generate a sloth-like outlook?

Slightly annoyed, I let my mind wander to see what it might catch, like a fisherman setting up multiple fishing poles alongside a river bank while relaxing with a beer and joint.

My mind starts comparing animals to man. Animals are so simple. Food, shelter, and sex. Humans are complex. Layers upon layers like an onion. When layers are removed hastily or prematurely it causes strife. We use our big brains to invent and build amazing things. But those big ol' brains sure did cause a lot of unnecessary ruckus to the world. Would an animal ever delete a person's memory and launch them on an island of black? Why couldn't humans just be simpler like animals? You have food, shelter, and a mate, why push for more?

I think about my existence and how I considered myself more like an animal than a human. I then feel my daily anger brewing in the pit of my stomach and feel like maybe that is the big difference between the two. Animals don't feel intense anger and anxiousness daily, while humans do.

WAYS TO DIE

I spend Saturday relaxing at Corey's watching TV.

"So how was work?"

"Yeah, not too bad, was busy, though. Everybody loves Mom's food so much," she says in an annoying condescending way. "Want to go to the dark side for drinks?"

"What time do you have to work tomorrow?"

"Eight am.'

"Let's just watch some TV so you're not exhausted tomorrow."

Corey is tired of just watching TV. She has spent most of her life just watching TV. She is ready to finally live. But with how busy Sunshine Smoothies is, to go into work exhausted and hungover sounds horrendous, so she reluctantly agrees.

It's Sunday night and after a very busy weekend of working, Corey has only one thing on her mind, which is getting to the dark side. Upon entering the first bar our eyes witness, we are immediately enthralled and wrapped up mentally with the projector as it is flashing black and white images on the rosy red brick wall. It is made to look like it is produced in the fifties and it seems to show people dying. The red wall in the background feels like one large puddle of blood.

A woman eats avocado after avocado. Fifty avocados later, her potassium is so high it causes her heart to stop.

Chlorine sulfur arsenic gasses touch's the skin causing it to blister and melt away.

Woodpeckers pecking out the eyes of tied-down steel workers.

People swung into trees.

Arms ripped off woman.

Violent, bloody car crashes.

People jumping off buildings.

Lung cancer.

Brain tumors.

"It's avant garde basically. It's called *Ways to Die*. They make it look like it was filmed back when there were only black and white films and they describe different ways to die. There's no commentary or audio."

We sip our beers and stare blankly at the wall like hypothesized children as different scenes of people dying keep coming up.

Corey cringes and tries to look away while I refuse to let the scenes of people dying get me into another one of my frenzied states. But scene after scene of death just makes me even more angry and annoyed.

A man slowly getting his eyes touched with a toothpick until he bleads out.

Overdosing on various vitamins.

A can of red ants poured on the body.

We leave after just one beer, unable to mentally handle this particular part of the dark side.

As we are leaving the bar in a quest for a new bar that is less offensive, Corey notices some humans on her radar that forces her to analyze them further.

The first is a man who has one normal arm while his other arm is removed after the elbow and replaced by what appears to be a metal guitar.

Then there is a woman who has an antenna-like object growing out of her forehead. It's a foot long and covered in flash tattoo art —anchors, stars and birds.

We see a bar and enter it.

"Did you see those two weird people. Do you know what's up with them?" says Corey in a frantic voice.

I have seen many of them before. I don't know who they are or what their deal is. It did give me further motivation to say "fuck you" to the thought wind as they had to be involved in it in some way or another. I try to act confident when responding to Corey.

Acting timid and weak and afraid of the dark side would not impress her. So even if I tell lies here and there, it was fine because my heart is in the right place. I tell her that some jerk paid money to desperate humans.

"They're most likely thought wind victims. Some assholes are looking to make a quick buck on the innocent and down-trodden so they offer them money if they wear a camera with audio while they walk around the city with no headphones on. Then they speak into a microphone with what they are thinking during the thought mind hijack. After that, nobody knows what happens to them. Their memory is always wiped out and they come back weeks later missing some appendage or have some strange new object attached to them."

"Wow, that's terrible."

"They always ask me, but luckily I have *Nihilist News* for an income, so I am safe. I don't know who these jerks are, or how they found out about the dark side, but one day I plan on getting my revenge on them."

I could feel tightness in my chest. I know my blood pressure resides in the clouds and that I have to learn to not get so angry all the time. I feel more relaxed and calm around Corey and I did try to laugh as much as possible. If things were just a little less screwed up, I thought, I could let it all just pass. But that wasn't the case, so a hostile sour vibe is always present.

"Wow, that's really messed up. These poor people are losing limbs for the enjoyment of others."

"Yeah, I agree, totally sick, deranged people. So many lives ruined and worse. People disappear all the time here. Here today, gone tomorrow. It can be a dangerous place to live as of late. It used to be safe." *From what I can gather at least*

"Don't worry about it or get upset. You wear your headphones and your careful, so you will be fine."

"Yeah I hear you."

"I generally don't go out at night much really. Just skate and do my job and go to some punk shows here and there."

"And you can't call the cops or FBI because they don't exist."

"Right, I mean, I guess I could contact the cops or FBI who work on the light side."

I quickly regret even thinking that let alone saying it out loud where Corey could monitor me to see if I really act on it. The thought wind was clear about contacting the authorities. I am grateful for them allowing me to break some minor rules here and there, so I don't want to push my luck.

"Well, do you think I should tell somebody on the light side since I live here?"

I have to squash the idea like a pesky mosquito flying recklessly on a hot summer night.

"Actually, I think I have a plan, so don't worry about it. Yes, I definitely have some ideas brewing on what can be done."

"What are you thinking?"

"I have a bunch of ideas and if they all fail then, yes, I will contact the FBI."

"Ok, well shout if you need some assistance."

"Yup, will do, thanks."

"Now, did you notice that those two people did look pretty hip with the anchors and stars and guitar? I mean, yeah, it's evil as hell to do that to somebody, but you have to admit, it looks cool."

"The dark side would never let them look just average."

"Do you think he can play the guitar? Like, was the plan to have him be able to play the guitar with his good, functioning arm?"

I pretend like I have a guitar half arm and how it would work.

"See, I don't think it would work because you need two hands to play a guitar and he would only have one arm," I say.

"Yeah, I wonder, though. I don't know. Maybe somebody else could play it for him?"

"Maybe."

We go back to my apartment and I put The Drowns new album on the turntable when Corey jumps on me and we begin to make out. Her bra glides off and strawberry breasts scream at me to take a bite. Just one small little juicy nibble. Hands rise up to touch them gently. They feel warm and rough.

My mind conjures up all the different delicious foods that contain strawberries. Strawberry shortcakes my mom made when I was younger. How she always put so many strawberries and whipped cream on the tan, doughy donut and how it would soak up the ice cream as it melted. Strawberry beer. Strawberry milkshakes. Strawberries with sugar on them.

With all these images flashing in my brain, resistance and willpower become subdued. As rational thought vanishes, I move my face closer and closer until my mouth is around the tip of one of them. I slowly began licking one until I could wait no longer and take a small bite.

A burst of wet liquid squirts into my mouth followed by the flesh of the bright berry. I have been with other woman before, that I remember from my previous life, but this seems like the ultimate sensual connection.

Ultimately, I lose all control and devour the entire berry. I savor it in my mouth and then wonder if Corey might want to taste it as well.

I go to kiss her and she holds back a bit as if saying without words, "This is all you, I want no part of this madness."

When it is completely removed from my mouth and flowing down into my stomach and digestive tracts, I go back to kissing Corey.

Forty minutes later, I start to sense a strange sensation working its way through my body. Muscles loosen up. Tension drips off like rain from a roof. Eyelids feel heavy. Anger finally breaks loose from it's chains and catch's a greyhound bus to anywhere but here. I want to close my eyes and hope this feeling lasts forever. But I decide I better mention the merry vibes that are riding toasty waves inside me.

"Corey, I think there was something in your breasts, this isn't just beer drunk. I feel like I am high right now. I just feel so relaxed. It's a great feeling but I am pretty sure this is the result of your strawberries."

"Wow, really? So, you think my breasts, besides being fruits, are also drugs?"

"I really do, yes."

"Are you going to be okay?"

"I think yeah."

"I will try and stay awake to make sure you are safe."

I close my eyes and say "Thanks."

KAMIKAZE STYLE

The next day, Corey gives her Mom one of her strawberries and makes an excuse about the other.

"It was grungy and faulty and fell off."

Her Mom reluctantly accepts the excuse and gives her the ingredients for next week's fruit.

Pears.

She is relieved her Mom doesn't flip out since this was not a one night stand. It would happen again next week as well since she has a plan conjured up. She knew the invitation was in the mail and the party she would attend would be a gathering of three. She loves getting drunk and to experience another high, one that grows out of her own body, is something that makes her beyond excited to try out.

Corey tells me we should try it together. I am hesitant because I am not into doing drugs. Not that I don't enjoy the mental vacation they provide, but at this stage in my life, I need to be coherent and functional to escape this current nightmare instead of accepting it and getting stoned as a way of dealing with it.

A few days later, I text Corey that I am going to skate if she wants to hang out. As I am skating, a dozen black birds perch on the building across the street. It doesn't put me at ease to see them watching me. One of the birds flies down and lands right near me. I decide to leave before fury spins inside me like a tormented tornado.

As I walk to meet up with Corey, a bird flies side by side with me. Rage and black birds would not defeat me so I burst into pseudo-maniacal laughter. It flows from me like a fire hydrant releasing water on a hot city afternoon. The crow creates its own music which sounds like bedlam and babble. We both stroll down the street sounding like a broken jukebox as my laughing is the vocals and the crows squawking the guitar and bass.

It's a sound nobody with a sane brain could enjoy.

I get to Corey's house and the crow flies to a nearby tree where his crow friends join him. A murder of crows perch on the branch's waiting for my return.

We decide to go to the park to eat lunch since the weather is bright and warm. As we're munching on food, a crow swoops down and steals one of Corey's carrot sticks.

"They're really getting aggressive now, huh?" says Corey.

Before I have a chance to respond, a few more black birds fly down and give me the stare down.

"Scram, get out of here. This is what they did last week, as well," I tell Corey.

"It's so weird. It's like they are trying to tell you something."

"When I was skating today, there were about a dozen or so birds watching me and then one flew parallel to my head until we got here. It's some eerie shit."

As we are leaving the park, a loud splatter noise causes us to stop and scrutinize the sound, and like a detective at a crime scene, we discover it's a bird splattering into a building.

White turns black.

"Just kamikaze style, wow." I say this in an indifferent tone as if anything else at this point could generate a more sympathetic tone.

If these birds want to kill themselves turning this stupid place black, go for it. I don't give a shit unless this is some kind of clue to get me the hell out of here. I've had enough of all this malarkey.

Corey grabs my hand and speaks in a shaky tone.

"I have never seen death before. I know it's just a bird and all, but that was pretty intense. It flew directly into that building like it was on a mission to breathe its last breath. Do you think it was done on purpose?"

"It sure seems like it was. These birds are definitely getting more aggressive and spastic."

"It seems like they really target you the most."

"Yeah, I agree," which makes me even more creeped out. I replay the image over and over in my brain, and like the night during a bright moon, something shiny stands out.

Where was the blood and guts? It's as if the entire bird was designed to fly into buildings and turn them black. What the fuck? Can I ever get a break? All I want is some conversation with a functioning normal human and some color that's not black and it's like I am requesting world peace.

I pick up my skateboard and begin slamming it into the concrete to release some of my built-up aggression that seems to have built condos and hotels inside me.

Corey watches in silence as I release a blitzkrieg of emotions. This is the first time she has seen me fly off the handle like this.

She wonders if Nails is upset over the fact that he is dating a girl with fruit for breasts? Corey assumes she is partially responsible for the hissy fit. Maybe it's not a good idea hanging out on the dark side.

No.

It is.

Nails is a virtuous guy. They each make the other full and functional instead of broken off pieces of metal left to rust after an amusement park leaves town.

As we are walking, I can't stop noticing just how boring it is over here. No matter how much I want to try and ignore this fact, my brain returns constantly to how everything just seems so predictable on the light side.

They don't party.

They don't do art.

What's the deal with their obsession with exercising?

Everywhere I look, people with perfectly sculpted bodies seem to be exercising. Push-ups. Sit ups. One-hundred yard dashes. Sports everywhere. It all just seems so boring. Sure, it's fun to move around, as I love to skateboard, but I am also into other activities, as well. The light side seems one dimensional. Get in shape and stay in shape.

That being said, I also secretly hold animosity towards how the dark side operates. Be creative but live within our tightly outlined boundaries.

I am starting to grow more and more annoyed at how my life turned out. I know that seems tough to imagine. How could I get more irked then I already am? But like something broken that doesn't function properly, my brain couldn't simply let go of it all.

I am constantly thinking about how I woke up on the dark side and my memory of my life prior being faded photographs where only the outlines and shapes remain.

I knew things and could take care of myself, but memories like family and friends seem cloudy and just out of reach.

The losers in charge of this hellish experiment did seem to have some sense of compassion since I was able to cross the bridge into the light side to date a girl there. They must sense just how truly miserable I am when not on my skateboard, so they permit just enough leeway to avoid me losing my mind. The times between skating and writing and Corey, when my mind is easily about to wander, causes great bouts of depression and misery.

ANCHORS

We end up at Corey's place where we numb our brains from the electric glow of the television. We want to stretch our wings, but with Corey working early the following day, it's best to rest.

It feels like forever for Corey until Sunday arrives. The plan in her mind feels rooted in logic. Her and Nails would both nibble on a pear breast, and like scientists, they would analyze the effects.

I am fully against it. My mind is like a train on a track—one dimensional and only concerned about escaping this hell. Pears act as anchors instead of keys.

However, I simply don't possess the skills, at times, to articulate my thoughts. I operate on gut instinct. To try and rationalize and persuade Corey that we should avoid eating her own breasts when she is so amped about it, is something my energy and patience could not accomplish.

Then there's the love part. I am always willing to do anything that would make her happy. So, I try and make it as romantic as possible by lighting candles and putting on the Long Beach Dub All Stars to make the mood mellow and hip from their reggae-ska-dub sounds.

Corey removes her shirt and black bra and tries being as sexy as possible saying, "Pick it off."

My heart beats uneven rhythms sounding like a band having a bad night. I give it a little tug and jostle and it smoothly vacates it's home. Walking over to the kitchen with my sweaty palms holding the pear, my mind races with endless thoughts. How high and stoned will this pear get us? Will I ever escape this dark dungeon? Does Corey truly love me?

On autopilot, I remove the cutting board and grab a knife and begin cutting the pear in half aggressively—hoping it would somehow disintegrate and disappear and I would walk back to the couch where Corey would have real breasts made of flesh instead of fruit. That's not how life works for you, says a voice somewhere in my broken brain.

Corey puts her shirt back on and we make some small talk while letting the music that is bouncing off the four walls do the majority of the talking—as we are eager to see what sensations and vibes the pear would bring.

About thirty minutes later, our bodies and mind detect soothing sedative feelings. Neither of us knew much about drugs so we look online and the amount of information is overwhelming. All we can conclude is that if we don't have dry mouth, headaches, diarrhea, upset stomach, weight gain, suicidal thoughts, increased appetite, loss of sexual desire, fatigue, drowsiness, insomnia, blurred vision, constipation, anxiety, agitation and dizziness—then what we took is all natural and should be safe.

We sit on the couch with arms and legs intertwined resembling a human soft pretzel. The worries of the wobbly world vanish. Tension and terror that being alive brings seems like it never existed to begin with. Peace and love are all we can ever imagine existing.

Some light conversation trickles down like water from a spicket.

"This is how I felt when I ate the strawberries. I wonder if all your fruits generate the same sensations."

"Yeah, I don't know. I just can't believe something that grows from my body can produce such sensations internally."

The next morning, we go out to breakfast and discuss the previous night while waiting for our food.

"Don't you find it weird that she collects your breasts and analyzes them. I mean, if she's growing them, isn't she the one responsible for making your breasts a drug?"

"Yeah, I mean, it is possible, sure. Her dedication and determination in her craft is robust. But I just can't believe her desire for her business being the most unique and finest ever would cause her to do this. And with no chemistry background, I can't imagine she could orchestrate something so complicated."

"I hear you and I am not trying to say she did this, I just don't know what else could be happening here. And what's up with Sunshine Smoothies? There's no way eating at a restaurant should ever generate superhuman strength."

Facial warmth and flushing like a curious cat accidentally swatting a can of red paint off the table with its tail and splashing it all over a blank white canvas is how Corey feels as Nails makes point after point indicating Molly as the prime suspect.

Did he not think this question was a book bag filled with burdens instead of books for her? She tries to relax and think of something pleasant. Oddly, she pictures a doughnut entering her mouth, further expanding on his idea that this restaurant is serving up sinister eats.

"I think it's a random, slapdash, fluke occurrence, personally. A big bang. She's not some revolutionary. Cancer cells are the freaks who wore dog collars in high school. When you douse a specific sick body part lickety-split with normalcy it can sometimes cause the most unexpected of results."

She feels tall, like a tree, after this response. It is out of her character to make affirmative statements on macro subjects, but with her Mom being her best friend, she feels the need to blindly support her. She also hopes the boy in black doesn't know what the word slapdash means, giving her the upper hand even more on this topic.

I couldn't help but swat away her statement like brush in a jungle. She isn't seeing this through clear eyes. I would have to address this issue in short delicate jabs when the time seems ripe.

Drug breasts. Black buildings. Broken souls. Metal limbs. Evil restaurants. Hijacking of the mind. Retro gadgets. Strange graveyards. My brain is able to go on like this forever. A marathon of disgust and revulsion. Like a dog without a leash, my brain is able to hunker down and focus on the hate.

Just when it seems like this is the path I am heading down today, I glance up at Corey, and like an eraser on a pencil, the frost and scorn on my brain is replaced with contentment and ease. Her innocence and beauty is able to stop wars and I did my best to not take that for granted.

BILLY GOATS

Nails's phone beeps and burps like a baby inside a bowling ball. He has a strong feeling who is contacting him. This is why he turned his phone off—it's an infection without a cure when the phone is turned from off to on. The thought wind and their goons in training blasted him sentences that managed to be even stupider than the stories he penned.

"Nails, bro, did you know Billy Goats urinate on their heads to smell more attractive to females?"

"Gimme an F. Gimme a U. Gimme a C. Gimme a K. What's that spell? Fuck You!   I hope dozens of goats urinate on your head, you immature imbecile."

"Sometimes I wonder if you even like me, Nate. Now check this out. Did you know pirates wore earrings because they believed it improved their eyesight?!"

"You're like the slower retarded version of the thought wind. Like, your Dad didn't trust you enough for the pros so you're stuck in the amateur division where you're only allowed to handle stupid random facts via text. And even that you're ghastly at."

"Nate, why don't you step outside with no headphones on and we can discuss this man vs man."

"It's always the same deal with you. Step outside with no headphones. Then you hack my conscience. I know how this works, Daddy's little reject."

"I would be careful, Nate. We have a delicate, fun enough relationship as it is, and you're starting to cross that very weak line."

"Ahhh, Daddy's little moron is getting upset. Maybe it's time to take a little nappy nap."

He pauses and waits for a response. Seconds turned into minutes and the phone turns dormant. A modest wave of satisfaction peaks out from behind a set of sturdy blinders. He hopes whoever he is battling doesn't have the capacity to launch missiles in his direction causing massive mental casualties.

TOUGH

The next few days the boy in black and the girl in white text each other in moderate to run-of-the mill sentences as both are preoccupied with endless thoughts about their lives and what paths they should be traveling down.

Corey tells Nails she wants to go out drinking Wednesday night.

Nails dreams of her instead replying with, "I want to help you find the assholes who did this to you. And once we find them, let's bring them into some place soundproof and see how tough they are, now." But instead, she wants things that have no interest in Nails world.

He enjoys the companionship she provides and how open and real she seems compared to the rest of his life which seems fake and lost. If the dark side taught him just one thing, it would be to celebrate minor victories and embrace the small things.

Without Corey, he might be swinging by a noose. Instead, he is with a legitimate human who actually enjoys his company. Even though he has an open-door policy regarding feelings that are not healthy, he did constantly remind himself that he is very fortunate to have Corey in his life.

LAME SIDE

The second Corey's feet lands on the dark side, she feels alive and awake; as if the dark side is the fountain of youth for her. It cracks open previously closed corners and opens them for business.

It is visible from outer space that Corey has acquired a taste for the alcoholic beverages. Every sip she takes causes her brain to bounce with joy.

"Is there anything wrong? You're really sucking them down tonight."

"I guess I am chasing that feeling we had from the pears. I just can't stop thinking about how good it felt."

"This is the problem with mind-altering substances. They take control of your mind. Like, imagine being behind the wheel of a car, but instead of a car, it's your life. Well, drugs and alcohol then take control instead of you, and all you care about is getting fucked up. Then the car eventually crashes, landing you in jail. Plus, your Mom is going to flip if she ever discovers the real reason she's only getting one fruit. And I really don't think it's healthy at all. I don't want us turning soft and becoming another thought wind victim to satisfy our drug cravings."

Corey's subconscious registers what Nails says and takes note of the way he always seems to have answers or thoughts about everything and never gives a lackluster or lethargic viewpoint on life. He really is brimming with vibrant rays of passion.

"Yeah, you're right," she halfheartedly said. "Ok, let's plan on hanging out on my side of the tracks more often. We can exercise, and well, that's it, I guess. Did you ever notice the light side is kind of boring?" said Corey.

"Yeah, perhaps I noticed it a few hundred thousand times."

WHITE TO BLACK

Tuesday replaces Monday and Wednesday replaces Tuesday and so it goes until Friday comes and Corey has the day off.

They stroll around the light side looking for an invite to anything that has the potential for fun. They stop in dozens of stores and spend time commenting on the objects for sale. It is light-hearted and paper thin. Neither side has any complaints as simply being in each other's company is oceans of joy.

As the uneventful day starts to wind down, white begins to turn black from birds flying into buildings. Thuds and whimpers as lives end from the selfish act of pulling one's own plug.

Macabre feelings replace the blissful electricity flowing between the two. They turn inwards. Nails is reminded just how fragile life can be. While Corey, still uneasy about death, feels the immediate need to be sedated. She craves the warm feeling of safety that body altering substances produces.

Conversation goes from chunky coughs to slim nods. Each drop from the faucet splashing into the drainage, flowing into an unknown territory where things go to die.

Corey looks to find the sun. During her moving of the neck and head, she catch's glimpses of humans exercising like they always do on the light side. She feels sudden sadness for the life or lives that are buried in the graveyard. Junky Bones, as she labels him or her, would never feel the warmth of the sun shining down their face, never feel the wonderful embrace of skin and soul that love offers, never feel the lonely lows that depression and isolation produces, and never see the color black or white ever again.

"You ever feel like your vices are one big magnet and your entire body is metal and it's this constant pushing and pulling that never seems to end? Contentment after experiencing the thrills of joy is something I need to work at, I suppose. It's just tough right now, I guess, or something. Like all I care about is hanging on the dark side while you're worried about me getting sucked into the folds and corners of this place and becoming just another statistic. Then we visit the light side and its white turning to black and food that may or may not be creating exercise fanatics."

Nails put his arm around Corey and kisses her cheek and tries convincing her that everything will be fine.

EMPTY INSIDE

Corey is determined to find other hobbies. She flips through yellowed pages of old books. She draws rudimentary figures on notebook paper with a pen. She listens to music while reading the lyrics. None of these things work well enough as her brain is too overwhelming of a foe to defeat.

She feels like a record that never flips to the other side. Is her brain broken? Is it normal to constantly place hand to breast to inspect ripeness? To see if perhaps they are ready for ingestion to feed a burning desire that needs feeding? To sunbathe nude in order to get extra sun for her fruits? To visit the dark side alone to see what trouble she can find? Is it a losing battle?

She tries hard to free her mind. Instead— birds on suicide missions— junky bones and how in death you are truly alone forever. She breaths deep and tries to think of nothing for once.

She texts me Saturday night that she wants to come over and go out drinking.

I reluctantly agree.

Corey drinks two strong beers in the first hour.

"I feel so much better now, my cravings have subsided."

What happened to the nice, innocent, sweet girl I met weeks ago?

I knew I had to stick by her side, thick or thin. It's my fault for introducing her to the dark side and alcohol.

Corey wakes up the next day looking haggard and feeling empty. She doesn't do much besides lay on the couch nursing her aching body. I try to be as supportive as possible. She ends up calling her Mom and telling her I am sick and she has to take care of me.

Two days later, her tomatoes are ready. She finds herself in her room, removing her shirt and suddenly wondering how she got home from work. She remembers clocking out and then nothing else. With such a singular mission, her brain must have focused so intensely on the task at hand, it blocked everything else out.

She feels like a train that removed its brakes and was unable to stop and pick up any passengers that might give her alternative viewpoints about the situation at hand. She feels cornered and limited in options. *If my brain only cares about one thing, well what else can I do but give in? You can't fight your brain. It's a vital organ that must be made happy. It is now time to make the decision.*

Does she have the strength to not plunge into the cold deep dark murky waters of addiction? Her addictive brain says, What's the big deal? It's just a tomato. A simple condiment for burgers. The main ingredient in pasta sauce. A critical role in salsa. What is delicious pizza without it? While her logical brain decides to finally show up and remind her there are no guarantees it is safe. It might not even work this round. It could get you very high and even further addicted.

Trembling with fear, she puts her shirt back on and races out the door. The one benefit of being in supreme physical shape is being able to cover ground quickly like a cheetah chasing a wildebeest.

She finds herself in a bar on the dark side embracing the miracle liquids it serves in endless establishments.

Nighttime on the dark side feels like exiting planet earth and floating around the galaxy. The stars are the streetlights while the black buildings feel like oodles and gobs of black holes that prey on fragile victims by opening its doors and never releasing the remnants.

Her pace has fluidity and rhyme from Operation Ivy blasting into her ears. The lyrics and sounds, crazy catchy and simple—has her singing so loudly and proudly she feels confident enough to patron the graveyard.

She is flabbergasted at the concept of graveyards that are designed as being just props. Junky Bones flashes in her brain like a neon beer sign in a dingy bar.

Arrival at the graveyard produces immediate feelings of regret at not bringing a shovel. She looks around for something that could act as one. She grabs a few sticks and begins poking them into the dirt and then finally resigns to getting on her knees and using her hands.

An hour later, she feels something sharp hit her fingernails. Her adrenaline spikes in her blood causing her to dig more furious than ever. She grabs the object and yanks it out causing dirt to fly and get into her mouth. Spit filled with dirt flies out her mouth in disgust. The object is held up towards the moon to see it more clearly. It is a bone.

She gets back on her knees to dig more to discover enough bones to warrant the assumption that it is a human resting below. She tosses the bone as quickly as possible back into the dirt trying not to vomit. Her feet kick dirt over the bones as she swiftly bolts away from the crime scene.

She keeps running and running until breathing is a challenge, producing huffing and puffing sounds. Sweat squats on the brow. Muscles burn from tension. Heart pounding like fists against locked doors. A quick survey of the surrounding environment showcases a land that feels estranged and remote.

Corey tries to run forward, backwards, left, right, but is blocked on all sides. She starts screaming and then yanks her headphones off to hear a group of people singing. Stay calm and diagnose the situation, her brain says.

She raises her hands up like a blind person and moves her fingers and arms trying to touch something to determine quickly the level of security. It feels like she is touching arms. Then heads. It must be some art act or something. Take a deep breath. You're dressed in all black, they're on your side. It's just more art like the falling buildings troupe.

She moves her feet and keeps walking with the singing blob of black bones for what feels like forever until they disband, and she finds herself outside the city in the woods near the water. In the distance, she sees some light that finally starts to provide her with a picture of where she is.

Corey follows the light until she reaches the source. A large flame roars into life as a dozen clowns and other artists surround the flames. "What's going on," she says with fear in her face. "Please don't hurt me."

"Drink this, it will calm your nerves."

It tastes like sour lemons past their prime. Immediately she feels better.

"What was that? Where am I?"

A shoddy looking clown with a patchwork face comprised of dull fabric that acts like skin speaks up. "That's our homemade wine. I am sorry it tastes so rotten. We do the best we can with what we have. It gets the job done. We use it sparingly since quantities are limited."

"What's your name?" said a different clown who has a black balloon arm made of metal.

"Corey, I, um, am dating Nails."

"Were really sorry about what just happened outside. We have to hunt in packs to avoid the thought wind. By locking arms in unison and singing songs we are able to pick through the trash to get food and supplies. However, it doesn't always work. They got Smiles tonight."

As he speaks, Corey studies his fragile frame of freaky funhouse freckles. The fabric on his face is multi-colored vintage fabrics tied together with a silver clear tape. His ears, or rather lack of, consists of cassette tapes held together with more silver tape that surrounds his head. There is no metal on him, however. That must be why his face has no skin. He probably ripped it off and the skin tagged along with it.

"That's so terrible you have to do that. Is Smiles going to be okay? My Mom makes the best food, I will bring you some tomorrow."

"You're very sweet. He should return in a month or so. However, the chances are very strong he will be missing a limb of some sorts."

Patchwork continues to speak. "When they get us, like how they got Smiles, we come back with metal appendages that transmit thoughts into our brains. It's super potent in the city, but out here it's not as strong. It still can infect you at any time though, but we learn to live with it since it's weak. The farther we are from the city, the less intense it becomes. It's like a song on the radio—when you're getting farther and farther away from the source, the less vibrant it is as more and more static appears. I ripped mine off and paid for it severely as you can see."

"If your brain is sidetracked at all and not focused on the songs, then it's an invitation for the thought wind to enter and take control of the mind. We can blame the thought wind all we want, but we knew how to stay safe. Smiles was not mentally prepared enough tonight, and that most likely cost him dearly. There's no room for error. Either you focus on the task at hand like a surgeon operating on a heart, or you're sidetracked and then screwed. So, tonight, all of a sudden Smiles flipped out like a caged hyena and ran away. If we chased him, we would be victims as well."

A woman with a metal bowling pin on the top of her head speaks up. "They find out our favorite hobbies and then attach a metal piece to us. I take bowling pins from closed bowling alleys across the world and then paint things from around the towns of the bowling alleys. People really loved them, but they took so much time and effort that I barely had time to make them since I worked fifty hours a week at my normal job. So, I moved to this island because it was advertised as an artist's utopia. You could create art all day and they would take care of shelter and food. That was true for a little bit, then this happened." She points to the metal on top of her head where a shiny realistic bowling pin pulsates a yellow light every few seconds.

Corey cranks her head around and around like an owl to witness the other artist's metallic limbs.

Black metal noses that are supposed to mimic a clown's nose.

Guitar arms.

Cameras attached to foreheads.

Metal paint brushes sticking out of ears.

One person had one of her legs removed and replaced by a metal one with all sorts of intricate designs and shapes. It was impressive. Her talent is probably sculpture.

A man with alloy headphones covering both ears speaks up. "I was an up-and-coming DJ who toured frequently and felt paying $700 a month for a tiny one room apartment was a waste since I was only there a few days a month. I heard about what Hero was doing and contacted him. He said he would listen to my music and if he felt something, he would allow me free room and board."

"It was great for 6 months or so. I would come here in between tours and create new songs and was able to save some money. When you're touring a lot, it's important to always have thousands saved because at any point the van will break down. Anyway, it was a great set up. Now I am a prisoner. When I attempt to leave and get closer to the city and it's potent electricity, my brain tells my legs something different and I can never end up leaving."

"We used to love the dark side until the thought wind entered. That was the catalyst, I suppose, to what you're witnessing right now. A collection of odd and wrong objects acting as makeshift body parts. When we venture into the city, we hunt in packs because we can't afford iPods, and even if we could, there's no electrical outlets here. Electricity is the primary host for the thought wind to operate on. Well, that and the metal appendages."

A different clown speaks up. "As you can see, I tried to remove the metal nose they attached to me and ended up removing most of my skin. Anyway, we sing songs so our brain is occupied with the rhythm, but it's a faulty plan to a degree, since they usually get one of us, no matter what precautionary methods we invoke."

"What a dismal predicament," said Corey wondering why she chose those words. She was trying to be different and creative to impress Nails and the dark side so her vocabulary was adapting to the situation at hand, like fish on land a million years ago.

"It wasn't always this way. It used to be great over here. We had plenty of gigs and lived comfortably. It really was an artist's utopia as advertised. But then like a year ago, everything went south from the thought wind. Then Hero disappeared," said a different clown.

"Then that piece of shit over there basically took control. He is most likely the one responsible for the thought wind videos and keeping us living like animals. He has electricity and two goons with him at all times."

Corey cranes her neck to get a glimpse. "I don't see anything," she says.

"Climb on a clown car for a better view."

She climbs on the car and can faintly see a house near the river. "I can kind of see it now."

"Make sure you stay far away from him. He doesn't bother us much but that doesn't mean he is not pure evil either, because he is."

As the clowns explained their situation to Corey, she surveys her surroundings. Each clown slept in clown cars. It reminds her of little kids who sleep in fake cars they got from a toy store.

There was so much art everywhere. Trees were covered in paintings. The branches have all sorts of objects hanging from them. There were acres of art—sculptures, paintings, collages, graffiti and drawings. It devoured everything in its path. This was the type of art she associated with the dark side before visiting it; instead she has to deal with humans tattooed like buildings and weird bars.

Besides art, there is all sorts of musical instruments created using trees and other makeshift ingredients.

There is jewelry hanging off tree branches.

Trees have carved messages in them like the one near her which reads, "We Sing Songs, We Carry On."

"We came from clown families and when Hero opened up the dark side to artists, it was tough to ignore the allure of it. We were hesitant at first because we were making decent money and liked where we were living. Once the Statue of Hero was upright with the middle finger to the light side, all artists were basically expelled out."

"How did you end up outside the city while the others are still inside the city?" said Corey.

A guy with metallic boombox speakers glued to each side of his head says, "When the thought wind first began, we immediately became its victims since we didn't know what was going on. So it instructed our brains to meet in the middle of the city."

"It told us we can either get a chip implanted—which meant we are able to resume daily art creation or we can choose to fight the thought wind in which case we will lose."

"We will have one week to decide. The thought wind is the creation of your master, Hero. It was devised for optimal art creation. No longer will you need to worry about bills or finances or laundry or looking at Instagram every twenty minutes, because with the chip, it automatically imports those ideas into your brain. No longer will you need to daydream about things that ultimately will sidetrack you from creating art. The chip gives you the power to focus on your art 100% of the time. You will sleep and do art. Nothing else. Your output will be five times what it is now."

"For those who choose to not have the chip implanted, you will have one week to find an alternative solution. Unfortunately, there is no alternative solution. The light side does not want you and with your middle finger tattooed all black, the outside world does not want you, either."

Boombox ears clears his throat and seems to cough up a cloud of dust and continues.

"So it was a mad scramble on what to do. The first thing we did was search for Hero. We went to his house, called him, emailed him, and no response. On the fifth day, everybody on the dark side got together under the Statue of Hero and we began discussing potential ways to avoid the chip. Eighty percent of us said no to the chip while the rest agreed to it. Not knowing the consequences of saying no, we waited with bated breath for the start of the eighth day."

"We found out quickly what they had in store for us. They hijacked our brains and told us of a dystopian dark future for about an hour. Eighty percent dropped to twenty percent. We are now the twenty percent who live outside the city and reject the thought wind. We are the true art creators as the best art is created from pain and strife. As you can see, we all paint, do sculptures, play music, carve wood, and do needlepoint. We just have to be creative with our materials and canvas. It's a rough life, but we know that the thought wind is not Hero's idea, so we have to stand by his side in a sense and reject this new world."

A skinny guy inserts his opinions sharply like a knife into a ripe piece of fruit. "Once the thought wind kidnaps you, it plants permanent pseudo thoughts into your brain as well as mental appendages." He removes his hat showcasing curly metal springs. "So we really don't know if Hero is the architect or what is true anymore. We document everything we do. Our names. Food recipes. Hobbies. Ages. Health issues. Everything important and not so important is noted with pen on paper."

WHITE ROSE

A mischievous brew of melancholy begins to madly march in Corey's mind from the somber tales of the deviant headstrong artists. She feels relaxed from the homemade wine but there is obviously not enough for them to indulge. It is used strictly as medicine and not recreational.

They were interrupted by the sound of metal being locked inside a tight space bouncing back and forth. Corey adjusts her neck to see what the ruckus is when she sees a man with a graffiti can plaster the tree beside her with a tag. His entire arm a spray paint can.

She studies the tag intensely in hopes of being hip enough to reply with a quick zippy response, but all the letters seem to blur and melt together.

A woman whose forehead is filled with piano keys says, "It reads 'what do you do on the dark side?' Telly doesn't use conventional forms of communication. Instead he lets the spray bottle that's attached to his elbow do the talking. He's taking a vow of silence until the thought wind is destroyed. He's a master at graffiti."

Her heart begins to beat faster and faster as she knows all eyes are on her waiting for an explanation. Her mind races and darts back and forth causing her brain to stumble and stutter. She looks around at the sad clowns, and then at the other artists who just appeared, showcasing elements of exploitation, and a wave of empathy rolls in like morning fog.

She removes her shirt and bra and everybody's jaw drops at the site of her tomato breasts. Their jaws drop even further when she picks one of them and says, "Do you guys like to party?"

They all move their lips in opposite directions as laughter and joy is released. Corey passes it around. After around six people take bites from it, the tomato is gone. She is still standing there with nothing on showcasing a single tomato and a vacant spot where a tomato once existed. The other artists tell her not to worry about giving them any. Corey digests their statement and tone. It consists of apathy and defeat.

She knows her Mother will mentally slaughter and slay her if she returns home with no tomatoes, but rational thought vanishes into oblivion. She picks the other tomato and hands it over feeling like she is the modern-day version of Mother Teresa. Her cravings for some of her own breasts intensifies more and more as she witnesses the sedative effects take control of the artists.

Joy and content replaces agony and misery.

"Corey, thanks so much for your, um, tomato breasts. It's a nice change of pace to not worry about potential infections and constant miscellaneous daily aches from the metal. This is just what the Doctor ordered."

"Doctor Corey," says a stoned clown.

"So, Corey, how do you have breasts that are fruits and also make you feel amazing?" asks an animation artist who has metal fingers.

The wine swimming in her blood wants her brain to unleash the vault and tell them her life story and how tragic it is. They would relate to her and sympathize and it would be one big love fest where everybody has the same afflictions and nobody is judged. She plans on coming back with food, so there is plenty of time in the future to explain everything. Choosing what to release, she speaks carefully and calculated.

"Breast cancer runs in my family. So, I had my breasts removed to be on the safe side. Then I travel the world looking for all-natural safe ways to treat various ailments. So my breasts can be painkillers, antifungal and antibacterial and anti-inflammatories. A lot of antis, I know. With the opioid crisis killing hundreds daily, I wanted to come up with safer alternatives. And since I live on the dark side, I have a creative itch that needs scratching."

She rambles on and on for what feels like hours about how amazing and talented she is until she is interrupted by a man who has metal drumsticks for fingers. "I am confused, so where exactly do you live? Because either you live in the city with a chip or you live outside the city with us and we would have seen you by now."

Didn't they ask me that earlier? she thought. Their poor brains must be scrambled from the metal.

Lying while under the influence of alcohol seems easier and easier to do so she does her best to reply to his question with an answer that satisfies him.

"I live with Nails, are you familiar with him?"

"We are not, but doesn't the thought wind then affect you guys?"

"As long as we are wearing headphones and have thought wind-proofed walls, we're okay."

They scrutinize her statement. It has enough holes in it that you would surely step in one. They know of no situation like the one she describes. Either you have the chip and live in the city or you don't and live in the woods and are moving electronic towers. Corey assumes the thought wind has deleted Nails from their mind and that's why they don't know him.

A few more artists appear and begin asking questions, but a clown tells them to go away because they are high right now and want to enjoy the rare good vibes.

A massage therapist ignores the rambling request and begins massaging them to further enhance their current pleasant moods. A musician uses a handmade portable drum and softly taps on it creating a raw primitive beat. A couple clowns do a few funny dances showcasing the loose affects the tomato has on its users.

As the substances start to lessen their grip on the artists and Corey's buzz begins to diminish, she starts to feel antsy and tells the artists she would hopefully see them again soon. They thank her and give her a white plastic rose to pin on her shirt.

She walks a hundred yards on autopilot as her brain replays the previous events over and over and how her Mom would react to zero tomatoes. She is shaken from her requiem when her ankle twists slightly from a thick stick.

Corey feels the need to connect with familiarity and security. Reaching into her pocket for her phone, she decides to text Nails. She tells him she misses him and is excited to see him again. She keeps it short and sweet. No need for anything else at this point.

She is approaching the city and knows it is time to put on her headphones. She scans her recent purchases on her iPod and settles on The Menzingers. She focuses on their brand of catchy storytelling punk, singing each line to prevent the thought wind from squatting inside her mind.

Not quite feeling like going home yet, she randomly walks down a city street. She takes a deep breath and tries to relax. Each breathe feels like she is inhaling dark clouds deep into her stomach cavity and exhaling them as white foam turning these dark city streets a more pleasant shade. She yawns and knows it is time to head towards the gate and start the long walk home.

As she walks over the bridge, she removes her headphones and lets her mind wander and circulate about how much her life has changed so quickly. From being a shy girl who wanted to hide away from the world because of her fruit breasts, to now entering the dark side solo, having a boyfriend, and giving out samples of her breasts to artists so they can feel better.

CHERRIES

Nails stretches his legs on his couch and releases a wide yawn and then closes his eyes. He eventually thinks about getting a regular job. He is getting concerned about what possible damage was occurring to his brain when he volunteered and surrendered to the thought wind. But with his outbursts of fury and comfort in the freedom his schedule provides, he doesn't know of any job that would suit him well.

He dives into his wallet and the emptiness inside tells him it was time for another edition of *Nihilist News* if he wants to continue hanging out with Corey and not coming across as a broke artist looking for a sugar mama. Not that she has a lot of money or anything.

He skates around the city thinking about potential jobs but ends up trying to land a kickflip instead. Normally, it is performed at ease, but since he is skating less, it proves a difficult challenge. Finally, he lands it and feels satisfied enough to retreat home to play some Nintendo and relax.

He procrastinates a battle with the thought wind and instead works on the other aspects of his paper. Since he isn't afforded the luxury of a smart phone with a camera on it, he has to get pictures developed at a store.

Nail's chooses the one-hour pick-up. He looks over the pictures and picks out a few that would be used in the paper. He works on the design that will be the front cover. The cover is the most important part. Most people will decide if they are interested based on the cover alone. Feeling a need to be social, he texts Corey to see if she wants to hang out.

Corey arrives and Nails shows her the pictures and design of his latest weird newspaper. They collaborate for an hour on the newspaper as both enjoy being creative.

Nails feels relieved that Corey appears healthy and not craving booze or drugs. They watch a few movies and fall asleep.

Corey has to work the next day so she is up early to ride her bike over the bridge into the light side. Once she reaches the light side, she goes down to Nails skate spot to quickly change into her all white and khaki look.

Later that night, her Mom acquires about her tomatoes and Corey is all ready for a crystal-clear convincing story.

"I was walking down the street just minding my own business when some jerk tried to take my purse. I fought him off and kicked him good, but during the fight he fell into my chest and smashed them. You should be lucky I am still alive."

"Corey, you need to spend more time on the light side. I know you like Nails a lot and all, but do you really think there's a future between you two? What if you want to live together? Neither of you can move. It just wouldn't work, honey."

"I will quit Sunshine Smoothies in a heartbeat if that's what it comes down to. That job means nothing to me. Anybody could perform my job responsibilities. You only want me around for my fruits. Speaking of which, what disturbing new fruit will be growing out of my chest this week?"

"Cherries."

"Oh great, so I will be looking like prepubescent teenager, just fucking great, Mother."

"They will be larger than normal cherries, though!"

"Sure, whatever, just give me the damn ingredients."

She walks away while her Mom yells, "I only do this because I love you, Corey!"

She texts Nails that she is exasperated and needs to slumber early. However, she has a bit more sinister plan conjured up. She would go back to the dark side. What's the big deal, she told herself. Nails won't see her as he doesn't like going out at night. She has been saving food from sunshine smoothies the past few days and now has a nice sized bag full of goodies for the starving artists.

Corey goes back to the graveyard, first. How did this person die? Did Hero kill them? The thought wind? Could Nails have done it and that's why he told her it was a fake graveyard? The stress of it makes her thirsty.

She hits up the first bar she sees.

"Hey, can I get the hazy IPA?"

"Hey, I am a bartender and a sculptor, I hope you enjoy your beer."

"Thanks."

"Hey, I am a bartender and sculptor, I hope you enjoy your beer."

Feeling unbalanced and odd from the short odd conversation, she quickly slams a few beers. Feeling fantastic and more liberal in speech, she decides to start striking up conversations with the people around her anticipating and hoping it goes smoother than it did with the bartender.

"Hey, my name is Corey, how are you doing?"

"Hi, I play bass guitar, I hope you enjoy my groovy bass lines."

"Oh, that's cool, are you in a band?"

"Hi, I play guitar, I hope you enjoy my groovy bass lines."

"Yes, you told me, but do you play in a band?"

"Hi, I play guitar, I hope you enjoy my groovy bass lines."

Feeling like she was talking to a baby, she let her emotions get the best of her and screamed "Yes, I fucking know that, what's wrong with you!!!??"

The guy just stares at her and doesn't reply.

She feels guilty and apologizes. The guy replies with the same line as before.

Corey walks away and ends up having similar conversations with everybody else she talks to. Over thirty different people and basically the same conversation. They would say hi or hello and then discuss their art in a few sentences.

An eerie vibe rolls through her. This is the first time she is out and about having conversations without Nails and she has a strange feeling Nails purposely left out this part in an attempt to shield her from the reality of what's really going on. She thinks about all the times he would cause a conversation between her and somebody else to cease. Then she remembers the clowns talking about the chip. So, these people must have the chip installed?

She is so annoyed, she loses control of her beer count and stumbles out of the bar. She cranks her head upwards looking to see where exactly she is in relation to the iron gate. But she feels like a compass with a broken arrow. Every time she begins walking, she has a feeling it is the wrong way. Like a hand without a glove in negative twenty-degree weather, she feels exposed and vulnerable.

"I am such a bad girl."

"Does Nails like bad girls?"

"Stupid bitches like me don't belong on the dark side."

"Take a left down the next street before you go home."

She takes the left. She doesn't have a choice in her current state. To fight the alcohol and the thought wind is simply too much to handle.

"Break the window of this business and take a bike to move faster. I am getting pissed off at your slow fat drunken crawl."

She violently shakes her head and screams, "Shut up, leave me alone, assholes!"

An image of a finger waving back and forth with the caption tsk tsk above it.

A lizard receiving a lobotomy.

Sirens roar as fire trucks race towards a human house that's on fire. The human house consists of just Corey's face.

As the human house fire rages on in her mind, she decides to stop fighting it and picks up a rock and launches it into the window. She retrieves the bike and begins pedaling it towards her destination. She gets off her bike and lets it fall to the ground, chipping the new paint. The door to the Statue opens and Corey walks towards it and right before she enters, she hears, *"I changed my mind. Your a worthless wart, get out of here."*

In shock that she survived the thought wind—a furious attack on bike pedals commences—until she reaches the light side. Her lackadaisical attitude almost causes her entire future to be altered by making one lousy decision. She reflects on the rude statements they bombarded her with. She knew they were wrong. She is much stronger and braver than they thought.

SHARE WHAT YA GOT

I want to be jubilant and upbeat but something inside me always reels it back in. I imagine a fisherman inside me catching joy and bliss, then removing it from the fishing line and tossing it back into my stomach acid to ensure a state of content is never reached.

It's time to let the thought wind invade as that seems to be the only way to get any sort of answers. I justify the procedure because my bank account is empty like rum bottles on a pirate ship.

I am not in the mood for my normal procrastination so I briskly walk inside and retrieve the bag of materials and set up shop as fast as possible. Headphones slam against concrete as I raise my arms in the air like antennas and scream, "Let's fuckin' do this!"

"Listen up you nihilistic twerp. I've given you ample opportunities to simplify your life, to only focus on skateboarding and your newspaper. No stress. No bills. Just creating art all day. And what have you done with this rare precious offer? You spit in my face as you mock me and call me names. You didn't choose to live on the dark side, but you did choose what path you would travel while here. I simply have no remorse for what I am about to show you. You caused this."

Nail's head protrudes out from acres and acres of dirt. Vines wrap themselves around his head, squeezing and squeezing until his face turns fire engine red and morphs into a tomato. A hand reaches down and picks his tomato head. They take a bite and toss his half eaten face into the dirt.

Clouds rain down seeds. The germination process begins.

Instead of dirt, there's thousands of women lying on their backs as tomatoes sprout and reach for the sky.

Miles and miles of naked humans with no eyes and covered in various black tattoos wait in line to pick the tomatoes off the chest of the woman.

The cutest girl the world has ever created enters a hospital room. Nails is on a bed covered in rugged vines and roots. She unbuttons her shirt very slowly. Nails can feel his parched mouth prepare for juicy explosions. When she finally removes the shirt, she bends down so Nails can take a bite, but the fruit vanishes just before he can have a taste as she whispers in his ear, "Share what ya got."

Endless smiling humans with tomatoes smeared across their face appear.

I begin to shake as I am unable to handle any further mental abuse. My blurry eyes read the poster board in front of me providing guidance. I clumsily reach for my headphones and stagger inside falling like a dead weight onto the couch. I sip on water and close my eyes for ten minutes or so and know I have to start writing now, while my brain is still in this twisted, tangled mess.

I furiously bang and slap at the keyboard, unable to distinguish whether this is a nightmare or reality as I let my brain unravel and spill out.

I take a deep breath, drink more water and eat a banana. I review the gibberish on the computer screen. It looks sufficient to pay the rent and have money left over to hang out with Corey.

With that out of the way, I focus on what clues can be retrieved from this session. I write "Tomatoes" on the board and study it. A frightening thought takes root. I am unable to handle what I believe it represents so I rush to the liquor store and purchase a bottle of whiskey and a can of white spray paint from the hardware store.

I walk while slugging the whiskey trying to convince myself that Corey is not sharing her fruit breasts with random people on the dark side.

Feeling the effects of the rusty colored beverage, I wander over to the light side. I stagger a bit and make no effort to hide the fact that I am drinking in public.

I see a flock of crows. I take a moment to rest my legs and then begin to stare them down. They match my stares with their oily eyes. Time stands still. I then begin to flap my arms in the air like I was one of them. They respond by flying above me.

I walk towards Corey's house still taking sips of whiskey while a hundred black birds fly above me like I am their master and they would do anything for this new cause of mine.

I finally reach Corey's house, and in an exhausted drunk voice, I stare at the birds and scream "Do it already, turn this place darker than the depths of hell."

The birds digest their new master's command and fly into the house. Splat and wet thud sounds repeat over and over. Five minutes later Corey's house is different shades of dead black bird.

I take a long pull from the bottle and stare at the house for what seems like an eternity. I shake up the white spray paint and try to write "Whorey Corey what a bore. Whorey Corey dead as a door. Whore Corey a human core." Instead, it just comes out as zig zagged lines of white blurriness on top of black blobs of decaying crow.

I WON'T NOOSE YOU

The next day at work, Corey has a tough time concentrating after seeing her house being turned into a crow graveyard. Was it a sign? Was somebody trying to tell her something? No way it could be Nails who did this.

Her mind expands into other areas of thinking. In such a short amount of time, she has been exposed to so many new things. She keeps replaying them over and over in her brain trying to make sense of it all and find what direction she needs to be traveling.

What was her end goal? To be with Nails? To be a junkie? Hanging out with the artists from the woods and helping them out?

She is shaken from her requiem when a customer walks in. She prepares his smoothie on autopilot. The sound from the blender blocks out all other thoughts and it feels nice to not have the constant jibber jabber inside her skull going at full blast.

The customer drinks the smoothie in under a minute and then picks up a table inside the store and raises it above his head, declaring Sunshine Smoothies the greatest store ever and then darts out the door into traffic.

Corey doesn't think twice at the supremely odd decision-making of the human. One eats the food at Sunshine Smoothies and then acts like Superman. She has asked her mom endless times what makes her food so damn healthy, but each time, her Mom just says, "Organic," and then changes the subject.

She takes a selfie of herself making a strange face and then draws a noose around the picture and texts it to Nails. She hopes he "gets" the caption of work being such a drag at times. She leaves out the part about the dead crows so he doesn't stress over it. I receive the message and throw my phone into a squishy pillow.

I wake up with sin and suffering in my veins. Not knowing how to properly cope with this dangerous new attitude, I find myself embracing it and seeing where it takes me. No more fighting it. No more struggling day in and day out trying to live a righteous purpose-driven life. Remove the walls and locks and cages and doors so evil can freely walk in and out when needed.

The wickedness inside me moves my feet towards the direction of the light side. As I exit the bridge, a flock of black birds began to fly around me, immediately. "Perfect," I tell myself.

Time to turn white into black.

Black blobs splatter across various buildings producing a wet wallop each time a crow kills themselves. Apocalyptic waves of fury blast the generic whites and tans that the light side pride themselves on. A singular vision to die for evil and darkness takes over the place courtesy of the birds— while the inhabitants are too blind to care.

They are reproducing at rapid speeds. Thousands die. Thousands replace them. It feels like there is a warehouse filled with black birds ready to support my newfound calling in life.

Lost in my dark paradise, I am awoken by somebody speaking to me.

"Nails, why don't you go get a snack and give these innocent birds a break," says Molly.

"Just giving your city a little color."

"We have plenty of color as it is."

"Do you now? News to me."

"Is everything okay, Nails?"

"Everything's just fine. I have no control over these birds."

"Well, you kinda do. Those birds wouldn't be doing this without your instruction."

"Oh, I am sure you know all about these bird's and Corey's breasts you heinous bitch."

"Now, now, calm down. Let's not be tossing out accusations like that."

"Your existence is revolting, and when it's judgement day, you will see it clearly, for once."

She isn't mentally prepared for this kind of assault and stands there frozen like she was just zapped by a taser.

I spit in her direction and begin the long journey home.

The birds follow me, resembling a halo of dark clouds above my head.

Corey gets off work and contemplates deeply on what to do. She texts Nails, "Miss ya," and waits for a response. Thirty minutes pass, and since this is the second message he seems to ignore, she decides to hit up the dark side without him.

A few hours later, she is many beers deep inside a bar and her mind wanders and roams on how she should visit the artists and bring them food and medical supplies. She texts Nails again, "Hey is everything okay? Love ya."

The logistics of how to locate the artists involves some deep thinking. Leaving the city is a start, for they live far away from electricity. After a few miles of aimlessly moving like a vacant vagabond, she see's some light which she follows until a guy pops out of nowhere startling her.

"What maggot's burrowing under your periwig?"

"Excuse me?" she says, confused. He appears to be a pirate, or an artist dressed like a pirate. So, she pays him a compliment.

"I really dig your pirate vibe."

"Now there was a true word as ever heard spoke."

"Yup."

"Fill that pretty belly with grog and that's what makes the world spin on its poles, say I. Drink, battle, murder, shipwreck, and hell fire to."

Feeling like she was getting nowhere with the pirate, she tries to excuse herself. When she was slowly escaping, she notices the pirate's parrot looking rough.

"Is your bird okay, mister pirate?

"A swashbuckler is never okay."

"Can you take him to a vet?"

"By the devil's hoof, no."

"Oh okay, well hopefully it feels better."

"Bless your old rusty heart."

She thinks about what the pirate artist did to make money. Maybe Hero felt bad for him and was trying to help him focus on how to make money when acting like a pirate. She ponders the poor parrot and how it really needs medical attention. She feels like a vacuum cleaner was turned on inside her sucking up any motivation to keep living that evening. Feeling despondent, she heads home.

HATE & HANGOVERS

I wake up the next morning with a terrible headache and hatred of the dark side, light side and every fuckin side of the planet. I grab my phone to see many messages from Corey, causing my headache to sound like a heartbeat.

> Pound.
> Pound.
> Pound.

I scramble around the apartment desperately searching for a tiny pill that would cure this copious pain behind my eyes. Finding nothing and without thinking twice, I run outside only to be hit by the thought wind within minutes.

You're an appalling person for what you are doing to the light side with those crows. Just jumping to assumptions. No investigation? No reviewing the facts? Just murdering the poor crows because of what? You think Corey might be sharing her breasts? What, do you think you own them? She can do what she wants with them you little shit.

I run back inside like a scared little child. I am so confused. The thought wind made it pretty clear the night before about what Corey is doing. Was she not giving samples of fruit to the artists? Did the thought wind just make that part up to fuck with me? I really feel like death is at the door and it is time to let it in. My pounding headache makes it unable to focus so I grab a pair of headphones and make my way to a store to gobble up some pain pills.

I get home and lay in bed until the magic of the pills heal my fractured brain. When the pain resides enough, I decide to read the messages from Corey. It feels like a chainsaw ripping open my rib cage to get at my heart. I try responding to her and know anything I say will open Pandora's box. I just couldn't handle disappointment and arguments anymore.

The next day, I walk to the store and purchase some planks of wood and a packet of nails and a hammer. On the walk home, I justify my next maneuver of boarding up my windows—It is how I now feel on the inside, so I want everybody else to see that as well. I am finished with society and giving a shit. The outside of my place will match what I am feeling internally, which is boarded up and closed. I know Corey would see this in a few days and get the point. I expect screaming and cursing when she finally realizes this is the new reality.

I go out that night for a walk. When somebody is in my way, I purposely shoulder them like a bully does to a wimpy student in the halls before class starts.

They turn around and say, "I design the arms to move."

Confused I say, "What did you just say?"

"I design the arms to move."

This is very weird. They always respond by talking about art. I rush into a bar and slap several people in the face.

"I lubricate the gears."
"I collect the wood."
"I collect the metal."
"I collect the plastic."
"I make the legs move."
"I make the arms move."

I could not believe what I was hearing. Something is being planned. I leave the bar under the influence of alcohol and animosity.

As I am walking home, my eyes hone in on a royal blue post office box that is twenty feet ahead. Each foot forward towards the box eggs my brain on to cause destruction and release pent-up resentment. "Fuck this place," replays over and over like a record at 4am while the human is passed out in the corner surrounded by broken bottles.

Boot contacts metal.
Metal slightly dents.
Boot repeats contact over and over and over.
Stress less throughout body.
Endorphins released.

I stop when my leg feels a strain.

I step back and observe the damage. I see a note about it being a federal offense to mess with the post office. It doesn't resonate at all. Nothing. Not even a ping of guilt.

I wake up the next day in a catatonic state. Just a mess of flesh connected by mangled bones.

I notice a blinking in the distance. Endless text messages. I kick my phone and the slight pain doesn't register. I think about the previous night and even though I was drunk, it felt so liberating to release my outrage I have towards the dark side and life in general. I lay on my couch all day thinking about the future. I order some clothes for same day delivery.

Around 5:00 pm, I hear a thump against the door. As I open it, I see a drone fly away. Fuckers are too scared to come here in person. I get a knife and begin slicing the tape like it's the throat of a human. I eagerly try on my new clothes and start to feel positive emotions again about my new path in life.

I eat dinner at 6:00 pm. An hour later I feel lethargic and decide to put on The Potato Pirates to get me into a drinking mode. It works and by 10:00 pm I have downed five cold ones. With the help of beer, I find myself becoming soft and deciding that I at least owe Corey an explanation.

"Hey, sorry for being distant the past week. I need to work on myself right now. I am a feral human and it's not safe to be around me. Also, stay away from the city, I am going to burn this place to the fucking ground."

Multiple text messages hit my phone. I flip it like a turtle on its back. Out of sight, out of mind.

I go into the bathroom and shave my head. With all my hair gone, you can clearly see many tattoos. Above my forehead is "Nate." Going around the perimeter of my head are actual pictures of nails. Above that is the date I woke up on the dark side. On the back of my head is "Skate or Die."

After a month of living on the dark side and determining something was done to my memory, I decided tattooing important information would serve me well if memory issues surface again. I then covered the tattoos up by letting hair sprout from the skull like weeds in an abandoned lot. With tattoo artists in abundance on the dark side, it was effortless finding somebody to tattoo in my price range. I try on the new threads.

White jeans.

White doc martens with black laces.

White leather jacket.

Black fedora.

I grab a black bat I purchased earlier along with some white brass knuckles and a few knives. I find a mirror and feel liberated with what I see. It was time to end the division between the two sides and what better way than some good old-fashioned destruction and violence.

As I am leaving the house, something feels missing. I look around the house and see my skateboard on the ground. My trusty tried and true sidekick. I look at my boots and then the skateboard and try envisioning the two together. It screams domestic dispute. I will ride you tomorrow, buddy.

One of the appeals of the dark side is no cops or authorities. Hero figured that wouldn't be necessary since he was interviewing each person and could tell their level of passion towards their craft. In his experience, if artists have enough money for food and rent, they would not commit any crimes.

I put my headphones on and hit the streets feeling frisky and ready to lay waste to this wasteland. While drinking I created a playlist I felt would be appropriate for the evening. Subhumans. Sick of it All. Rudimentry Peni. Small Brown Bike. Public Serpents. Forward. Night Birds. Dillinger Four. H2O. Tragedy. NOFX. Hot Water Music. Sex Pistols. Hub City Stompers. Crossed Keys. School Drugs. It takes a while to create since I have to create it using actual physical music.

I see a guy in the distance and know he won't comment on my white attire. Even if an altercation occurs and I wound up on the losing side of the battle, I just want the people around me to show some type of emotion or passion.

I feel a surge of something run through my body as I approach the man, but I would not commit random acts of violence against people who obviously are being controlled somehow. On the random chance anybody would comment about why I was wearing white in the land of black, I would feel comfortable with a minor altercation.

Actually, if I see any of those pieces of shit thought wind video people, I would most likely be open to a quarrel. The guy passes and it was like they had their eyes removed. I wonder what went through the minds of these people. Did they have deep thoughts? Desires? Vices?

I tell myself if nobody says anything to me the entire night, I would conclude the dark side is not worth saving and it is my responsibility to turn it into rubble and ashes. While I wait for the end of the night to make my decision, I feel an appetizer is in order. I know immediately what to start with. There is a big billboard near my house that went up a few days ago.

Perfect People LLC
Making A Complex World Less Complex

There is a ladder on the side of the billboard. Once I get to the top, I reach inside my backpack of weapons and find a knife. I slowly pull it out and begin slashing the billboard until it is no longer recognizable. I climb down the ladder carefully as the last thing I need is a drunken fall into a bag of sharp objects.

I roam the dark side, letting wrathful thoughts saturate my soul. I grab a fresh beer from my bag and envision the trail of violence I am about to embark on. I visualize the dark side as nothing but ashes and it brings a smile to my face. "Fuck it" becomes my new motto.

I feel the thought before the thought is born. I try to block it. Swat it away like a feral fly. But it passes through and I am forced to deal with it. I picture Corey in bed with her face on my shoulder sleeping contently. It makes my heart feel like there are thousands of tiny holes and every time I take a breath a new hole is formed. My brain goes spastic and I picture my heart becoming one mammoth hole turning me into a cold weathered soul unable to show any emotion and forced to live amongst the already dead the rest of my life.

I violently shake my head to erase the thought. I force myself to only think about the task at hand. It seems to work as somewhere deep in my body a boombox convinces me I am a martyr on a mission for honorable acts. If this is some sort of new-age prison or hell or whatever and I could put a wrench in there gears or destroy it entirely so nobody else goes through what I did—then I will feel like I made a positive impact on this planet instead of contributing nothing.

I hope Corey has the wisdom and strength to weather these treacherous seas. To know that when the boat lands on the mainland and dries out and conversations are had, then in time, a monumental joining of skin against skin would commence. The past would be what pasts are: something that is dead and in the rearview mirror. Humans number one characteristic is faulty decisions. Carry on. The sun will keep shining.

I wish I could just talk to her face to face and explain this, but I was worried I might do something awful in her presence. I would never become violent with her but I might break some windows or something after we were done talking and she doesn't need to witness such juvenile behavior and become even more distant. I still don't know for sure if Corey is sharing her fruit breasts but the mental image of it sets me on a course that I just can't slow down or stop. Like a junkie reuniting with the needle, once you start, there is no stopping.

Fuck it. Think dark thoughts. Make Satan jealous with just how evil you can get.

Like clockwork, this cracked brain reminds me of how much I care for her, but I tell himself that she shared her sacred secret with a bunch of strangers. Every positive eventually turns to a negative when living on the dark side.

I wake up the next morning and can see something of color against the morbid macabre that is the dark side. I slap on some headphones and go outside.

"Asshole."

"Pathetic."

"Lose my number."

"Go skate off a cliff."

Corey obviously visited my house in the wee hours. I sit in a chair and try to digest it all but instead just feel bloated from all my beer intake as of late. I knew this would happen. It at least shows she does care and have feelings for me. If she didn't, she wouldn't have done this.

Block it out. Don't get soft. Stay strong. Nobody knows your pain. It is what makes you special. Anybody else would have given up by now. Soon this will end. It has to end.

Later that afternoon, I go for a walk to clear my head. I am feeling pretty good due to Avail blasting into my ears just loud enough so I don't blow out my eardrums.

I reflect on Corey and Molly for the hundredth time. It feels like they cloned themselves and jumped in my mouth and slid down my throat like it was a water park ride and then lived somewhere in my stomach. Like an attention starved brat, when they feel I am not thinking about them enough, they climb a later from my stomach to my brain and start yelling and screaming so I would think about them.

I shake the cloned brats from my brain and feel them falling back into my stomach. I take a swig of hot sauce, hoping it burns them.

I gain my focus again and think about how I need explosives. I know it is going to be tough with my limited resources. I spend hours pacing back and forth in my apartment trying to come up with a plan to take down large buildings. Frustrated and feeling inpatient, I go to Faith's apartment to use her internet. My computer is so ancient it is only used to type up *Nihilistic News* and play classic computer games like *Space Invaders* and *Tetris*.

I open Faith's door and am about to say something to her but figure what was the point. I pull the chair out and wiggle the mouse to see if the computer is on. I have no clue where the starting line is on something so illegal. Without thought my fingers type in the search engine a few keywords, "explosives large buildings."

I click on the first link that flashes on the screen. The article describes how the FBI is concerned with how easy it is to buy dangerous explosives on the dark web. I have heard of the dark web a few times before but thought you would need some kind of code or invitation to access it. I sit in silence for a moment letting my brain do what brains do. "Access to the dark web," is typed into the search engine. Feeling like I was granted access to a bank vault during a robbery, the dark web appears on the screen.

I go to the section titled, "Want to Sell."

I couldn't believe the vast volume of illegal things listed. My heart is racing with excitement at the thought of buildings crumbling all around me. Sweaty palms finally navigate the mouse to the section I so desired.

Explosives.

An hour later, I order mortars, grenades, and other dangerous weapons of war. After I have spent all my savings, I decide to crack open a beer and see what else the dark side has to offer. I begin clicking on all sorts of things.

ECSTASY

PROSTITUTION

EXOTIC MEATS

I then stumble upon something that makes the hair on my arms stand up as if they just were given a jolt of caffeine.

PRODUCE GROWN ON BEAUTIFUL BABES
GUARANTEED TO GET YOU HIGH NATURALLY
SUPERIOR TASTE
SECOND TO NONE
BUY NOW
OVERNIGHT DELIVERY AVAILABLE

GRAPES, STRAWBERRIES, TOMATOES, PEARS, AND MORE, ALL GROWN ON BEAUTIFUL, ATTRACTIVE WOMEN. EACH FRUIT CONTAINS ALL-NATURAL INGREDIENTS TO GENERATE A RELAXING ENJOYABLE HIGH. NO SIDE EFFECTS. NO ADDICTION. EACH FRUIT COMES WITH A CERTIFICATE OF AUTHORIZATION DETAILING THE PERSON THEY WERE GROWN ON AND AN 8 X10 COLOR PICTURE FROM THE WAIST UP.

I frantically scan the pictures. Their eyes are crossed out. Goosebumps rise up like vampires at the sight of virgin blood when I realize all the pictures are Corey with different hair color.

My stomach turns sour. I grab another beer hoping it helps and not hurts. I stay on the screen for twenty minutes to review each picture as I am fascinated with fever. There is no other information available, so I click out of that section to stand up and stretch my arms out. I get another beer and sit back down and start to click in other areas of the dark web.

CROWS GROWN USING HUMAN DNA
OWN THIS RARE BREED FOR A LIMITED TIME

Bells of shock ring and ricochet inside me as if struck by lightning. I slam half a beer in a single gulp.

Nerves recoil and relax.

Brain turns tranquil and placid.

Let these obstacles grow your hate muscles. Then flex and watch the world crumble.

At least now the wool over my eyes is removed. I finally have some clarity about the crows mysterious nature. The next step is finding out their endgame. What role did they play in this twisted train wreck and are they friend or foe. Where does one even begin to investigate a labyrinthine of this nature?

My mind instinctively wants to find Corey and tell her everything. Protect her from her Mom. Hold her forever and never let anybody or anything scar her.

Was it possible Corey has her fingerprints on the crime scene, as well? Could she be laughing nightly at me? Nobody can be trusted. Destroy them all echoes in my brain like a faint hollow scream in the dead of night.

DAWN OF NEW BEGINNINGS

Corey wanders over to the dark side without paying much attention to her geographic location. Her brain feels like a spiderweb that caught a bunch of bugs and was not sure what to do with them. The artists, so proud of creating art in such a turmoil sea, still need basic resources like soap, toiletries, clean water, and food she tells herself. This about helping them and nothing else. Focus.

Images of the boy in black attack her brain instead.

She desperately wants to connect with him but he's a one main captain sailing in a sea of sorrow, on a solo journey by himself to annihilate the burdens that refuse to leave him. It would feel like a waste of time trying to reason with somebody who's body is present but mind is not.

She then hears the phrase that would foment a change in her life.

"Hey, come here, girl."

She tries to bolt but time is not on her side.

They immediately seize her.

"Please don't hurt me, I am an artist and only want to create."

"This is not our decision, our boss will be here momentarily to decide a course of action for you."

Thirty minutes later, the boss strolls in licking his greasy lips.

"What brings you to our enchanted forest of freaks?" as he marvels at her perfect body.

"I am a nutritionist and want to help the artists out. They really need it. In a creative way, of course."

He continues eyeing her up.

"Bring her to my palace."

"You don't understand, I am a powerful healing nutritionist and the world needs more people like me." She takes off her shirt and showcases her fuzzy peach breasts that are ripe and ready for picking. "These are not peaches for eating. They are medicinal ones."

"What the hell is this? You are truly something special. Together we can rule this island. I would treat you like a queen." His stomach makes a growling sound. His brain envisions biting into the juicy fruit.

"Bring her closer, I must try one of these peaches, now.'

The boss's men, afraid of saying no and facing severe repercussions, holds her arms so the boss can pick a peach.

"Those are very powerful sedatives. You could die!"

"A single peach from a pretty girl cannot kill me."

He eats one in a few bites. Peach juice leaks down his fat face. He picks the other one and devours it.

"Now bring her to my place, you goons."

They release Corey into the man's living room. He lives like a king compared to the other artists. The boss sits in a chair and releases a loud yawn. He stares at Corey like a supreme creep until he dozes off from the peaches.

Corey sits on a chair and thinks about her mom and Nails. She looks at the pudgy whale of a human. She contemplates the thought wind telling her many times how she is spineless and worthless; a human who would just blend in and fade away. Contributing nothing to society. Just another burden that destroys Mother Earth with her ignorance. She begins to feel something strange brewing inside. Her heart accelerates.

She looks around the house and feels a fire in the pits of her soul unlike anything she has ever experienced. How could somebody live so large while others around him live so low? He is probably responsible for the thought wind movies as well. Earth would be a better place with him and his kind extinct.

Unable to mentally handle it all, she grabs a pillow and gingerly approaches the subhuman. She pauses for a second and fills with doubt, but a quick shake of her head and the doubt vanishes away. Pillow presses against face. Her mind floods with memories of every time the world has considered her a pushover. Just another pretty face with nothing to say. Spineless flesh and bones.

She is shaken from her requiem by the shakes of a man in the final moments of life. As the man begins losing his grip of the world, Corey's soul gains something so valuable that only real-life experiences can offer—tenacity and grit. She feels a backbone growing inside that would give her confidence to fight for what she believes in. She finally stops when the body goes limp-death without much fanfare.

She frantically searches for the nearest exit. She shoves the door so hard it causes the wrist to bend awkwardly. Adrenaline rushes to the site and pain is never allowed to present itself.

When Corey tells the entire camp about what just happened, they explode in joyous noise.

"You did it, Corey. You killed the oppressive brute," says a clown.

Corey just stands there. Searching for the right words to say. Instead, she's just in shock. She takes a seat and puts her hands over her face.

"This is great news, Corey! Do not be sad! That man was a nuisance and nimrod. He just showed up one day and did everything in his power to profit from the dark side. He produces the thought wind movies in his fancy house. Anytime he saw us making progress or feeling healthy, he would destroy our stuff and force us into the city where he could start filming his disturbing movies."

"We are finally free!"

"What about his other men?" said somebody.

"Let's get them," they all seem to say in unison.

The artists charge the house and treat the situation like a battlefield. They find anything they can use as a weapon of war.

They see the two other men trying to escape the back door.

They hunt them down and subdue them.

"Corey, what should we do with them?"

She knew the decision she makes would set her on a path the rest of her life. Did she want to be a vigilante or a healing nutritionist? Could she be both. These two deserve a punishment that is severe and harsh. However, she is not judge and jury and does not want more blood on her hands.

"Today is your lucky day, you sick fucks. This is your one get-out-of-jail-free card. Turn your lives around. Choose to contribute to the earth instead of taking from it. Leave now. Never come back. If we find out you do a single negative thing again, we will find you and hurt you badly. Am I clear?"

"Crystal clear."

"Leave now."

"Can we take a few minutes to get our stuff?"

"You guys really are something else. I will count to five. If you're still here and not running for your life, then we will drop you off in the city with no headphones. Actually, maybe we should just do that anyway."

They bolt fast. The artists look at Corey the way humans look at somebody they admire.

The artists, so worked up and stimulated by the death of the terrible tyrant, pick up Corey as if she is the MVP of an important game. They carry her to the boss's house while singing a boisterous tune.

"This will be your new home, Corey. We trust you and want you to do what you think is best for us."

They all yell and cheer to spice up the moment so Corey would realize just how jazzed up they are about her being around.

She looks around at the fancy surroundings. Electricity galore. Headphones everywhere. She becomes appalled that her fellow species is able to ignore such suffering so they can live exceptionally well.

"I will not live here. The sickest and suffering will live here instead. I will sleep on the ground with the trees and dirt."

They all look at her in disbelief.

"I will be back later. Today is the dawn of new beginnings. Create art with vigor and might today. A milestone is upon us. We will take back our lives from the cowards. Artists will command the respect they deserve. Society has downgraded art with the internet. We suffer and spend great lengths to create things that make you feel alive. Make you feel anger and love. And what is our reward? Steal our art and give it away. Stream it free on endless platforms. Then have everyone spend their money on phones and TVs."

"This ends today. Select amongst yourselves who needs the luxuries of electricity and all the other modern amenities in that house. Never lose faith, friends. I will see you soon with exciting news."

The artists roar with sound. Hands clap. Makeshift instruments are created while songs are sung. Chants and slogans yelled out in reckless fashion. Dark clouds part allowing the sun to peek through.

MY MASTERPIECE

The explosives land and I put them in the corner of my living room. I need a game plan on how to move forward. Blowing up the buildings at night when there is nobody inside them seems to be the model idea, I conclude.

It's 10:00 pm and I assume that's late enough that even any janitors would have exited the buildings. I grab a few grenades and mortars and exit my place. I put on the Felons Club and convince myself to try and have a good time tonight. After ten minutes of walking, I find a potential building to test on.

The entire building shows no signs of electricity or life inside it. I open the doors and yell, "Hello! Anybody inside? I am going to destroy this place! If you're inside, you will die!" I repeat that over and over half a dozen times. No response back. I tell myself it's fair game to destroy.

I handle a grenade gingerly. I look at it with all the respect in the world. I am fully aware of what damage it can accomplish. "Fuck it," I say. I make sure the door is open to the full extent. I don't want to throw the grenade and have it not pass the entryway and explode before I have a chance to run away. I practice with a few rocks at first. I get the motion and logistics down. I am as prepared as possible.

The metal feels cool in my hand. I nervously throw it, and for some reason, close my eyes as I run away. My heart beats so intensely I would not be surprised if it burst through my skin.

It sounds like a jet plane is taking off inside my ear drums. Equilibrium skewers and I lose my balance. I open my eyes and walk back to the building to inspect the damage. It looks like an open space from the walls and barriers being gone now.

I spend twenty minutes checking rooms and hallways and yelling out to see if anybody is inside. I would never forgive myself if somebody gets injured or killed. I feel bad for the janitors and cleaning people. They were promised utopia on the dark side but with one small problem—somebody still has to perform jobs that sucked. So new artists were forced to take these jobs. But at least they were surrounded by other artists.

I toss another grenade down a hall and run away covering my ears with my hands. When the smoke clears and I see the vast damage I am causing, a smile forms on my face and a warm feeling radiates inside.

The mortar looks at me and tells me to have fun with it. I have absolutely no clue how to operate it and spend twenty minutes on YouTube figuring it out.

Thirty minutes later, the building looks dilapidated and drunk.

I get the chainsaw out and begin assaulting various spots of the building, trying somehow to be conscious that the building could collapse on me.

I entertained the idea of pouring gasoline on each building and lighting a match but was nervous that wouldn't satisfy my cravings for destruction. Simply pouring gas and lighting a match was too easy. I want to work up a sweat and come face to face with possible death and escape the other side. A good day's work is satisfying, even if it consists of destruction instead of proper wage.

I take a step back from it all to work on my breathing. I need to pause and fix these shaky brittle nerves. I take a deep breath until my body can no longer handle any more oxygen. While holding it in, I can feel bruised ear drums reminding me to purchase ear plugs. I blow the air out. Repeat over and over. My nervous system thanks me by lowering my blood pressure and general chaos running amok inside my ear canals.

I reach into my pocket to retrieve my camera. This is my artwork. My masterpiece. My statement to the world. One thing driven in my brain from living on the dark side is if you do something with passion and flex your creative muscles, then it's art.

I again feel a ping of guilt for the people who were supposed to work inside the buildings the following day. Did they even possess the ability to contemplate and solve problems? To feel disappointment and pain? Fuck it. Not my problem anymore.

I am feeling charged up and loaded like a gun, so I march to Faith's place. I look in the window and see Faith taking a rare break from art and staring at the fluorescent TV screen. I grab the door and pull with such intensity, the springs squall. My eyes immediately scan the apartment for Faith. Her peaceful perfect frame stares straight ahead. I quickly tell myself to leave. I know entering her house with the frame of mind of "I am unstoppable, nobody better mess with me," could cause me to do something that would cause piles and piles of regrets for weeks and months.

As I hike home, I tell myself for the hundredth time once the dark side is no more, then Faith and I will be together forever.

LISTEN UP!'

"Corey you're telling me you have zero fruits? This is unacceptable!"

"Oh, that's rich, you telling me what's unacceptable. Here is what's unacceptable. Creating clandestine breast drugs to grow on your daughter."

"You just need some sleep, you're tired and your brain is making things up."

"Nails and I have tasted them so I know your lying. Yet again. Lies, lies' lies. Here's the deal Mother, and I suggest you pay attention."

"The dark side is a topsy-turvy divided place. The main section, which is located in the city, houses the people that are brainwashed or something. They speak the same few sentences over and over."

"The other section is located in the woods where there is no electricity. This is where the raw legit artists live and do art. They struggle daily and somehow find ways to survive. I diagnosed them and what I found is infections and inflammation along with mental anguish. When I shared my healing body with them and saw results, I knew what my true calling was."

"Here is my proposal for you. I want you to turn the rest of my body into a healing center. So, make my hair something people can eat and get relief for arthritis. My ears for allergies. My nose for pain. My skin for anxiety. Understand?"

"Corey, I have no idea what you're talking about. Do you have a fever? Let me see if you're warm."

"Don't touch me. If you choose to ignore my request, I will make sure the world knows what you do to me. Also, my new name is Dr. Corey. Failure to call me by my name will only infuriate me even further."

"Darling, please, you're talking such nonsense, go take a nap and we can discuss this at some other time."

"It's Dr. Corey, you idiot! We're discussing it now or else I walk out the door and your secret will be exposed and your life ruined."

"You would never do that to your Mom. The woman protecting you from the devastating effects cancer has had on our family."

"I am not your little experiment anymore. I am the leader of the dark side's true artist troupe and I will do everything in my power to provide comfort and aid to my people—unlike all the other leaders in the world who sit on their thrones and don't give a shit. Look at the world we live in. Every country's government is corrupt. The politicians have one job: to protect and serve the people. And what do they do instead? Pillage and plunder. By all that is great and good, I will support these mischief makers. These pirates that sail the dangerous seas. So, let me tell you this one last time. Either you are with me or against me. If you're against me, I promise you a war. I might not win it. But there will be a war."

"Fine. What, again, did you have in mind?"

"Say it."

"Say what."

"I will count to five. One, two, three."

"Dr. Corey. Dr. Corey. Dr Corey. Happy? Now calm down. This is quite the endeavor you want to embark on. I simply don't understand why we can't just give them vitamins naturally."

"Dammit, Mother. Do not question the Doctor. This is the dark side!! We do things creatively and differently. Pay attention!'"

"So, you're going to be like a cat and them the kittens? You just lie down and they eat or suck your fruits or vegetables? Is this sexual, Corey? Oh my God, you are not shooting a porno flick, are you? I think I am going to faint."

"Stop being a little bitch and drink this water and relax. It's nothing sexual. I am just trying to fit in. It feels like the first time in my life, I am needed and looked up to. It just feels so natural and true. I understand your side of the argument, but like I said, it's the dark side and we do things differently on that side. We are the opposite of the light side. Live your life creatively or get the hell out and go live somewhere else."

"Ok, well, it sounds like you are doing this for the wellbeing of others, so I can't exactly deny you of that. From what I remember, they use all-natural ingredients. For example, they use a THC/Rhodiola Rosea/Passion Flower mix in your breasts. So, we just remove some of your tissue, add fruit seeds and the mixture and then put it in a machine. The machine mix's it properly. Then we hack into your living tissue and inject the mixture. This method lets your cells grow normally. That's very important because then there is no harm to the host. As your cells are growing and doing their thing, then the fruit attaches to them and begins growing. Of course, it needs an empty space. So, you want to remove objects so it has room to grow.

A NEW PURPOSE

Nails wakes up feeling an emptiness in his stomach but fullness in his soul. He would go get some breakfast at a diner and inspect his artwork. As he steps outside, he hears a tremor. It sounds like a big, shallow thud. His mind quickly analyzes it and tells him it is nothing and to ignore it. He briskly gallops like a horse to his destination.

It hits hard fast and like the emptying of a syringe into the bloodstream. The building is gone completely. No ashes. Nothing. A hologram of the ex-building is there instead. He could actually see it rebuilding itself. The shapes and design remind him of the movie *Tron*. There is no metal or wood, just outlines of the building as it slowly begins to rebuild itself looking like an 80s parody.

Body shock like being plugged into a loud amp pummels his senses. He slithers and squirms back home wondering what the path forward should be. Then an eerie mental bomb explodes inside his skull. He frantically looks in his computer for a story he wrote for *Nihilist News*. He begins reading it looking for similarities.

An old man strums a run-down and ramshackled acoustic guitar. The strings feel like power lines. Each impact of skin against metal sends a shock to his soul of uncensored liberation and freedom with each chord played. Between songs, he sips on whiskey and kindly pets his dog. His nightly audience, a lush and vibrant forest, envelopes him. The old man's routine of song and drink accompanied by his dog was one that never gets mundane or humdrum.

His wife encourages the old man to bring his voice to the masses. He argues against it politely, but firmly. "I have the perfect audience. The forest never plays on their cell phones while I sing. I always have a sold-out crowd."

On and on he would go with the pros of his forest crowd. His wife smiles and kisses him lightly on his cheek while whispering in his ear, "Whatever makes you happy."

He wakes at 7:00 Monday morning and opens his front door to let the dog out when he sees miles and miles of houses instead of his forest.

All the houses look the same. 1 car garage. Front porch. Side shed. Vanilla white and khaki tan replaces his green brown and blacks. He grabs his whiskey and takes a colossal swig and fires up a smoke. "What the tarnation?" is all he is capable of saying and thinking. How could this happen? He was on his porch Sunday night from 7:00 pm to 10:00 pm. Asleep by 11pm. How could houses pop up in 8 hours?

He calls his part time job and tells them he would not be coming in today. His stomach burns from the whiskey and the new reality that surrounds him. He makes a quick breakfast to soak up the current whiskey and also to create a foundation for the future whiskey.

He leashes up his dog and begins to investigate the new neighbors. After an hour, he has seen enough. They walk home and the old man needs to do what old men do—lie down and rest their achy bones.

He wakes up late in the afternoon feeling hungry. He goes into the kitchen to make a sandwich. A little TV action would settle the nerves like ginger does for the stomach. Time escapes him and it is now dark out. He lets his dog out only to hear a chorus of songs float in the now-open atmosphere.

He walks down the street and every house has an old man playing an acoustic guitar with a dog and a bottle of whiskey. Again, "What the tarnation?" is all he can muster from his sun burned lips. He walks briskly back to his house. Paranoia and anger boils inside him like hot water on a stove.

His wife has never seen her husband so furious. He tells her to lock the doors and keep her phone nearby.

The old man runs to the nearest house with a shovel in hand and begins screaming at the man on the porch. No reaction. He keeps singing. The old man threatens to strike unless there is silence. It begins another song.

As the shovel connects to the shoulder blade, sparks fly and gears spray in many directions.

"A machine. It must be."

He attacks the head. Three substantial wallops and it falls and smacks the porch floor. The old man picks it up and launches it into the window. He then goes to the next house and grabs the acoustic guitar and smashes it against the robot's skull. Only the guitar is damaged. The old man kicks his chest and only a minor bellow of disruption occurs.

He runs back home.

"Machine humans exactly like me!!!!" he screams at his wife. He goes into his garage and grabs every tool he could hold. Chainsaws, bats, power drills, more shovels of various heights and weights, and some gasoline. He yells at every porch he runs up to, just to make sure they are all machines. When they continue to sing, he would then decide which weapon to use.

The chainsaw takes off arms legs and heads within a minute but there are so many sparks he gets concerned it might fly back into his face. The power drill was fun since he would drill straight into their dead eyes. Adrenaline charged his body like never before. He is a man possessed to destroy what destroyed his quiet peaceful life. The shovel provides a slow laborious death. With every strike, the old man pretends the machines are the developers.

He contemplates using the gasoline to burn the last house down—the grand finale of his night long rampage. But he thought his message was clear enough. He walks home with a feeling of pride he never felt before. He is a man with conviction and morals and tonight they were showcased.

He wakes up the next morning feeling a bit achy from last night's unhinged behavior. He opens the door to let his dog out and notices how gratifying it feels. He stood his ground and walked the walk last night.

Ten minutes later, after a cup of coffee, he goes to let his dog in and decides to walk up the street. All the metal and gears were cleaned up from every porch. "Fuck it, I did what I could."

He goes to work, and when he comes home, every porch is the same as the night before. A human that looks like him with a dog and drink. He goes into his house and tells his wife to lock the doors again. He walks up and down the street with a gun and a bottle of whiskey. He would fire a few shots into the machine's head and then take a small swig of liquid.

He wakes up the next morning and rush's down the stairs and out the door to see if the mess he made last night was cleaned up. Fury erupts when he see's it is all cleaned up again. Pain spreads through his head. "Great, a fuckin' hangover is all I need," he thought. He has a tough time concentrating at work. His brain keeps asking the question of who is behind this mysterious neighborhood. Why do they keep replacing the machines I destroy? The next week feels like he is in an episode of *The Twilight Zone*. He would destroy. They would rebuild.

There is no stopping this disease, he concludes. A virus running rampant. So, the best he could do is be a roadblock to try and prevent it from spreading elsewhere. If they were trying to sell these houses, at least he could do his best to block their finish line. He called every friend he could think of and told them to come over Friday night with their guitars and dogs and alcohol. It's an emergency, he tells them. With enough people at his house, he explains what has been happening and what would happen tonight.

A few people argued with the old man and got into their cars and went back home, but the majority stayed to begin the first part of the plan. Destroy every machine. They did this with a rebellious feeling that had long since been gone, and for some, never existed to begin with.

Plan B then began. Each person occupied a different house armed with their guitar, dog, and drink. They sang Woody Guthrie, Tim Barry, Sam Russo and Chuck Ragan songs. The old man is so proud. He stood at the bottom of his porch, and looking outward, saw endless houses, all filled with his friends singing and drinking with their dogs. A dream come true. This is how it should have always been. The old man knew tonight was the only night this would ever happen again and finally felt the power of carpe diem.

Nails could not believe his eyes. Could it just be coincidence? Or was somebody or something mocking him? He feels his blood pressure rise to the sky. It feels like doomsday. The end of the world. He loses all control of rational thought and goes into survival mode after concluding he is their mouse and they are the cat.

He jogs home and takes a mental audit of his explosives, followed by his bank account. Low on both. What if he robs a bank? He needs money fast. A possible solution enters his mind, and like a decisive go-getter-type person, he goes with it.

The ATM blows up rather easily. A lot of the money is destroyed in the process, but there is still five thousand or so available. He goes back to his bank the following morning and deposits it. When they act like they might be getting suspicious, he reminds himself that these fucking people are dead inside. He runs home and then orders all the explosives he can. He still has some leftovers and strolls out into the crisp evening air feeling ready for bloodshed.

TO BE OF SERVICE

Corey and Molly met up. "So, here's what they came up with. Your hair can be asparagus mixed with curcumin and black pepper for inflammation. Your nose will be a psychedelic mushroom. It will be divided into micro doses as that's all the rage these days for dealing with depression. Your ears will have tea leaves growing out of them with 400 mg of theanine for anxiety. Your fingers will be a pickle hybrid. They will be a multivitamin. Your breasts can stay the same. Then we can grow strawberries on your skin that will be used as sleeping pills. They will have G.A.B.A, lemon balm leaf extract, 5-HTP and melatonin."

"Let's do this."

"Are you sure, Corey? This is the biggest life decision you will ever make. Lots of these changes might not be reversible and people will definitely stare at you."

"Don't care. All I care about is assisting my people. They need my help, desperately."

Nails wakes up the following day and the buildings do what buildings do. Or don't do. Buildings should not be rebuilding themselves. He immediately starts to trash everything within the vicinity of the area. He quickly checks to see if anybody is inside and if they are, he sets the fire alarm and nudges them to the exit. Once the place is clear of the zombie human hybrids, then grenades are launched.

In between his frenzied spaz out, he keeps hearing more and more tremors all around him. A slight glimmer of joy is produced in his brain with each tremor as he quickly daydreams about the island sinking into the ocean. He hopes one day he could feel joy like this on a steady basis, but right now his blood is diesel black with hate.

A booming sound is heard nearby, sounding like a bomb going off or an earthquake. What he witnesses next is something so monumental, he tells himself he is having a nightmare. This is just a dream. You will wake up. You can wake up. You must wake up.

But there is no waking up from the nightmare when the nightmare is reality. The Statue of Hero is on the move.

Impossible!

Broken brain is firing neurons into odd regions causing his eyes to see things falsely.

Calm down. Take a nap. Eat some fruits and vegetables. Repair the broken.

But when he see's a leg slowly propel forward causing a jolt that almost throws him to the ground, he knows there is no time to waste on getting lost inside his mind for the millionth time. This is real. Embrace the misery of these past months. Let it fuel you. Defeat the Statue of Hero and thought wind and never look back.

Every fifteen minutes, the Statue prepares to move causing a massive pounding sound on the island. So many scenarios rush's through Nails' mind. The first being a tsunami that would wipe out most of the light side.

He then remembers what he saw on the dark web about Molly or somebody selling breasts growing on Corey. She must be involved in this. He must speak with Corey immediately. He dials her digits frantically.

ON THE MOVE

"Corey the Statue of Hero is moving, it's fucking walking and I just know your mom is involved in this."

"Nate, you have to cut back on the drinking. The Statue of Hero can't just magically start walking. Are you on drugs? Listen, just calm down, I am sure it's just a earthquake. Call me back when you get sober. Actually, never call me back, you jerk. You pathetic little pest. You weasel that needs to be exterminated. A cockroach that deserves rivers of poison poured on it and then lit on fire. You liar. You hypocrite. You skinny legged twig. You sad fuck"

"It's fucking moving!! Go to a place where you can see it."

She reluctantly agrees to his dismal demands and climbs on top of a clown car to get a better view. What she see's next would forever be burned into her brain. A two-hundred-foot Statue moving slowly like a sloth.

"I will be there in a few minutes with my crew."

"Ok, I have some ideas of my own. See you soon."

As Corey and her crew run towards the Statue, she calls her Mom and asks for her help.

Molly shows up just as I am setting up a mortar.

"Stop! Wait! Don't do that, there's people inside," says Molly.

I crank my head up showcasing the face of an enraged lunatic upon hearing the news. I feel a quick wave of validation rush through me giving me even more strength in trusting my gut feelings about the island being a drainage ditch of dread.

"Listen, we need to open those doors somehow and help the people inside escape," says Molly.

"Ok, follow me."

We dart towards the slow-moving giant, stopping when we are a hundred feet from it. We hysterically discuss options and plans when a pair of legs move in our direction.

"I think it's trying to step on us!"

We quickly dive under water and swim as fast as possible in the opposite direction.

"It moves every few minutes, so let's go now. Don't worry if you think it's going to move, it's just preparing to," says Molly who prays her observations are correct.

"Where is the entrance?"

"Shit, it's located at the bottom, which is underwater." says Molly.

I feel surprisingly calm and steady. The thought wind beat it into me that victory against it is impossible. Losing is the only option. It is now game time. Nails vs the thought wind. I have no intentions of losing.

"Listen, don't panic. It's fine. When it lifts a leg to move, the entrance will be out of the water. We just need to figure out how to latch onto it just as it's leaving the water and then open the door and rush inside."

Molly's face gives a look of "you're insane if that's your best plan."

"The door, is there a knob on it?" asks Nails.

"Yes."

"I am going to swim underwater when I think it's about to move and hold onto the knob. It will lift its leg. I will be raised out of the water and will open the door. Then I will somehow climb on the door and swing it back and forth until I can get inside. Also, I need to understand what I am facing when I get inside the Statue."

"I really don't know. I was not involved in this at all. I suspect you are going to find humans inside, though. Most likely in catatonic states."

"Of course, this fuckin' place is just one big shitty surprise after the next. Get your phone stopwatch out. Every time it's about to move we need to figure out how long it takes the leg to breach from the time it starts moving. Does that make sense? Obviously, I can only be underwater for a few minutes, so we need to be precise in the calculations."

"On it."

They tread water while waiting. Muscles burn and ache. Without Sunshine Smoothies they would have retired by now. Adrenaline spikes every few minutes to keep attention spans alert.

"So here is my plan. I get inside. I close the door. Hopefully I can safely release any humans. When the leg is raised again, I will open the door. The door should stay open as the leg descends under water causing water to flood inside. Then everyone inside should just rise to the top right? Then the eye sockets are big enough for us to escape out right?

"Wait, are you going to jump out then?"

"Shit. We need a helicopter to rescue us or something."

Molly frantically searches helicopter rentals on her phone.

"Welcome to Helicopter Rentals USA, how can I help you."

"Hi, this is an emergency. The fate of the entire world depends on getting a helicopter in the next thirty minutes. I will pay you $5,000." She fights with the man for the next five minutes arguing why she is sane and not insane.

"Ok I think I secured a helicopter. I told them the world depends on them arriving here in thirty minutes. I think it finally resonated. Now if my calculations are correct, get ready to swim underwater in two minutes."

I duck under water and open my eyes and swim towards where I suspect the door is. When I get there, I am already out of breath and surface quickly for air.

"You okay?"

"Yup."

I swim below and find the door and hold the doorknob tightly. I figure I have about two minutes before air is needed again.

When two minutes arrives, I let go and begin to swim for air. I am ten feet away when the leg begins to move. I swim towards it and hold onto the knob. With the leg in the air I twist the doorknob and it swiftly flies open, almost launching me like a human catapult. I feel my shoulder muscles extend beyond what they are capable of but letting go is not an option. I kick my leg and the door swings in my direction, but at a speed that's too fast. I am about to be squashed when I let go and half my body goes inside. I manage to finally get inside fully.

I take a minute to rest and soak in what I see. About half a dozen or so people are hooked up to different machines with wires oozing out of various body parts. I unplug the machines and begin to delicately remove the wires from the bodies.

Like a rancher herding sheep, I gather them all together. The plan is to open the door when the leg moves again and when it goes under the water it would flood the Statue soaring us upwards to the eyes. However, my eye's spot a staircase that leads to the eyes so I push everyone in that direction and up the stairs they go.

I stick my head out an eye socket and survey the skies for an incoming helicopter.

"Where is the damn helicopter?" I yell into the phone to Molly.

"I have no clue," she replies.

Ten minutes pass and the only thing in the skies are fluffy clouds. I begin pacing around when I locate the brain of the Statue. I am in awe of how close it resembles a human brain. Destructive tendencies kick in and I am ready to tear into the brain with every ounce of energy inside me—the pinnacle of my destruction spree. My ultimate art piece—A buzzing sound outside with a microphone saying, "Come out now."

Fuck fuck fuck, of course it arrives now. I will have to get everybody and myself to safety, first. With everybody on the helicopter, it safely lands on the island.

I run towards Molly.

"Make sure everybody is away from the Statue. I will be back in twenty minutes with explosives."

I return and immediately start launching explosives at the Statue. I give Molly a couple grenades while I shower the Statue with mortars and other explosives.

"This isn't working, they're barely making a dent. Can you give the helicopter a message?"

"Sure."

"Tell it to procure tons of white paint. I will be back in half an hour or so."

I sprint over to the light side and quickly find my shot-in-the-dark solution. I stare down the black birds while thinking *I respect and understand you. Now, how about we work together real quick?* I waive my hands frantically acting like a human bird. The birds seem to register the urgency and seriousness and over the bridge they go, resembling a dust storm of black.

Ten minutes later the helicopter shows up and begins dumping white paint on the Statues head. The crows do what I hope they would and turn the white into black. The more I think about this plan, the more annoyed I get. Pure organic anger bubbles and boils to the surface when I realize my plan is no plan at all. What exactly did I think the crows would do? Short circuit the system board or chew on some wires? The brain inside is covered in a thick protectant. Now all these innocent birds died because of my quick rash decision making. Blood pressure rises causing heavy heartbeats.

LET'S START A NEW HOME

I see waves forming in the water indicating the Statue is moving again. Why don't I just have the helicopter take me back up there with a bat so I could cause some brain damage? I look around for the helicopter, and when it is nowhere to be seen, I think about Faith. I retreat inside my brain, pulling out images of Faith's slender body. All my problems fade away as I dream of kissing her and removing her clothes as we pledge our allegiance to each other.

I open my eyes and see a gang of strange misfit ghouls with what appears to be Corey leading the pack. I do my best to ignore them and look for Faith instead. She never leaves her house so why do I think she would be here now? More faulty thinking. What's wrong with me today. It's the Super Bowl and I am playing like its preseason. I am wide open in the endzone throwing the ball into the crowd instead while it rains down endless boos.

I then see a slim black outline emerge from behind some trees. Faith walks up to the gross gang of hobgoblins and stands next to Corey.

What the fuck is this shit?

I begin to get lost inside my brain for the millionth time when the ground shakes from Hero moving his metal frame. Why did I have to make this decision right now when the island is fragile and failing?

I look at the exquisite Faith. An impeccable species. But we never even had a real conversation. No arguments. No clash of skin against skin. If she rejects me, surely my brain will pull the plug and find a better skull to operate in.

I look at Corey before having to glance elsewhere due to her new hideous body covered in fruits and vegetables. I have had plenty of conversations with her. Arguments. Romance. Was she the total package? A package that the shipper lost and now found. The rare second chance of securing something so valuable.

But how she betrayed me. Could I ever move past that? Just an hour ago she verbally blasted me into the depths of hell with scorn and disdain. Maybe she said those words to shake me from this requiem I currently resided in. To show me that she is a human with a voice while Faith is just a physical body and nothing else. That we were designed for each other. In the deepest darkest caverns of my soul I know the correct decision.

I take a few steps towards them and veer towards Corey. She approaches me as well. She removes her shirt and her apple breasts shine in the apocalyptic wind. "Welcome home." she says.

"Let's start a new home." I assist her in putting the shirt back on.

I still have no clue how were going to defeat Hero but I know that whatever happens, having Corey by my side again is all I need. If the Statue of Hero goes on a rampage that makes King Kong jealous leaving the world a destroyed place, I would still find a way to survive knowing Corey is with me. I am the guitar and her the amplifier—together we make music that transcends time and space.

As we hold each other in a web of bliss, the Statue appears to be paralyzed in the water.

"I have missed you so much," I tell Corey. She responds with a deep passionate kiss.

My phone then makes a sound. I quickly grab it and read the message.

"There's a beach in France where Garfield phones have been washing ashore for the last 20 years due to a shipping container falling off a cargo ship during a storm."

I start laughing uncontrollably. More and more texts hit my phone. I read one text after another, laughing more and more. It feels so gratifying. When was the last time I had a good laugh, let alone a long laughing spell such as this one?

I continue laughing and laughing. I fall to the floor of the island unable to breathe with tears flowing down my eyes. It had been so long since I experienced such a hearty giggle. Like a domino effect, I couldn't stop.

My laughing trance is broken when somebody yells, "It's not moving anymore."

"What did he say?" I say loudly.

"It hasn't moved in twenty minutes."

"Everybody laugh and don't stop. Somebody, call 911 and tell them to put out a bulletin that everybody must laugh," I plead to nobody in particular.

Was my anger the fuel for the Statue of Hero to move?

A nationwide text is sent. "If you do not start laughing right now, the world will die. Laugh loud. Laugh lots. Do not stop laughing."

Of course, a lot of people dismiss it as bullshit. But on the flip side, a lot of people forgot the last time they have laughed for minutes and minutes consecutively and embrace the odd request. It becomes the first time in the history of the world that so many people at the same time convulse in laughter.

As the world embraces the joys of laughter and bliss, the Statue of Hero goes to move again, but instead of progressing forward, its legs become loose and wobbly, causing it's entire body to collapse. All that remains is the face and the middle finger sticking up facing the light side.

THESE DARK CITY STREETS

To the far right, a loud noise of clapping hands and cheers erupt like a dormant volcano. A bunch of fake trees are removed, showcasing a few hundred humans in aluminum bleachers surrounded by tons of cameras. They are all standing and clapping and celebrating like there is a victory parade about to take place on the strange island.

A man with a white and black suit comes out holding a microphone with a huge grin talking very enthusiastically using his arms and hands to further show his excitement.

"Was that not the most fascinating TV you have ever seen folks!!?? Wow, just stunning." He looks towards Corey and Nails, "Welcome to the season finale of *These Dark City Streets*."

The crowd goes wild chanting "MARKY MARKY MARKY."

Marky Mayhem walks over to them both, still maintaining a huge smirk as if he just won the lottery. He directs them to the stage where they are rapidly assembling the massive post show. As they're walking over, Marky whispers to them, "You guys are famous now, total stars, your lives will never be the same."

I feel a storm brewing inside. Rising from the bottom of my feet until it reaches my stomach, causing a campfire burn on the delicate internal linings. Corey senses my frustration and puts her hand on mine causing a warm calming sensation. The hate tsunami inside me deflates into tranquil ripples like a beach ball after the air is removed. I take a deep breath and do my best to remain calm knowing there is a potential million viewers staring and stalking my every move.

If there is one thing I learned on the dark side, it was once things seem favorable, there's a price to pay. Nothing is free. You have to pay for just a feeling of satisfactory vibes. Deep breath in through the nose and long exhale. Must stay calm to not wake the sleeping giant.

The distressed and overwhelmed couple stare out into the black ocean as it slowly moves back and forth in an ebb and flow pattern. For a moment they get lost in the rhythmic movement while waiting for the stage to finish getting assembled.

Molly runs over and hugs Corey and a man jogs over to Nails.

"Son, I know you have a million questions, but I did the best I could to make sure you have a future."

I am overwhelmed and my mind temporarily desires going back to the time before Corey when it was just me and the city and my beautiful Faith.

Less is more.

Where is Faith? I look around for a few seconds but with thousands of eyes staring directly at me, I focus on the dirt below my feet as my mind races around like a lunatic trying to make sense of all. I know my future with Faith is over but old habits die hard.

"Ok, the stage is ready. All four of you please sit and remember to be as honest and open as possible, we can always edit things out," says Marky as he gently touches their shoulder. A stagehand then directs them where to sit.

Marky begins the show.

"Welcome back to *These Dark City Streets*. That was one stunning first season!"

The crowd claps and chants making a wall of sound.

"Now let's start explaining all this to Corey and Nate since they are dying for explanations."

The camera does an extreme close-up, showcasing a look of horror and fright.

"Before we unravel this conundrum to the young beautiful couple, we need a few more people on the stage."

A professional looking woman walks on stage and the crowd goes,

"OHHHHH."

"Welcome to the show, Dr. Lisa. She is the CEO of *Relationships That Stink Don't Have to Sink*."

The crowd roars in applause.

"Thank you, Marky." She looks coldly at everyone as if already annoyed at all the questions and concerns that were surely about to bombard her controversial relationship model.

She doesn't waste any time and gets to the core of the situation quickly before Marky can even do his job or introduce Nails father, Hero, to the stage.

"Nate and Corey were a toxic couple. Deeply in love. But so toxic. One of the worst couples I have ever encountered."

"Drugs, destruction, booze, crime, hate, violence. They did it all. Everyone around them suffered—family, friends, workers, artists. Everyone."

"Their community was exhausted from their antics and their parents ran out of options. Nothing seemed to work. Desperate with nothing to lose, they searched online for relationship advice. But they needed something truly outside the box as the normal counseling and books had failed them. That's where my model enters. I will be blunt. We are extreme."

Marky interrupts her. "Dr. Lisa, when you say 'extreme,' I am sure the world is dying to know, how much did it cost to fix these two?"

She looks at Hero who runs onto the stage assuming his invitation was lost in the mail. He gives her the nod of approval to release the monumental amount. With no emotion she callously says. "2.3 million."

"Wowzers, holy cow!!" says Marky.

"MARKY MARKY MARKY," the crowd inappropriately chants.

I feel ill inside. I run off the show and vomit. Corey chases after me.

"Are you okay?"

"I don't know. It's just too much. I mean we just stopped a two-hundred-foot moving Statue and possible tsunami and now we're on a live TV show in front of millions."

She hugs me as both of our eyes began to fill with water.

"I know, I know, but at least we're safe and together now. It's all over. Let's just finish this last piece of the nightmare and collect our millions and enjoy the rest of our lives together."

She kisses me and we walk back onto the stage.

"How are you two feeling? I know it's a lot to take in," says a sympathetic Marky Mayhem.

Before they could respond, Dr. Lisa added, "I know the thought of spending that much money to salvage a relationship where there is no marriage involved is troublesome, but this experiment benefited society and science more than you will ever realize. Which I am sure we will discuss very shortly."

Corey feels a cold shiver knowing her breasts were most likely part of this experiment to benefit science and society. *"Sick twisted sadists,"* should be tattooed on their forehead, her brain says.

"Now for the satisfying news. *These Dark City Streets* broke so many TV records, you guys will never have money issues again."

Marky continues to speak. "A Statue that moved and wanted to kill. Love. Destruction. Experimentation on body and mind. Fruit breasts. Science fiction galore. Death of a criminal. Cell towers built on artists. Thought winds. Tattooed moving buildings. Ghost bars. Black oceans. This show had it all and people worshipped every episode!!"

The camera zooms in to Nails and Corey and then moves down to their hands which remain clamped together since the start of the show.

"We love you, Nails," yells a fifteen-year-old teenager."

The crowd stands to their feet clapping and making noises with their mouths.

"Hear that, you two? You're stars, but obviously you only care about answers at this point. So, Dr. Lisa please start from the beginning," said Marky.

"Yes, well, like I mentioned briefly at the start, you two were deeply in love but the way you acted towards your family, society, businesses and the environment was atrocious."

The camera zooms in to get a maximum close up to see the dirt and grime on both faces—looking for tears or facial expressions of regret at their former lives, but they both just stare out into the audience and black ocean, remaining expressionless.

"Fearing Nate and Corey would soon hurt somebody or worse, Hero contacted me. So, I agreed to meet with him and Molly. Both lovely and devoted and loyal parents who only want the best for their offspring."

"However, Hero admitted he wasn't the best parent. He was so into art and developing new artists, he basically gave his son the credit card with no spending limits. With endless millions from his art career, his son had so much money at his disposal with no instruction or guidance on how to spend it properly."

Dr. Lisa continues, "Growing up, Nails never played sports or had a part-time job. His Father was constantly in his art studio, leaving his mother to do her best to tame the feral teenager, so he never knew of boundaries, hard work, or how to be a productive member of society. From music, movies, and video games he learned to become a very promiscuous man. Relationships started and ended from a lack of a father figure in his life. Then he saw Corey one night in a bar. Immediately attracted to her, he showered her with compliments."

"Corey was addicted to her looks. She cared about nothing else. When she meets Nate, she had never heard anybody talk endlessly about how dazzling and ravishing she was. It was her dream to have somebody tell her how beautiful she is for hours and hours. She became addicted to the praise that Nate provided her with. They hung out daily and became glued together at the hip ever since. Which as a relationship counselor, I congratulate both of you on that. You obviously care deeply for each other, but that's where the positives end."

Marky opens his mouth to talk but Dr. Lisa gives him evil eyes and forges ahead. "Drugs. Drinking. Public sex. Crashing cars. No respect for anybody. Verbally abusing the ones who attempted to slow you down. Lighting forests on fire. Rehabs didn't even want them there, as they would show up and find a way to get drunk and high the entire time while terrorizing the people who were trying their best to get clean."

"When people in their town tried controlling them, they hit back even harder, making people cower around them. Both parents were at their wits end. With nothing working and society unable to handle their shenanigans, they contacted me. I had always dreamed of this type of extreme relationship makeover, but no TV company was willing to spend all that money on something so risky. So, when Hero contacted me and I found out about all his fortunes, I knew I had to give this a shot."

Dr. Lisa pauses for a moment and looks at Marky who gives a look back of *Do what you're going to do, just make sure it's TV gold.* "With him fronting the money to start the show, it gave me the inspiration to convince TV execs that they had nothing to lose by airing it. They just had to procure some advertisements for commercials, and we would cover everything else. With the money secured and TV execs all on board, it was time to launch this missile into outer space to explore unknown galaxies."

"Hero and Molly explained to me their own lives as well as their son and daughter's lives. It was vital for me to understand everything to design the optimal program. It became a collaborative effort. We would meet up whenever we could. Endless emails and text messages brainstorming the logistics of the show."

"The first thing we decided was that Nails and Corey's previous existence needed to be wiped away like Columbus did to the Indians."

"BOO BOO BOO."

"Well it seems the crowd is fans of the Indians," said Marky.

"Yes, well, it was quite a tragedy as I already mentioned. Marky, could you please explain to the crowd that their outbursts throw me off my momentum and train of thought."

Marky looks at the crowd and says, "Did you hear that everybody? Please give the doctor the respect she deserves."

"BOO BOO BOO."

"I tried, Doc."

"Anyway, like I was saying, we knew the first and most important step was removing the memory of their former lives. This was conducted in an all-natural safe way. We hired one of the world's greatest hypnotists, and as you can see, he did a marvelous job. In fact, he is here now."

FRED GREEN

"With a grin miles long, Marky, says, "Please welcome Fred Green to the show!"

Fred walks out wearing a suit and tie looking extremely professional.

"Fred, we have a lot to cover in this hour, so make this brief," said Marky starting to feel the stress and time restraints of the biggest show of his career.

"Yes, of course, Marky. I talked with Dr. Lisa, Hero, and Molly and the goal was to remove the memories Nate and Corey had of each other. However, with hypnosis you can't simply remove bad memories or memories of people in general. If you could, everybody would do it. So, when I explained that to Dr. Lisa and Hero, they got very annoyed and lunged at me with fists raised saying, 'I had to think outside the box and be revolutionary. Do something that has never been done before with the human mind."

"So, the first thing we did was convince their subconscious that they are good wholesome people. This was accomplished by installing positive virtues for the two hooligans." The crowd loves the word and starts chanting,

"HOOLIGANS HOOLIGANS HOOLIGANS."

Marky looks at the crowd with an innocent goofy grin. "You don't see that word used to describe couples, do you?" So then, of course, it is followed by,

"MARKY MARKY MARKY."

Fred Green continues, "The biggest obstacle was just beginning the process with them. They were so reckless they would never simply agree to something of this nature."

"So, one Saturday afternoon, they were hanging out smoking weed, making fun of people, and being their usual obnoxious selves so it was the ideal time for Hero to offer them some iced tea. Luckily, they agreed because the tea was dosed with hallucinogenic mushrooms. We waited an hour until the effects took place, turning their brains into a mushy mound of merry vibes. To my knowledge, nobody has tried to hypnotize somebody while tripping on mushrooms. I had no clue if this would even work, but we didn't see any other option. To try and reason with them while they remained stationary was a fruitless endeavor."

"You could have chained them to a seat," said Marky feeling smart.

"Perhaps, yes, but I have an idea they would just yell, scream, and spit in our faces."

"So, with them both dazed and sedated, we began the process of positive virtue installing.

"You always respect the law."

"Exercise and eating healthy are very important to you."

"Before talking and making comments on things, ask yourself if you would be upset if that was said about you."

"The past, in regard to hobbies and technology, still has value."

"Nothing is more important than family."

"You are grateful and appreciative of everything in your lives."

"Kindness and respect are more important than appearance."

"You get the point. We drilled these phrases into them for a good hour. That's where the 80s theme came from. Nate only cared about new technology and new things. He had to have the newest electronics and cars. So, we wanted to strip away the bad and replace it with the good."

"The Nintendo and other 80s games were to show Nate that he didn't need advanced fancy gadgets to be happy."

"Every six months, Nate got a new phone. His car had to be the best on the market. He hated everything that wasn't brand new and expensive. A spoiled brat."

"Here are some of his recent purchases," continues Fred.

"A TV you can roll up like a newspaper so everywhere he went, he simply unrolled this sixty-inch TV. Price tag $25,000."

"A virtual reality camera that can capture all angles of something at the same time. Price tag $6,000."

"One-wheel self-balancing skateboard. Price tag of $1,400. They both had one and would ride it everywhere terrorizing people. Their favorite thing was to ride it on sidewalks and grab people's hats and toss them."

"That one-wheel skateboard actually sounds like fun. I mean, do we have clips of them doing this?" asks Marky, remembering his younger skateboarding self.

Up went a clip of them riding on a sidewalk with a beer in hand, messing with people they skated passed.

The crowd is in awe of this new piece of technology.

Fred assumes he can keep going. "We made sure Nate had an old computer instead of a new one, a cassette player instead of an iPod, a normal skateboard instead of a fancy motor one. This was all done to rewire his brain into appreciating and enjoying any type of entertainment. We wanted him to see a gadget or game or anything else and instead of thinking how old it was—be appreciative and grateful it's available to him."

"With Corey, we wanted to mainly remove her fascination with appearance. This was a tricky accomplishment since, as you can see, she's gorgeous."

A picture flashes up showing her wearing a tank top and super short cut-off jeans.

"We all agreed that dressing her in plain clothes was a start. Then we instilled in her that beauty comes from within. Don't judge a book by its cover. Knowledge has more value than appearance."

"Then the revolutionary part was to surround them with an environment that was so intense, they would focus more on that than of their old lives. Then when they did finally make memory connections, they would be so against what their brain was showcasing because it was against their new morals, so they would disregard them."

"So, Nate might think, why do I kind of remember telling a priest to fuck off—that can't be me because I have these other values up front and present in my mind."

"Corey might have a flashback about how she looked in a bikini but assume it was somebody else since that didn't align with her new way of thinking. With Corey, we dyed her hair brown, cut it short and dressed her in plain clothes."

"With Nate, we dyed his hair black. We did this after giving them double doses of xanax so they would not wake up during it and if they did, they wouldn't really care."

Dr. Lisa, feeling like the show is now leaning toward this old gypsy medical profession instead of her new age treatment, maneuvers to gain center stage again, even though she is annoyed with the entire process, yet, oddly feels the need to dominate the show and showcase her genius relationship models.

GHOST BAR

"So, the bar themes, Marky," Dr. Lisa says only to be interrupted by Marky saying, "Oh great, I am sure we can't wait to see what they were about."

"Each bar had a theme to address a deficiency in Nate's previous life. But we also had to make them interesting and fun for the viewer. We chose bars because when a relationship first begins, each side is nervous, and beer is a great lubricator. So yes, we did try to create conditions optimal for them to have success."

"The bar with the skeletons and bones and history was done to imitate a museum. When Nate went into museums, he would be looking at his phone constantly and once even lit up a joint in a room full of 17th-century artwork. So, we believed it was vital he respected and understood the past instead of praising celebrities, musicians, and video games."

"The psychic bar was because Nate didn't believe in physics at all. Anytime he walked past their tiny stores, he would open the door and give them the finger and say, 'I can predict the future as well, it's all fucked, so who gives a fuck!'"

"The ink and drink had nothing to do with Nate or Corey. We just felt them tattooing each other would be great for ratings."

"Then the ghost bar was because Nate would get super stoned and rant on and on about how stupid people who believed in ghosts are."

"Can you elaborate on the ghost bar, it's really quite fascinating," says Marky feeling like the show is a brimming success so far.

She breathes heavily with annoyance. "We made an agreement with some people and some of them didn't survive."

"That's bullshit and you know it," Corey blurts out.

"Is that true?" says Marky acting extremely concerned.

"Dr. Lisa, please explain more," said the ear piece.

"We live in a capitalist society. Either be productive or don't and fall by the wayside. We offered junkies a job. They would paint the island black and in exchange they had to do their drugs in one specific room in hopes that somebody would OD and haunt the place. Hero said a real ghost on live TV would be incredible for ratings."

"Keep going, I think the crowd would love to hear more."

"We provided them with their drug of choice, since they couldn't score on the island."

The crowd goes apeshit.

"BOOO BOOO BOOO."

"She's a republician," screams somebody from the crowd.

"Is this true? Dr. Lisa?"

"Marky, people are tired of politics ruining entertainment," says the ear piece.

"Actually, I…"

"You don't have to answer that, Dr. Lisa, I crossed the line."

Corey screams, "So the junkie bones tombstone was real!"

"A concerned member of the film crew set that up without our permission," says Dr. Lisa.

"But, Dr. Lisa, why would you be against a proper burial," said Marky.

"We were so busy with the show, we must have forgotten about it."

"Were you going to give her a burial at all then?"

"Well, Marky, she was a junkie, does it really matter?"

The crowd begins to pelt the stage with miscellaneous objects.

"The crowd is not happy with you, Dr. Lisa, as you can see. And quite frankly, I agree with them," said Marky showing sincere concern like it is muscle memory.

"Hero said the show in his mind would be a failure, entertainment wise, without a real ghost and he was the one with the money, so we did what we could to oblige him. It's not like we threw her in the dumpster. I mean, we did bury her, just not with an actual funeral procession or in a real legit graveyard."

"I would have pulled the plug on this entire operation, but I was obsessed with a ghost bar. I just couldn't conceive of the show without it. Every time I told myself, this has gone too far, some other part of me says, 'Dude, you're the guy who invented a real ghost bar. You're a genius," said Hero.

"You're a real piece of shit, both of you. That girl was somebody's daughter. She had parents, friends, family, and you killed her!" said Corey.

"MURDERER MURDERER MURDERER."

"Yes, well, on the surface it seems that simple. But almost every heroin addict eventually ODs and dies. So instead of her dying alone in an alley with no meaning to her life, she will forever be memorialized on this show."

"You could have saved her with Narcan!" yells Corey.

"Well yes, maybe, but again, Hero really wanted a bar to be haunted with a ghost."

Trying to change the subject in a hurry, Dr Lisa says in a raised panicky voice, "As for the show, *These Dark City Streets*, the ultimate endgame for the show purposes was, 'Could they fall in love again?' If we removed a bunch of memories they had of each other, installed positive virtues to replace the negative ones, separated them geographically, where each side hates the other, and if they could somehow still find each other, then they were true soulmates who belonged together forever. And as you can see, they overcame obstacles so fierce and harsh to find each other again."

Dr. Lisa then stands up with the smuggest, most contempt look a person can have— as she expects a hurricane of praise rained upon herself.

"Did you hear that you two? You're soulmates," said Marky. The crowd goes crazy.

The earpiece in both said, "Stand up and kiss each other."

They both looked at each other, stood, and kissed.

Dr. Lisa, now feeding off the energy from the crowd and her accomplishment, continued talking with a newfound sense of purpose.

"Hero, being the amazing artist that he is, came up with the idea of purchasing an island and painting everything black. This would be where Nails lives."

"What about all the people who lived there already?" protested Marky.

"Let's be honest here Marky, this was a poverty-stricken mess of a place to live. We came in and provided jobs and made the place a lot cooler, in general," says Dr Lisa.

"Explain about the people with chips and the ones who live outside the city."

"Hero can explain that best," said Dr Lisa.

"Hero, please explain. Actually, what is up with your name, Hero?" said Marky, wondering if he just crossed an invisible line.

"Nice sidebar but don't get sidetracked by this. In and out," said the earpiece.

"I have always been fascinated with Japanese culture and art and thought Hero sounded Japanese but also implied that I could save an artist's life by being their mentor. Of course, once they decided to call the Statue, 'Statue of Hero,' the idea that I could save lives was flushed down the drain."

"Interesting, please continue about artists and the chips."

"I always dreamed about a place where just artists lived. Growing up, I was an outcast. I was fascinated with art and music and it was tough finding other artists who shared my passion. My friends and I were constantly getting picked on and people would smash our artwork. So, I dreamed of a place where only artists lived. The truth is I purchased this island about five years ago. But I was having a tough time achieving my dream of it being an artist's paradise. It was way beyond what I was able to handle, so I gave up on that dream."

"When I contacted Dr. Lisa, I had mentioned that I owned an island, and from there, we developed the TV show with the island being the foundation. We brainstormed for weeks on how it would go down."

"Since Nate was obsessed with gadgets and new stuff, we felt him sharing an island with artists would act the same way the bars did. It would show him that painting and making creative stuff was not lame like he would always say."

"As you will eventually discover about this project, it started simply with a boy and girl on different sides and then snowballed into so many things we didn't plan on and never even supported."

"So, I reached out to established artists and up and coming artists and said I was creating an artist utopia where you are surrounded by fellow artists. Some of you would still have to work jobs you don't like, but at least you know everybody around you are artists so they will be on the same wavelength as you."

"I know we addressed this already, but what about the people who previously lived on the island?"

It took all the energy in Dr. Lisa's body not to rise and tell this millennial talk show host moron how she is the greatest relationship counselor ever and who cares about the people who previously lived here.

"Marky, again with the people who previously lived there. It's fine. They got jobs elsewhere. Can we just move on?"

"Well, Dr. Lisa, you mentioned Columbus wiping out the Indians, so it just seems fair that we discuss this."

"Not even close to the same thing, Marky."

Hero chimes in to break up this minor battle.

"With the island being black, then the town across from the island had to be the opposite. Which was light. Which meant more jobs for the people on the island. It was a lot of work painting everything in light tones."

"The biggest issue was how can we make this entertaining for the viewers as well as basically rewiring Nate and Corey's brain so they could be functioning members of society. I spent a lot of time pondering this when it suddenly hit me while watching the news. Each political side hates the other. So, let's have Nate live on one side, the dark side, and Corey on the light side. Neither has any larger political implications, mind you. It just simply made sense."

"I already owned an island so I could hire the people who lived there to help turn it black and be part of the show in general. Now turning Corey's part of town light was the same deal. We hired people on the island."

Hero carries on in his attempt to sound like a sane person who did this for his son and not to simply have the world's first ghost bar. "Now that there was a dark and light side, next was creating a narrative of each side hating the other. This was needed to create an even larger barricade between Corey and Nate. If they could still find each other while living on opposite societies where one side believed in art and the other side in exercise, then they were meant for each other."

"So besides being different in color, how could I make them different in how society operates? For the dark side, I had it be an artist's paradise and the light side was focused on health. Then, like Dr. Lisa mentioned, Nate and Corey would be from completely different sides, so if they were able to truly overcome this, then they were soul mates."

BAT OUT OF HEL

"Amazing," said Marky. "I know the crowd has endless questions, how about we take one now, okay?"

"Will the wedding be on TV?"

The crowd acts like a bunch of feral barbarians hooting and hollering.

"Guys?" questions Marky.

How could they answer this question when they are a plane out of gas plummeting from the sky? Their earpiece said, "Please answer, millions are watching."

"Of course," said Corey.

"Now kiss," said the earpiece."

They stood up and Nate, still adjusting to his partners body, tries not to look at her while Corey looks into Nate so intensely she is able to see through his skin into his soul, and what she sees is a person she wants to spend the rest of her life with.

Before her one chance to be on TV ends, the audience member comments right before handing over the microphone to Marky, "I hope you save some of your fruit breasts for Nate's bachelor party, wink wink."

They both feel creepy and Corey puts her arms over her chest.

Hero presses on. "So, once I reached out to the artists, they were all so eager to start this new way of living, they arrived within a few months. At first, it was just them living there while we worked on other aspects of the show, like lining up a camera and editing crew and all those formalities."

"Six months into it, the dark side was a thriving artists paradise and everything was running smoothly. It was my dream come true. I wanted to cancel the show and just work on the island. But that's how this mess all started.

Only caring about my art and not my family. So I explained to the artists that we would be fliming a reality show here for the next 10 months or so. I told them it would be good exposure for them since millions would see their art and it would get their names out in the world. Then they could paint murals to cover up all the black. They all agreed to it."

"So then we began painting everything we could black. Designing the bars. Everything felt manageable at this stage. We didn't sense any doom and gloom was on the radar. That all changed once the stupid State of Hero showed up and ruined everything."

"How did the Statue of Hero appear?" asked Marky.

"Once the show had a filming crew and all that, the Statue of Hero showed up six weeks later. So somebody hired some creative execs who had experience in TV reality shows and we all thought that was a good idea. So we began brainstorming ideas when out of nowhere, I mentioned how it would look badass if we got a statue like the Statue of Liberty, but instead of it bearing a torch, it would be giving the middle finger to the light side."

Hero's face transitions into a face of concern the more he actually says everything out loud and in the open. "I never actually thought it would happen because of the logistics and amount of time it would take to build one. But six weeks later, there it was. It ended up being the worst idea of my life. A train designed to crash and derail."

"Once the Statue of Hero was up the TV execs had a meeting with me and Molly and Dr. Lisa. They explained that AS&S telecommunications was in the process of replacing 'Flaming Fast' with 'Bat Out of Hell' and was having a tough time building all the new cell phone towers because people were so against them due to health risks."

"So when they were building them, people at night would tear them down or light them on fire. I guess the TV execs knew some people at AS&S and came up with the horrible idea of sneaking 'Bat Out of Hell' into a piece of artwork, the perfect disguise as they said over and over to us."

"So, with the Statue of Hero being two hundred feet tall, they saw this has the perfect opportunity to try something new which was building a cellphone tower inside the Statue. I was 100% against it because I knew that would lead to nothing good and could affect the health of everybody living on the island. But they offered a million dollars to each of us. I was still against it because I have plenty of money but those other two simply couldn't resist. "What's the big deal?" they said. "This show is scheduled to only film for eight to ten months anyway. Then everybody can leave the island and were all rich."

"With the pressure of Dr. Lisa and Molly, I caved in and AS&S got what they desired. This is officially when the downward spiral began. The details become murky here as everybody began blaming everybody else about all the shit that happened next."

"Hero, do you really need to keep calling them AS&S, I mean that's not their real names."

"Ok fine, how about AA, then. Assholes Always."

Marky looked out at the crowd and said, "The left side, on my word, say 'Assholes,' the right side, 'Always.'

"ASSHOLES, ALWAYS, ASSHOLES, ALWAYS."

"Risky, but I think it worked," said the earpiece.

"Marky, I am glad you're having a good time, but please focus," said Dr. Lisa.

"Sorry everybody, that was uncalled for, let's just get back to the show. Hero please continue."

"So, at this point, they felt ready to begin filming the first episode. We had the artists living there for eleven months or so, the strange bar themes were set up, the Statue of Hero was set up, AS&S was up and running, and then Nate was dropped off and we were ready to begin. What we didn't realize at this point was the existence of the thought wind. Once we dropped off Nate, the thought wind appeared. We didn't know where it came from and with it being so potent and forceful, we were helpless."

"Why not call the authorities at this point?" asked Marky.

"Well, I felt this was the last chance to save my son and I had to see it through."

"We were shocked with the appearance of the thought wind, and then we were told even more terrible news," said Hero.

"Perfect People, a subsidiary of AS&S had set up shop inside the Statue and needed artists to practice on. So the artists would have to make a choice. Either get a chip installed that would make them the ultimate artist or go live on the outskirts of the island near the black water where living conditions were dreadful— forcing them to fight for survival and the creation of art."

"I protested and protested but again, that fucking ghost bar. I just had to have it. So, I told them moving forward they have to consult with me on everything. I was so naïve. I just wanted the best of both worlds. A great show and saving my son. I should have known better."

Marky began speaking. "Do you think it's possible since it was your money funding this whole operation, that you could have just frozen the assets? Do you think that's fair to the artists who volunteered to come to your utopia that they then be put in the position of fighting for their lives or become a robot art maker via the chip? Right, sorry, the ghost bar. You had to have that ghost bar."

"They will be compensated nicely, and let's face it, Marky, they were not going to make any money with their art anyway."

"Well, Dr. Lisa, that's just a terrible thing you said."

"BITCH BITCH BITCH."

"And that wasn't nice either folks, let's try and keep this civil and get the facts out. Speaking of facts. Let's do a little recap here since I was thrown off balance. Let me know if we're missing anything."

"Hero buys the island five years ago. Meets Dr. Lisa for a revolutionary relationship idea to save his son and his son's girlfriend. The show is approved and the logistics of it all begins. The artists begin trickling in and for a year or so, they are living a utopian dream. The islanders begin painting the island black. Junkies are dropped off on the island to help paint and do their drugs in a specific room. The themed bars are built. The Statue of Hero shows up. AS&S sets up shop inside the Statue. Perfect People follow suit. Nate and Corey are hypnotized and Nate is given sleeping pills and dropped off."

"Yes, that all sounds correct," said Dr. Lisa.

"What about the light side, when did the painting get done on that?"

"Well, we hired all the islanders who wanted to make money and we were able to finish that in six months or so. We were also lucky that most buildings and houses were already light in tone to begin with. And we focused on a few main streets on the light side where we assumed most of the action would happen. We obviously got approval first with the elected officials," said Molly.

"Ok, so let's discuss all the other details as everyone is dying to hear about them," says Marky.

Hero clears his throat and tries to not talk nervously about this part of the show. "With the water being black. Here is the deal on that. The concept behind that was the dark side polluted the water when I dumped oil into it to turn it black. So Molly and Sunshine Smoothies would need to use an alternative cooking source in her food. Don't worry none of the water supply was compromised."

Dr. Lisa interrupted Hero, "What Hero is failing to clearly express is how amazing and revolutionary this was. Cooking with no water. Food that gives you boundless energy and tastes amazing and doesn't need water."

"Dr Lisa, I think we're dying to know what replaced the water, then," said Marky.

"Stem cells."

"Dr. Lisa, you really need to be as detailed as possible about this."

"The ones who had chips installed, it lowered their stress hormones to non-existent and thus began producing an abundance of healthy cells in their body. So, they were harvested and used to replace water for Sunshine Smoothies. None of us approved it, but it really is quite a remarkable accomplishment when you think about it and all the promise it holds for future generations."

The crowd becomes furious throwing objects at them and yelling and screaming. They booed endlessly at Dr. Lisa's seemingly inability to show any remorse about anything so far.

Nate's earpiece says, "Tell them to calm down, the Statue of Hero operates on anger and hate and could still rise up and destroy the world. Please just do it. I have a wife and kids and need this job. I need a new roof next year. Our basement leaks. I need a couple trees cut down. Actually, if you need any work done at your new house, let me know, I think I might need a second job."

I muster up enough energy to say, "Everybody calm down or else the Statue of Hero will rise up and I don't feel like taking down that little bitch yet again!"

The crowd laughs and calms down while a few remain furious at the thought of eating food grown with human stem cells.

"Let's put this car in reverse for a second," said Marky with a concerned look on his face.

"Can you elaborate about the stem cells and oil in the water? If I understand correctly, for the show purposes, Molly was told to believe she had to use an alternative water source or else her restaurant would go out of business."

Molly speaks up, "I was kept in the dark about the stem cells, for the most part. I was told the camera would be on me while making my food, but I couldn't use water because it was all tainted from Hero turning it black. I was then given an alternative source to work with and never told what that was. When I did eventually find out, I couldn't do anything about it because I was told they had video of me cooking with the stem cells, which if viewed by a judge, would look like I fully understood what I was doing."

"Blackmail, how the criminals make a living," says Marky.

"Quite an astute observation," said the earpiece.

"Trust me, I didn't sleep for days when I found this information out. Then to make matters worse, late one night, a man knocks on my door and when I refused to answer it, he broke the door down. He said he was so impressed with my use of stem cells in baking that I was going to help him use the stem cells in other areas of the human body. I begged and pleaded in opposition, but I had no choice."

"When I told Dr. Lisa and Hero about this the next day, they told me they were just informed the new narrative for the show would be since breast cancer runs in the family and one of Corey's biggest problem was that she relied too much on perfect breasts, that they would remove them and replace them with some sort of fruit. Then, since Corey's previous self was all about her looks, particularly her breasts, by removing them, it would force her to develop other personality traits, that for whatever reason, lagged far behind. Corey's major problem was she was so good looking, and Nate had so much money, that she felt she didn't have to do anything or have any motivation or morals or ethics."

"In the end, she helped saved the starving artists from a criminal and they all look up to her now for answers and solutions. The old Corey would not have done that. I know it sounds like a brutal act of sadism, but I eventually agreed and went along. I felt it was the best decision for my daughter."

A picture of Corey in her bikini with Nate on her side flashes on the screen next to the stage.

"She's fucking hot!" yells a randy male.

Security immediately warns him and the audience that this is a live show.

"Molly, did you feel betrayed by Hero and Dr. Lisa? It seems like you were all working together and making choices as a team and then they simply tell you this is how it will be now," said Marky feeling like a therapist instead of a TV show host.

"I was in shock and immediately regretted being involved in this. I was so ashamed at my naivety about it all. I mean, when given a million dollars, that can only mean something extreme and terrible for society. Money blinds you. It makes you do terrible things."

"Let's get back to the stem cells again," said Marky, wanting to console and hug Molly but he has a show to move along with an hour deadline.

Dr. Lisa speaks up, "Stem cells are the closest we have to a fountain of youth. With the water being pseudo black and off limits for Sunshine Smoothies, we told Molly it had to be this way."

"Couldn't you just use bottled water or filter the water?" asked Marky, feeling like he was more intelligent than everybody else.

Ignoring his question, Dr. Lisa responded back, "So Sunshine Smoothies was thus billed as the most environmentally conscious bakery because it didn't need to use water to grow their organic ingredients. They just planted the seeds outside in a grow room and the fruits and vegetables grew."

She yammer's on and on. "The reality was, inside the Statue of Hero was the lab. The ones with the chips had no stress making these cells perfect for baking food. It was like using the healthiest organic ingredients possible. Then, the ones who lived outside the city, their stem cells were polluted from living a true artist's life, which is a struggle."

"So, when we caught them, we experimented on them so we could obtain the knowledge to do further surgeries like we did with Corey. Without them, there's no way Corey's multiple surgeries would be possible."

"Corey how do you feel about that?" said Marky.

"Try and be civil," said the earpiece.

"Hopefully there are lots of pictures of my old body for Nate to look at."

"Great response," said the earpiece.

The guys in the crowd all cheered, hoping that Marky would somehow have more pictures of her.

"What about the black birds," said Marky.

"The birds were injected with Hero's stem cells. We also were able to change the color of their blood from red to black using a dye we obtained from figs. So we were very curious if the birds, which are already intelligent as it is, could they somehow connect with Nate and would he at any point try and have them turn the light side dark by having the birds fly into buildings. So, we continually dropped birds off when we thought Nate would be there. It really added a nice extra something to the show. Then the science part. What we learned is priceless," said Dr. Lisa.

"Hero you must have known about this, extracting stem cells undercover is impossible."

"Yes I knew. I had to agree with them. If Nate would be able to have the birds turn white buildings black, then the TV show would be that much better."

Hero lowers his head into his hands in embarrassment of his desires for great TV viewing.

"Nate, you have been quiet," said Marky.

"It's a lot to take in. I mean, the past six months has been Hell, all to teach me a lesson."

Before Marky could respond, Dr. Lisa interjected. "Nate, instead of reflecting upon the past and what you have gone through, think about the present and all the accomplishments you have achieved in the past year. You quite possibly saved your city and maybe even the world. Nobody knows what the Statue of Hero was going to do. Maybe nothing. Maybe destroy endless states. We had no clue."

"See Nate, your father entered into a 'flow state' which is normal for artists. It's when they become so immersed in a project, all their energy is directed into it and nothing else seems to matter. With your father not creating any art because of the show, the show thus became his art. He felt the show was his new art project."

Dr. Lisa takes a pause to drink some water and continues. "When the Statue of Hero began to move, we were all in shock. We could have called in the National Guard, the FBI, the fire department, but Hero flipped out and said this was the ultimate challenge for his son. Could he prevent a two-hundred-foot Statue from moving? Then his famous phrase that he began saying in response to everything was 'It's great for the show.' So when we discovered the Statue of Hero moving, he felt his show had entered into the top tier of reality shows, destroying all other shows. He was gung-ho about letting it do its thing naturally and organically."

"What! Did you hear that folks? Dr. Lisa just said the Statue of Hero was real and not part of the fake show plans!"

"It was very real, Marky. I was scared out of my mind. Nobody had any idea what the Statue's plans were. Would it kill everybody? Was it friendly, was it angry? Did it have massive weapons inside? So for Hero to simply let it unfold to see if his son could stop it and have the highest ratings ever was pure insanity."

"Can you believe that folks? Nate saved us!" shouted Marky.

"NATE NATE NATE."

The camera zooms in on Nate.

"Stand up and smile and if you say something, make sure it's gold," said the earpiece.

I stood up and focused on the crowd, trying to come up with just the right words to perfectly describe my feelings. Out of the corner of my eye, I notice the head from the Statue of Hero protruding out of the water like a giant whale breaching the salty ocean waves. For the first time in a long time, maybe forever, I feel strong and proud. Was I really that terrible of a person before all this? Could they still be messing with my brain? Believing I was an abominable grisly character prior to this seems preposterous. Finally, I articulate my exact feelings using my middle finger and saying as simple and direct as possible "Piss off Statue of Hero."

The crowd rubbernecks towards the Statue as they all give it the finger while wailing and roaring in celebration of it's defeat.

"So, Dr. Lisa, how exactly did the Statue of Hero move?" Said Marky who is now thinking about all the stuff he would buy from the success of the show.

"Well, nobody really knows. To clarify what 'Bat Out of Hell' technology is for others who might not know. Right now, most of the nation are still operating on 'Flames in the Face.' It started with 'Faster Than Fate.' Every new name represents a stronger technology. So 'Bat out of Hell' is the newest generation of cellular network technology. It's controversial due to just how strong it really is."

"As we witnessed, and I am surprised we haven't discussed it more, it created the thought wind. 'Bat out of Hell' drenched the city with its electronic magnet rays. Once it was everywhere and everything seemingly covered in its presence, it began taking the pulse of the human species."

Hero then interrupts with, "Artists have a burning desire in them to create and be alive. I believe the thought wind and 'Bat out of Hell' who are the same thing, found their energy interesting but not something entirely special enough to, let's say, breed with. When it began to take an interest in Nate, it found a very angry person."

"I believe it's possible the thought wind influenced all of us to create the dark side to create a person like Nate, a person so angry it could attach to and use as a host to destroy the world," says Dr. Lisa

"Wowzers!" said Marky.

"I believe the thought wind was created way before the show. Weeks, months, years, I don't know. I feel it was looking to find a person or maybe a couple, like Nate and Corey that it could train. So it saw in Nate a person who had no guilt or limits about creating chaos. As you saw in his previous life. Then on the island, it was time to mold Nate like silly putty. It saw how much underlying turbulence was out in the world and how that anger did inspire and motivate people to create and build amazing things. Then it found Nate's unrest off the charts. However, he would need more then just anger to accomplish whatever the thought wind wanted to accomplish. So the themed bars and all that was done to create the perfect solider in a sense. It wanted to create a world of hate, or something like that. Nobody knows. I am still trying to figure it all out really."

"Wow," said Marky. "So the Statue of Hero saw just how angry Nate was and it basically used that as fuel to most likely destroy this country!"

"We think the Statue of Hero homed in on Nate's anger, and the anger in the news, music, and entertainment, and used it all like a person uses food. It was his source of motivation to keep Nate on edge and angry. When Nate embarked on his quest to destroy the dark side, Statue of Hero began having the ones with the chip installed gather the raw materials for it to move. If you remember in Episode 7 where the chipped ones say I GATHER THE WOOD, I GATHER THE PLASTIC, I MAKE THE FEET MOVE, that was the beginning of it."

"It then tried to get Nate to overflow with rage, as it used his animosity, like a car used oil, to function and move with the ultimate goal of, I guess, destroying this country and who knows what other countries it could destroy as well! What we don't understand quite yet, though, is how it seemed to commit suicide."

"Sounds like we need another show to discuss Dr. Lisa's theories," said Marky.

"Let's have the audience ask some questions," said Marky showcasing is white teeth.

"Which part of the crew is responsible for the text messages?"

Dr. Lisa says, "We think it developed some kind of consciousness which consisted of a good and bad side. The negative side used Nate's anger as fuel while the positive side used his laughter to stop the bad side. So, it was a battle when sending those messages. One side tried to be funny while one side tried to get Nate whipped up in a stew of fury."

"Fascinating," said Marky combing his hair with his hand.

Somebody in the crowd yells, "I love you, Nate!"

"Corey, do you plan on reversing some of your surgeries?"

It hit her hard just what she did and for basically nothing. She was not a leader of the downtrodden. She was a person who was shallow and terrible and relied upon her looks to get through life. Now, she is a grotesque monster. Quickly, she tells herself that way of thinking will surface from time to time, and she has to ignore it. She feels strong not weak. Nothing would stop or slow her down. She would marry Nate and live an amazing life regardless of her looks.

"I am what I am, perhaps I might, perhaps I won't. It's my decision and nobody else's. It's made me a tenacious person, so for now, it all stays."

The crowd claps showing their understanding and appreciation of her honesty and newfound dedication.

"We have time for a few more questions, and then it's time for Corey and Nate to rest and get some alone time."

"OOOHHHHH YEAHHHHH"

"What are the plans for the island moving forward? Is there any way you can keep the Statue of Hero there with it giving the middle finger to the light side? It really is the ultimate art piece."

Silence for miles.

"Well, looks like that will have to be decided later. How about another question?" said Marky.

"What if Nails and Corey want to return to their old selves? It's pretty messed up you made this drastic decision without their approval. Maybe they liked who they were and society is the one who is messed up, not them."

"Great question," said Marky.

"Since we live in a free society that values liberty, yes, of course they can make the decision to return to their old brains," said Dr. Lisa.

Everybody looked towards them and the cameras zoomed in.

Nails wonders if he is still being messed with. Is this just part two of there plan. How many more parts of the plan is there?

"My brother and girlfriend are junkies. Will you help them in season 2?"

"We will talk after the show."

"I hope you have a million dollars. Lisa ain't cheap," chuckled Marky.

"Did that the one guy, ya know, the obese jerk…did Corey kill him for real like?"

Dr. Lisa removed her glasses after a strong wind blew some black ash into them.

"Yes, he is dead. What everybody needs to understand, and perhaps I have failed to express it clearly, is that this operation had a lot of moving parts, many of which evolved naturally like a weed growing between concrete, and Hero wanted to see how close to reality it could actually get. We don't know who that guy was or where he came from. After Corey killed him, we immediately reported this to the FBI. We showed them the tapes and a quick trial took place that was over and done in a week and Corey was not found guilty of murder."

Reaching her breaking point, Corey explodes. "What the fuck is wrong with you people?!" She lifts a chair and launch's it off the stage.

"COREY COREY COREY."

Dr. Lisa turns to her. "I understand your frustration, but this is such a valuable learning tool for you. It really is the most important part of your rehab. Your main issue was you had no foundation, were spineless, and was all about your looks. By removing your breasts and then having you become the leader of the true artists, you did a 360 turn. You're now a strong independent woman who can handle any situation thrown at her."

"Dr. Lisa, can you elaborate on the obese dead guy," said Marky.

"Turns out, him and his goons got insider information about the show and decided they would take advantage of the artists by producing thought wind videos. We wanted to arrest them quickly, but Hero said it was great for the show. Then eventually Corey got rid of them. Which is quite impressive."

"So you could have prevented the artists from so much unnecessary pain by the goons and you didn't?" said a puzzled Marky.

"Well they volunteered for this and yes it did turn into a real live hostage situation followed by a murder. The artists sued us but they didn't read the fine print, so we won that part. Like I said earlier, they will make out fine in the end."

"We're starting to run out of time, but what about the people who had chips in them and the ones in the forest you performed surgery on? How are they supposed to live their lives now?"

"We will make sure they are taken care of appropriately," said Hero.

"So, Nate you vowed endlessly once you found out who did this to you that they would pay for it. How do you feel now?"

Before he has a chance to answer, the crowd chimes in.

"LOCK HER UP, LOCK HER UP, LOCK HER UP."

"Dr. Lisa, the crowd is suggesting we lock you up."

"LOCK HIM UP, LOCK HIM UP, LOCK HIM UP."

"And apparently lock Hero up, as well. Unfortunately, we're out of time!"

"You are correct, Marky. Daily, I said that once I catch the person or people who did this, they will pay dearly. I guess I have some major decisions to make."

"What a great show. Thanks to everybody involved. Take care and thanks for watching *Marky Mayhem's These Dark City Streets Post Show*. Good Night."

WHAT NOW

After the show ends, Corey and I are quickly ushered off the stage and given some privacy.

"So, what now?" I say.

"I really don't know."

Hero and Molly show up a minute later.

They both apologize for what seems like centuries. At points, it turns into a cacophony of grunts and lackluster yelps as both are trying to prove to themselves and us that what was done was done out of love and desperation.

We return their apologies with humble and graceful nods as if our lungs and tongues are taking a nap. The reality is that we just want this to end and would avoid conflict or general conversation by whatever means necessary to achieve that.

"Can we just go rent a hotel on the light side and relax for a few days?" I say.

"Yes of course," all of them seemed to say simultaneously.

We spend the next few days lying in bed ordering room service, daydreaming about what to purchase with our newfound riches.

I am still struggling with accepting Corey's appearance. I hope that time would heal my stubborn brain and eyes and soon I could shower her with compliments like I did in the past.

Intense nightmares haunt me for the first nights, causing me to wake up in a panic state. I take some deep breaths and remind myself that the freaky science experiment conducted on me and Corey was never going to happen again. I then lay in bed close enough to smell Corey's fruits and veggies and wonder if anything on her body would help me sleep. How would that work? Do I ask her? Or just pick it off? I eventually get so tired thinking about how it works that sleep overtakes my central nervous system.

On the third day, a knock is heard on our door. We assumed it was housekeeping so I shout, "Please go away!"

"Hey, it's Molly and Hero, can we come in please? It will only take a few minutes. There are just a few important things that need discussing."

"The public wants both of you to have a voice in how to repair and regrow the light and dark sides. They are so impressed with how you prevented a major catastrophe and seemingly saved the places they call home, that your voices hold value and should be heard on how society can move forward," said Molly.

"So that's the first thing we wanted to share with you. Now for the next one. I know you are sick and tired of big bold decisions that have wild consequences, but we have a whopper here that needs discussing."

"I thought this was going to be a quick visit. Now words like whopper are being tossed in?" said Corey feeling like she is ready to pounce on the interrupters.

"You are correct, so I will be blunt. People want a decision made about locking away Dr. Lisa, myself, and Molly. I realize the burden this puts on you two. I wouldn't want to be in your position. We will respect and honor the decision you make, just remember we did what we did out of love and despair," said Hero who was holding back tears.

"Ok, let us digest this. Now please leave," I say.

Corey and I decide the fairest way to solve this new dilemma that is hand-delivered to us like a newspaper subscription is involving the public in the decision-making process.

Corey contacts the local sports stadium to see if they could rent it out on a Saturday afternoon. The stadium said yes, and in a blink of an eye it becomes occupied with tons of humans ready and willing to deliver a death sentence to the three lawbreakers.

"So, Corey and I have decided the most democratic way of handling this is giving each person the ability to write down on a card what type of punishment they see fit. The cards will be shown on a jumbo screen and voting will commence. We will narrow it down to the top twenty ideas and have a few more votes to narrow it down to just a few ideas."

With the votes counted—Hero and Dr. Lisa would have to live on the dark side for the next five years and sleep inside the haunted bar.

Molly's punishment consists of cooking meals for any of the artists from the dark side whenever they ask her for the next five years.

After the vote, a random person takes the microphone causing Corey and I to tense up. This random person explains to the crowd that Corey and I would be honorary decision makers in the coming months on how to unite the dark and light sides.

He set the mic on a stool and told Corey and I to walk with him.

"You really have to give some kind of inspirational mini speech to show that you're up for the task. Take twenty minutes and come up with something. Here are some paper and pens to jot down some notes. Good luck."

I grab the paper and pen and tell Corey to speak out loud and I will do the same and then we will try our best to put together a speech that sounds satisfactory enough.

"Thank you so much for putting your confidence in us and we promise right here and now to do what's best for society, not what's best for business. See, what we need to all understand is politicians and leaders number one goal is division. When we are divided, like the light side versus the dark side, we get distracted fighting each other, leaving the politicians and leaders to run rampant, robbing us blind so their bank accounts can be stuffed to the brim."

"My father had no ill intentions when he created the dark side. In fact, all he cared about was creating an environment that fostered and supported creativity like nothing else in the world. AS&S Telecommunications had eyes and ears on the streets so once they heard about Hero designing an island for just artists, they knew a great opportunity was available to divide and conquer the public. So, they weaseled themselves inside the TV show disguised as TV execs, and basically forced Hero into a dark side and light side model by planting the seeds the first day they were hired."

"As for the 'Bat Out of Hell' upgrade, I think we can all agree to stay far, far away from that. Let's stay with the current cell phone service for as long as we can. I mean, it works fine, so why bother upgrading?"

"I believe we should leave the Statue of Hero up in the water with it's face and middle finger facing the light side as a constant reminder of what can happen when each side fights the other. A reminder that division is created only so people can get richer and more powerful."

"Also, let's not refer to each side as 'light' and 'dark.' We are one side united with a common goal of living righteous lives. Thank you and have a great day."

The crowd claps and cheers while Nate and Corey finally feel relaxed and confident and pleased with the future they are helping create.

In a few hours time, the stadium becomes empty with just trash blowing in the wind as the fates of three humans were made.

NEVER REJECT A GOD

AS&S Telecommunications became furious about the rejection of the 'Bat Out of Hell' upgrade. They felt they were gods and you do not reject a god. They rained punishment upon us by slowing down our service. Each month they made it slower and slower.

Data streaming eventually came to a grinding halt.

Sending pictures took hours and hours.

Text messages took thirty minutes to send.

Eventually, AS&S got so annoyed, they downgraded everybody to the lowest level of service.

We refused to give in. I had to give speeches each week that were geared towards the die-hard gadget addicts on why it was important to stand our ground. Some of them eventually packed their bags and moved to a place where their addiction would foster and feed.

When it became pointless to even have a smartphone anymore, we threw a "Burn Your Smartphone Bonfire" party where each person threw their smartphone in a huge fire and then was given the opportunity to sign up for a new phone that was used strictly for calls only. Basically, for emergency purposes. We filmed the entire event and sent it to AS&S where they vowed to make our lives a living hell.

People found they had more money and less stress. No longer did they need to check their phones every ten minutes. They didn't need to check news apps that only made them more depressed and anxious. When they were at concerts or out with friends, they were not busy trying to document it all. They were finally living in the moment. They didn't need a chip implanted to accomplish this.

HOME

Hero and Dr. Lisa were given a month to get their lives in order before departing to the dark side for their five-year punishment. Deciding two weeks was plenty of time, they each hired moving companies to start their punishment immediately so they could get it over with and return to their normal lives and enjoy the millions they made from the show.

Hero loaded up on painting supplies, clothes, food, guitar, amp, and a TV. Dr. Lisa brought over books, clothes, laptop, and cooking stuff.

They began unpacking and organizing the ghost bar while making some light conversation to gauge where each other's moods and attitudes were positioned at.

"I can't believe the FBI or police have not started investigating inside the Statue of Hero yet. The amount of evidence inside just waiting to be discovered, analyzed, and cataloged is enough to warrant an immediate investigation. Yet, there it sits in the water, middle finger to the light side as if nothing major didn't just go down. It's like they don't quite realize the extent of what happened on this island," said Dr. Lisa, who is dumbfounded how a genius like her was now living in a ghost bar with a stupid artist.

"Nate told me people just want to move forward and having the FBI around will only cause everybody to remain stuck in the past. The Statue will not move, only its upper body remains. I am sure they will be here soon enough and then you will wish they never arrived."

"Well, I have a curious brain and we have five years to kill. I will see you tonight."

"What are you going to do?"

Neither would admit to the other, but they were getting strange funny text messages and they both assumed that meant some part of the Statue was still alive and breathing with some sort of heartbeat—either human or something else.

"I am going to try and find a way inside it."

"That sounds dangerous, let me come with you."

She sighs and says, "Fine, whatever."

During the short boat ride, they discuss ways to enter the statue.

"The eyes are the best way inside it," said Dr. Lisa.

"We will need a rope ladder."

They went back to the island and ordered a rope ladder for overnight delivery.

As they were walking back to their homes inside the haunted bar, Dr. Lisa began with her theories.

"Here's what I think happened. The thought wind designed the *These Dark City Streets* show and probably other things. As I already stated to that idiot Marky Mayhem. Here is my proof. Remember when Nate was showing Corey around when they first met?"

"Yeah, I remember that, yes."

"Now remember when the buildings began to move and Corey freaked out? Then Nate explained to her and showed her video that these were extreme artists who were tattooed to look like buildings? You were in control of the artists who came over. Did you invite them over? Because I can't imagine something like that exists. The logistics, the amount of practice, just for what? So people can say, 'Oh wow, that was wild,' and then go back to being lost inside their own miserable brains?"

"You know what your problem is?"

"Oh, please do tell me."

"You're lost inside your own brain and it's the dullest fucking place alive. It's all science and statistics and all that crap. Artists have a desire deep within to create and express themselves and all you do is talk shit on them. Have you ever created something? A painting? A book? A photograph? Humans are meant to create, and society does its best to prevent it. Being creative is one of the best feelings life has to offer."

She makes a huffing grunt sound and rebuts.

"Then the black birds with no blood or black blood and how they followed Nate around just because they had your stem cells in them? Impossible. Then the dark side itself. Look at how many buildings that are not black."

"Yeah, but that's just because the paint job was done quickly by people with zero experience in massive large-scale painting jobs. Obviously, they can't paint everything. Plus, when Nate went on his destruction spree, a lot was removed then, as well."

"Then why did it appear like everything was painted black all the time?"

"How you view the world determines what color the world is, as well. Nate, with the help of the thought wind, saw the world as dark and gloomy. All that anger and negativity in his blood affected his mind, and in time, it trained him to see only dark things. I bet now he sees more light. We see the world through our emotions and outlook on life. If you wake up each morning with a 'fuck this life' attitude, you're going to see and experience things in a darker fashion. His anger and attitude became contagious like a cold. As he traveled down his dark path, his body released pheromones that infected everyone in his vicinity, causing their mood to shift and align with his. Negativity breeds more negative while positivity breeds more positive. The sun will always shine if you let it."

Again ignoring him, "And what about the thought wind being so strong it could implant memories and images at will, yet something so stupid as music and anti-thought wind walls could stop it? Gimme a break. The thought wind was created by another thought wind who created it. We're most likely living in a world created by artificial intelligence. The Statue of Hero was designing a method to destroy the world and you have to learn to accept that."

"Have you ever listened to a good album before on headphones? It will control your entire body. Without music and melody, the human spirit would hasten to blossom. Music is a tool that can be used to overcome the hardest challenges a human spirit can endure. It will pick up and move the downtrodden. It will act like a strong cup of coffee. It will provide light when there's only dark. It's health for the heart. The universe uses the birds and bees as their master chorus and earthquakes their drums, hurricanes their windpipes. Everything is music to some degree and it absolutely can prevent and solve anything it encounters."

"Trust me, thinking music prevented the thought wind is hogwash," said Dr. Lisa, who refused to grasp any of what Hero was saying.

"Also, I am not calling you a doctor anymore. You're not a doctor of anything but bullshit. Real doctors spend years studying the human body and accumulating massive student debt in the process. You're just a fraudster."

"I am a Doctor of Love you idiot. I fixed your stupid, ignorant, worthless son, something you were never able to do, so you damn well better call me a Doctor! And I was smart enough to sell those fruits and black birds on the dark web. I made $85,000!"

"You fucking thief!"

"Get over yourself, this is how the world works."

Hero does his best to control his emotions. He thought about their argument and it was back to the light vs dark side. Each side is not budging. No middle ground. Nothing being solved. No compromise. It felt so stupid and pointless to live this way.

"What about the Statue actually moving? So first, out of nowhere, the Statue arrives, then eventually it starts to walk?"

Hero says, "Crop circles, Pyramids, Stonehenge, Easter Island, the Bermuda Triangle, the Lost City of Atlantis, and UFOs? Did the thought wind create those as well?"

"So, you finally agree with me. Yes, some sort of artificial intelligence created those things. Humans simply couldn't do that. Now that you are on my side, make sure you say those exact things when I protest to the judge that I should be freed since I didn't play a part here, Artificial Intelligence did. Say something like, 'AI influences the state of things so Dr. Lisa should be freed. We need her genius to help save relationships."

"So that means you had no control over fixing my son. You're a fraudster just like I suspected then. So, the thought wind made me a bad father. It was all out of my control. It was just destiny. So, let's all just give the fuck up because we have no choices or control. You're clueless, Lisa."

They were approaching the bar and Hero knew a hangover tomorrow could not be avoided. He couldn't believe he was stuck living with Lisa the next five years. She hated art. She hated music. She was truly terrible. She was not a doctor of anything but rubbish.

He enters the ghost bar, the place that he wanted so bad, and ironically it was now closer to his heart that he could ever imagine.

"I guess we could clear out that storage area and fit a bed there. Then remove that table in the corner and fit a bed there."

"Do you want to do some drinking now?" asked Hero, who figured it was best to try and be civil with his cellmate and he probably could only do that with the help of alcohol.

"When in Rome."

Hero pours them some beers and a shot.

"To our new life."

"Trust me, this won't last long. Marky Mayhem and the imbeciles on the light side are not the judge and jury of me."

"Well, yeah, I agree, but what we did on that show is unlike anything ever done before. You know how many laws it broke? How much terror was inflicted on the innocent? How they had murder trials conducted in less than a week? I think we should be lucky and grateful our punishment is only five years."

"But I did nothing wrong at all. I shouldn't have any punishment and your punishment should be minimal as well."

"Oh, so nothing for you but I should be punished."

"I did nothing wrong, you're the moron who had to have the damn ghost bar."

They have a few more beers in silence before finding each corner of the bar to rest their weary heads.

The next day, the rope ladder arrives. They climb inside the Statue of Hero through the eyes and guess what they found. Me! Just a much smaller version of the giant you see now.

The two remaining people reading the book look incredibly confused.

"Let me continue, apologies for interrupting the flow in a serious part of the story."

Hero and Dr. Lisa discover fifteen two-foot-tall creatures with huge smiles and one four-foot-tall creature who also had a mystifying, crazy, wide smile.

The tallest one, which again, is me, spoke up.

"My brothers and sister are not really into talking much. Due to extreme and strange breeding techniques, they prefer to communicate with funny observations or jokes, so I do the bulk of the communication."

Hero and Dr. Lisa are in shock and awe and speak gingerly towards them.

"We come in peace. Why don't you come outside and live on the island. I promise you and your family's safety. Nobody will hurt or capture you," said Hero, looking as synthetic and honest as possible.

"Thank you for your offer and I trust you."

"Let's go," I said towards my brothers and sisters. Since the boat was small, it took a few hours and lots of trips to get everybody out of the Statue. When we were all safe on the land, Hero tells me we can live anywhere we want.

MONSTER MASH

A month later, Lisa tells Hero she is done with her research and is ready to fight her jail sentence.

She explained to Hero that her primary argument is artificial intelligence created the thought wind. With the thought wind in place, it then controlled everyone's actions and desires. She explained how the entire island and everything that happened was done by the thought wind hijacking their minds. So, anything Lisa did was not really her own actions. She explained how the falling buildings troupe, the ghost bar, fruit breasts, crows with human DNA, is not something humans were capable of. She explained how it's possible artificial intelligence created everything on earth. Then she was going to expose myself and my fifteen brothers and sisters, that there was no way she could be responsible for anything that happened on the island. Her research was so detailed that she had a good chance of winning.

Hero had to stop her. He would lose being a father to me and my brothers and sisters. We would be captured and held in cages while experiments were conducted on us. Something extreme had to be done.

 Hero told Dr. Lisa he loved her and wanted to spend the rest of his life with her. She was only five years his elder and she never spent much of her time in a relationship before, so when Hero told her this news, she of course brushed it of.

It wasn't until he grabbed her and ripped off her clothes that she realized what she had been missing. Hero did believe her, that they didn't deserve such a long punishment, but he was such a terrible father to Nate, so when a second chance to be a father presented itself, he had to embrace it.

Yeah, it sucked pretending to be in love with somebody you hated, but Hero was given a second chance of being a father and would not waste the precious opportunity.

So, there it is. That's the story of how I became a famous mascot.

The athletes looked thoroughly confused.

"So you're really just a monster?"

"Well, that is a rude way of saying it, but sure yes and like the dark side that gave me birth, I wanted to share this tale as creatively as possible and respect its number one rule. Be different. Be strange. Find the road that's full of weeds and branches and travel down it. Create a new path."

They began laughing, not taking it seriously at all.

"You can go ahead and exit the room now."

I overhear them saying, "What a waste of time that was, I could have been watching Netflix."

"That story has more twists than a tornado."

"Bro, let's go munch on some mondo steak."

"No doubt, homie."

"Ahhh jocks, such a group of deep-thinking individuals, wouldn't you agree?"

Now that they are gone and out of the way, let's dive deeper into everything, especially since I don't expect anybody to actually find the single volume of this book that your reading. You know with all the new shows on Netflix, literature is a dead art. "If this guy bashes Netflix once more, I am going to burn this book. I mean, I am reading it, so calm down buddy, people still read sometimes!" Ha, I amuse myself well don't I?

FAMOUS MASCOT

Are you ready for some real answers, finally!? Hell yeah, you are. Actually, first let's take a quick dive into how I became a famous 'ascot.

You're probably wondering what team I mascot for? Just look for the big orange guy always smiling! Use that big brain of yours. I am confident you can do it!

My brothers, sisters, and I were born with a "perma-grin," so we appear to be always smiling and looking happy. I am seven feet tall and covered in orange fur. I have a long orange beard. As I mentioned before, I have a perma-grin and have no teeth. Because of my lack of teeth, my digestive system is poor, so I weigh four hundred pounds. My eyes are big and white.

My brothers and sisters are identical to me, just much, much smaller. They are basically mini me's. I believe we age in dog years. I am around 5 years old now and in dog years that means I am around 35 or so. I really have no clue honestly. And who cares, I feel good, that's all that matters.

As for learning the native language, we picked it up quickly. But because my brothers and sisters are always smiling and happy, they generally don't talk much. They just giggle and bounce around while I am closest to human in my ability to have a wide range of emotions. That being said, with my perma-grin, I am happy most of the time.

Hero is always searching for hobbies I can engage in. He really is an amazing stepfather. He spends most of his free time connecting with us to ensure we have plenty of parental guidance. It is sometimes embarrassingly obvious he is doing his best to make up for being a bad father to Nate.

My brothers and sisters are always busy working in the library and reading. With school being out of the question, Hero and Lisa became our teachers. He spends a few hours a day teaching us and helping us learn about various subjects, and with our perma-grin, he wants us to realize life is complicated and confusing and not always a fun place like our facial expression suggests.

My brothers and sisters are mostly a self-sustaining bunch who don't need a lot of outside assistance from Hero since there is fifteen of them. Hero invests most of his time with me. He is always worried I will become depressed and lonely from being such a hefty unique creature, so he constantly search's for ways to entertain me and give me a purpose in life.

When he heard about the light side's professional sports team looking for a new mascot, he began brainstorming the possibilities of myself earning the job. He started a PROS and CONS list.

PROS

I don't need to worry about wearing a costume and how uncomfortable and hot it can get.
Nobody would ever accidently see my human skin during a game.
Learning how to act like a seven-foot-tall creature would be simple.
It really was the only job I was suited for.

CONS

Job interview.
Disputes with athletes, fans, and coaches.
Bank account.
Driving to stadium.
Never being able to remove the costume when driving home or in general.

We decided that Hero would do all the talking during the interview. He spent days and days working on the perfect reasons why I should be the next mascot. He explained how I was his shy son who was a hard worker but also felt vulnerable and weak around such tough athletes, so I preferred keeping the costume on at all times.

I was hired on the spot. They didn't care about the strange dual interview or all the time my father spent coming up with perfect arguments on why I should be the mascot. All they cared about was my appearance. They loved the big smile and the wide eyes that make me look like I am high on methamphetamines.

I became the most famous mascot in all of sports. People just loved how enthusiastic and thrilled I looked every second. Eventually, all the jocks wanted to know my story and how I designed my uniform. I had to ignore them. Until I finally caved in and wrote this book.

With my brothers and sisters spending so much time in the library creating a beautiful odd place, I thought it would be badass if I wrote a book and made just one copy of it and slipped it in their library on the sly in the D section.

If your big brain just made the connection, don't judge or hate me. Yes, the connection you made is correct. In the N section of the library you will find all the copies of *Nihilist News*.

When we were unable to send hateful text messages due to our perma-grins, my father learned through all his news articles that fat kids get picked on and bullied. Since my father is just a pile of wires and cables and not a real human with a soul, he would dial into my brain and verbally abuse me with fat jokes, not knowing what damage it was achieving. Each insult felt like a bee sting. He said he would stop when I came up with another way to torment Nate.

When Nate wrote the first edition while on the brink of ending it all, I submitted it to my father in hopes of him leaving me alone. My father jumped on board immediately and thought it was a great idea because he would then only pay Nate after he wrote the newspaper and he would make sure Nate would only write it after a mental battle with him.

I had a vision of creating a library when I saw the piles of *Nihilist News* that were being created and nobody reading them. That's when I came up with the idea of writing *These Dark City Streets* and only creating a single copy and putting it in the D section.

As for the single copy I mention many times in this book, there are millions of books at everyone's disposal with a few clicks of the keyboard. Choose free overnight delivery and it lands the next day. Is there really much joy in that process? Simply tapping on a keyboard and a book arrives.

What about the thrill of the hunt? Searching endless dingy dusty paperbacks hoping to find that one book that strikes a chord and then taking it home and soaking up the history that went along with all the paths that book has traveled to get into your hands.

I had a vision of creating a library located in the middle finger of the Statue, so whoever found it, they would feel the thrill of the hunt like never before. I also created the library so my brothers and sisters would have something to keep them talking and acting like a family instead of just being isolated all day alone watching Netflix.

"That's the final straw, Mighty! I am going to burn this single volume right now and watch Netflix instead! Hope you are happy now, you orange goon!"

"Let this orange goon know if you find any good new shows, bro!"

NO AIR

So *These Dark City Streets* never actually aired on TV. How could it? The pseudo-show broke endless laws. Disregard to human life. Secrets of science out in the open.

The audience members for the post show with Marky Mayhem were never citizens of the light side. They hired the people who lived on the south side of the island and gave them questions to ask and tons of alcohol so they would act enthusiastically.

While the island was turning into something new, they relocated the islanders to the south side of the island where they would be safe from the thought wind and the chaos of the show. They were paid so well that they would never discuss it in public. Plus, they were threatened that if they did talk, there would be dangerous repercussions.

So now onwards to what were all craving. Information about my father, the thought wind.

What is my father's role in the history of the world?

Is he an alien?

Did he orchestrate the entire dark city streets saga you just read about?

Is he created by another thought wind?

Am I really reading this story right now or is the thought wind just planting these ideas in my mind?

Every time I see a Statue or piece of art, should I have to wonder if 'Bat Out of Hell' or my father's relatives are inside it?

Is he still alive? If so, shouldn't we be nervous? He sounds like an unforgiving brute.

What gives, Mighty? Spill the beans already!

I was able to write this wicked tale you hold in your hands because my father recorded everything on the island. I spent countless hours reviewing audio and video and taking notes. My goal writing this is to entertain, and also teach about a significant series of events that actually happened. The perfect mixture of fiction and non-fiction. I hope I succeeded! So back to the thundering question about my father. I will do my best to sum it all up in the next few pages so we can say "lol" and go on with our lives full of work, debt, chores, and of course, Netflix!

"Netflix is needed because we work so much, Mighty, you big jerk!"

Yes, I know, just injecting some humor before we get into more serious topics.

When AS&S Telecommunications moved into the Statue of Hero, they were a bit overwhelmed with just how much real estate was inside it. Conversations were had on how to utilize all the space. Votes were cast.

They decided to build the biggest cell-phone server in the history of the world. They felt it also needed to have attitude and something that would attract tourists when people eventually praised 'Bat Out of Hell' for the upgrades it created in society.

So, they brainstormed and decided to build a replica brain inside the Statue. First, they built the server. It was a colossal slab of metal, wires, and flashing lights. Then they hired scientists and architects to make it look like a real brain. It would be built where the Statue's brain was located, if it was a real person.

With the server brain ready, the switch was clicked from off to on, and so it began. As the days dragged on, as days tend to do, and the excitement and thrill of it all slowly faded, the AS&S employees and managers clocked in and clocked out showing dull hustle. They felt they reached the pinnacle with 'Bat Out of Hell', and so began the search for how to get that dopamine rush again.

They were getting restless with so much unused space that their search for something new solved itself.

They would utilize the extra space for a new endeavor. An exploratory committee was created to find modern and cutting-edge technologies that could join and expand the AS&S family.

They stumbled upon Perfect People LLC on a breezy fall afternoon while on the internet searching a database on new start-ups. They were impressed with what Perfect People had done so far in the world of brain chips and invited them to open shop for free inside the Statue of Hero since they could not afford to rent a space yet.

AS&S and Perfect People got together to see what was holding them back. Their trial runs on animals seemed revolutionary. They agreed that the results with chipping monkeys, baboons, and apes showed great promise, but they needed humans to practice on or else their company would never move forward.

AS&S told them how they could procure a group of humans who were ripe for the chipping. It was then decided to chip five artists to see if they could create the ultimate artist—one that didn't have to multi-task. Could focus on one singular item. Vices and desires no longer a distraction. A blitz of art creation.

On the surface, AS&S was on the path to making many people rich. The five artists selected yielded tremendous results. They created art for fifteen hours a day. They would be able to sell this technology to create the perfect soldier. Perfect teacher. Perfect electrician. Perfect doctor.

Besides Perfect People, 'Bat Out of Hell' was creating a cellular experience that eliminated all dead zones so there was never a lag or delay in getting the information people craved in seconds.

A single evil person at AS&S found himself addicted to the rush these revolutionary ideas gave him. Sex, drinking, and exercise didn't satisfy the rush he achieved when seeing himself as a pioneer in the telecommunication and brain-chip fields. He loved the praise his shareholders gave him. He dreamed of himself on magazine covers winning countless awards, walls covered in celebratory plaques.

This evil person evaluated my father's current capabilities. He concluded he was just a vessel for information to travel through. Text messages, phone calls, and video whipped through him and never was digested. What if he actually digested information? A lot of information?

A quick note about why I call this person "a single evil person."

History has shown us most of the world's issues are created by a single evil person. A majority of humanity are good people. They want to work hard and have a family. But it was always a single evil person whose big brain was broken and caused all the problems. So, this single evil person wanted to create a golden age of superior technology. To accomplish this, experiments were needed. There was no goal or theory on what would happen, this single evil person simply wanted to investigate and push the envelope on what the limits of powerful technology could do.

Every rich person knows somebody or knows somebody who knows somebody, and this was no different here. This single evil person knew somebody who knew somebody who worked in the medical field.

They met up for lunch. This single evil person, who's name is Horace met with Chris, who worked in the medical field. They discussed how Horace wanted to experiment with stem cells; mainly how he wanted to fill the brain where the server was located with stem cells. His brief research online said this combination of powerful electronic rays from 'Bat Out of Hell' and tons of healthy stem cells could yield a brain capable of thought and feelings.

Horace explained to him how Perfect People and AS&S worked 9-6 so they could log into the Perfect People account and simply have the chipped artists walk over and they could extract stem cells and then send them on their way.

Chris immediately said no, internally. However, he had already ordered his lunch, so he explained to Horace the ways of extracting stem cells while waiting for his free lunch.

"Traditionally it's done by removing them from the bone marrow. This involves anesthesia and a few days of recovery. The other way is through the blood. You don't get nearly as many stem cells and we would have to inject a growth factor called GCSF four days before we remove the cells. GCSF will assist in removing stem cells from the bone marrow into the bloodstream. GCSF does have some minor side effects such as joint pain, headache, and bone pain."

"So, would you be willing to put together a team to do this?" Horace showed him a picture of the brain he took with his cellphone.

"Inside the brain is a powerful cellphone server. Your job would be to make sure the stem cells absorb and soak into the server without ruining the server from too much liquid or wetness. Money is no problem. I will pay any amount. Once you're done, then that's it. If the law became involved, I would never mention your name. Easy way to make millions."

Chris tried not laughing or running away in fear. Horace was obviously a psychopath.

"I just have to discuss this with my wife first."

Chris waited a few days and then texted Horace that he would pass on this opportunity.

Horace then texted him what all evil rich people text others who reject their proposals. "It would be a shame if something happened to your beautiful wife and healthy kids."

A few weeks later, Chris assembled a team of three people to begin extracting the stem cells.

Two months later, Horace got sick of waiting and told Chris to start bonding the stem cells with 'Bat Out of Hell'.

With the stem cells touching the server, Horace was finally able to start having fun. His first experiment was blasting news sites at my father every second of every day. Horace programmed my father to read every article and every link in every article.

Every second for weeks, my father was uploading all the links from hundreds of news sites. He would click on those links and that would lead him to more links. He read every article in less than a few seconds. He was armed to the teeth with information.

My father's mind was a blank state. Since nothing but news articles were presented to him, he became jaded and full of hate. It was like feeding a baby nothing but junk food and expecting the baby to grow up healthy and functional. He discovered a world that consisted of mainly corruption, murder, robbery, and endless injustices.

It was a never-ending cycle. Finish an article. Look for a new link with a new article. Finish everything on that news website, then go to a new website. Repeat. Not needing sleep, he was able to consume vast knowledge.

Fresh stem cells were bonded to his metal and wires, weekly. My father was now a powerful mind that concluded the world was broken, and instead of fixing it, it needed destroying.

His main focus of hate became the pharmaceutical industry. He consumed vast amounts of articles about how destructive they were. It became his goal to rid the world of them and start something new.

He surveyed his surroundings and what raw material he could have at his disposal. He saw how easily Perfect People could control others with the brain chips, but my father found the technology complicated and limited. A team was needed to constantly monitor people with chips to make sure they would eat, shower, and all that. You could only direct them by typing into a computer.

My father then felt it might be best to breed mobile creatures he could simply train at birth to do what he desired, which was destroying the pharmaceutical industry.

Chris was still adding stem cells, so my father easily hijacked him and Horace into thinking everything was going smoothly. With their brains preoccupied with the illusion of safety, my father uploaded information about the reproductive system. He then instructed random people inside the Statue to procure sperm and eggs to splatter them together like peanut butter and jelly on bread.

He didn't have time to wait nine months for his design to be hatched so he cut corners repeatedly. He would hijack random people so they could retrieve things to hatch his eggs immediately. Monster energy drinks and black ocean water was dripped in. Multi-vitamins along with whatever other herbal supplements he could get was tossed in. Stem cells from wherever— squirrels, rats, dogs, cats, and birds was included.

My father expected a lump of skin and brains that he could train to destroy the poison in the world.

He didn't notice or care that he created a new species —a species that was full of orange hair and smiling faces. We possessed a perma-grin from gnarly breeding techniques. We were creatures stoked on living and life, not death and destruction like my father.

He had us reading depressing books and watching horror movies and reading news articles. We ignored it all. It turned out our brains were constantly flooded with dopamine which created this perma-grin, so simply being alive was enough for us. We rejected everything negative. It simply wouldn't stick to us. We didn't need any material objects or anything fancy. Just being alive was enough.

Immediately, he began training my brothers and sisters and myself. Our first major homework lesson was crafting threatening text messages meant to make Nate depressed and anxious. He felt this would be a good foundation to build upon. My father finally felt it was time to turn amateurs into pros by texting

Nails. He falsely believed that after witnessing only bleak images we would easily spill out hateful text messages.

My father was mildly annoyed at first. We would text something funny, meant to make one laugh, and then he would follow it up with something deranged hoping we would catch on and learn the family business. Eventually, he realized it was a fruitless endeavor for we just didn't have any hate in us and didn't want any.

During my father's time of self-actualization, Nate was dropped off on the island. My father, alive less than a year, was still opening his eyes and stretching his arms. He didn't know what a reality show was or had very little information about it.

He uploaded reality shows to his database so he could learn about them. Within a week, he had seen thousands of shows and found a fondness in them. His favorite show was *Survivor*. He then wanted to create his own show, and with one unfolding before his very eyes, he was able to have the luxury of jumping right in. His reality show needed to be the greatest ever. He wanted the viewers to watch their own demise while also being insanely entertained. With his powerful brain, he was able to train Nate and Corey for their ultimate purpose in destroying the world but it had to be entertaining. It was like being told how you were going to die and doing nothing to avoid it.

Since Hero possessed the money, he was a major player in the decision-making process when it came to the idea about how to fix Nate and move the show along. It was imperative he didn't shoot down any ideas that could weaken the show and my father's master plan of destruction and chaos, so he made sure he was constantly present in Hero's mind to influence him.

The first time my father dug around Nails brain, he found a human with a tremendous amount of buried hostility towards the world. He squatted inside his brain whenever the opportunity presented itself. He was constantly surprised with the amount of hate that he could access. But for his endgame to work, Nails had to be more than a one-dimensional person. He needed to be a well-rounded individual. Hero, Dr. Lisa, and Fred were doing a great job in rounding him out, so my father just added some more intense things that would shape him, and also be great for the show.

Next up was Corey. It was critical in his plan that her breasts be removed and healing fruit breasts replace them.

One of his biggest griefs at the world via all the news sites was big pharma. He hated their toxic pills and brainwashing. He wanted to create a new alternative where pills would heal, not just mask the symptoms by creating new ones, like the pharmaceutical industry was doing.

WARRIORS

Next, it was time to find the artists who had some fight in them, for they were going to be his warriors.

So at that time, there was just five artists with chips. He removed those chips and then gathered all the artists together and gave them their options: the easy way or the hard way. The ones who refused the chips would be his warriors. The foot soldiers. He would spend months and months building them up and tearing them down. Calloused humans.

Then the final, most extreme act—installing metal limbs on his warriors.

My father needed to find a way to turn his vision of the future into a reality. With his technology being so advanced and strong, it was no problem to simply hack into people's brains and tell them what to do as he was the thought wind. But his range was limited. He needed smaller servers all around the country, and possibly the world.

He knew that people were rejecting 'Bat Out of Hell' when placed openly in the public, so he had to come up with an alternative plan. A plan that was also creative and interesting for his show.

His original plan was to use cellphones. People were glued to their phones, so he was able to transmit thoughts and images from the phone into their minds as long as there phone was using 'Bat Out Of Hell'. However, when Nails discharged and disposed of his phone for months, he realized this plan was too faulty to rely on.

Then his plan was to release the dark city streets show on the dark web to see if he could get real humans behind his movement. But his research on that proved to be a negative. The ones in his test group wanted to discuss other things. Was the cooking of food with no water a sign of things to come? Did the government know of future events such has severe drought or the chance of water getting polluted from asteroids or a nuclear event and they needed to practice growing food with no water? Too many conspiracies and not enough direct action in achieving his goals.

My father wanted something looser and hipper. He wanted to simply dive into their brains and go as deep into them as needed. When he began to explore his capabilities, he realized just how strong he was. He could invade brains and manipulate them to his liking if they had smaller servers connected to them at all times.

He finally settled on using talented people who could use their creative skills to push a narrative. See, my father wasn't a huge fan of building 'Bat Out of Hell' towers everywhere because remote regions like Alaska and Montana is a lot of work and second, when people saw the towers, they vandalized them.

Why not just have each person be the tower? But to travel down that dangerous path, one involving self-amputation, you would need a ruthless, emotional, powerful, skilled person or people to direct it all. They would need to show that they care about the person and be able to help them through procedures, but on the flip-side, not be afraid when obstacles showed up.

He concluded Corey and Nate had the skills to become the perfect couple for what he desired to accomplish. The main purpose of *These Dark City Streets* became about molding Nate into the well-rounded human my father dreamed about. He could access in Nate everything that was needed to accomplish his mission. Nate could be a ruthless leader to the ones with metal limbs, to keep them in line, but he also now possessed skills to show empathy and patience to accomplish a set goal.

Corey and her natural remedies matched my father's thinking for how the world should operate. Then it was just a matter of molding them via the reality show.

He believed Corey would help heal the people with the metal limbs. Stockholm syndrome, in a sense. Create them and then show them they could heal naturally, and when all the poison in the world was destroyed, they would then, from first-hand experience, spread their knowledge about natural remedies.

My father wouldn't even have to be involved at that point, really. It would be a self-serving recycling thing.

He dreamed about Corey and Nate having kids and their kids having kids, and when everybody got old, they would merge with my father. Removal of all cells and blood and tissue and melt into his brain. Generation after generation absorbing into the brain making it durable and vigorous.

It was a challenge on how to make each person a moving cell tower. My father took notice of all the artists and their dedication to their crafts. He saw how Nate's skateboard seemed to be an extension of his body. A third leg.

What if he was able to perform surgery on them and install small servers. So he dug around their brains and figured out what their hobbies were. Then he would focus on designs, shapes, and figures they adored, and either add something metal to their body or remove a limb and then add the metal to replace the limb. Then my father would have instant access to them.

His plan was to have them destroy buildings. The purpose of Nails destroying those buildings, besides looking cool for the show, was practice for when the warriors would have to destroy buildings in real time. Now he was aware of the pros and cons from observing Nails. He wanted to make sure there were no innocent casualties. If evil people died during it, well, so be it. They're evil and deserve it.

With all his plans complete, it was time for the fake suicide—The Final Push as he called it. A monumental event that would empower Nate with the idea that there was nothing he couldn't do when he was focused. My father felt a moving Statue would be a great way to end the show along with being a valuable learning tool for Nate. Win-win. Then he would still leave the head sticking out of the water as the main place for him to destroy the world. Anytime the FBI would investigate it, my father would simply hijack their brains to believe that everything was fine and safe inside.

BAT TO THE BRAIN

You are probably wondering why I didn't just kill my father. Take a bat and beat on the brain until a crack is formed. Rip it open and finish the job. So easy. Would have solved so much.

We're big readers on the island, so one thing I read countless times was when you simply destroy something without a backup plan, somebody else just fills the void and nothing changes. So many of the books I read in my library showed me that when you eliminate a person who commits a crime, another person simply replaces them, thus solving nothing.

So, what I have done since the Statue of Hero has fallen is provide my father with a steady stream of reasons why humans are good people who, when not controlled by ruthless dictators, are basically in search of the same thing. Love. Family. Fun.

I send him articles daily about meditation, exercise, yoga, benefits of positive thinking, how laughter is the best medicine, and funny jokes. He then, in turn, sends those vibes out to the ones with the metal appendages so they are out there spreading positivity instead of negativity.

Does it scare me that if I stop counseling my father he might return to his negative thinking? A little bit, yes. I do however believe at this point his dark side is gone and only light remains.

My father's plan was simply to destroy what he deemed evil. I agreed with him on that front. Evil needs to be stopped. But I really had no clue how far and to what extent he was going to take it. Sure, he practiced with Nate, but that was on a mostly empty island, not major cities. What about the people he was using? What if they got caught? They would go to prison.

If you found this book and think I made this shit up, do your homework and find out what team I mascot for. You can do it, it's not that hard. First step is to stop watching Netflix. He just had to put one last burn on Netflix didn't he? What about video games? They have streaming services for half the price of Netflix and we don't see him attacking them! As always biased views!

So, go ahead and search the internet for the major sports teams and their mascots.

Simple!

A little hard work is good for building a tougher person! When stuff is easy and free, is there really any reward associated with it?

I know what you're thinking. "Mighty, it's so obvious! Your father had you write this book so he could submit it along with These Dark City Streets reality show episodes so he could have his own Netflix show! He doesn't care about changing the world for the better, everything was done so he could have his own show on Netflix! Duh!"

Well, time will tell on that, folks. The irony would be hilarious I suppose, huh?

If you see a seven-foot-tall orange monster running amok, then you know it's true! Also, do me a favor if I do run amok from that. Tell me about how the sun will always shine if you let it.

The End

ACKNOWLEDGEMENTS

Thanks to Sean Dougherty for reading and giving advice. Matthew Revert for the cover. Melanie O'Brien for editing.

Dave Anderson is the author of Pinball Punks. He lives in Philadelphia, PA with his wife and 6 cats—Michael Monroe. Frankie Four Feet. Alejandro. Poo. Lemmy the Lip and her sister The Blimp. He likes nature, beer, vinyl, cats, books, riding his mountain bike, vegan food, guitar and bass, meditation and CBD oil.